THE EYE

CONVERGENCE WAR
BOOK 3

M.R. FORBES

Published by Quirky Algorithms
Seattle, Washington

Cover illustration by Tom Edwards
Edited by Merrylee Lanehart

CHAPTER 1

As the bright flash faded from the viewscreen and the familiar emptiness of folded space greeted them, a collective sigh of relief swept through the Wraith's bridge.

"Fold successful, Captain," Bobby reported, his voice steady despite the lingering tension of the fight they had just escaped at this universe's Omega Station. "We've cleared the battle zone and are now on course for the Eye."

Out of the frying pan and into the fire.

"We made it," Jack said, a note of disbelief in his voice. "I wasn't sure we would, for a minute there."

"I wasn't either, but we did," Soren agreed, allowing himself a brief moment to collect his thoughts before addressing the crew. "Excellent work, everyone. Ethan, damage report?"

"No significant damage, Captain," Ethan replied after a brief pause. "The shields took a few hits during our escape, but nothing to worry about. We're in remarkably good shape, considering our entire starboard side was exposed during that mess."

"That's good to hear, Ethan. Make whatever repairs are needed."

"Aye, Captain."

Soren turned toward the helm. "Good work, Sang. If you were still active Navy, I would put you in for another commendation."

"If I were still officially a Naval officer, I probably wouldn't be out here with you, having so much fun, Captain," Sang replied, drawing a grin from Soren.

"I'm grateful the Galileo made it out of there, too," Jack added. "I just wish Omega Station had survived the attack. We lost a lot of lives back there."

"The cost was high indeed." Soren's mind flashed back to the destruction and the lives lost in those final, desperate moments. The other Jack Harper had sacrificed himself and his crew to buy them time to jump away from certain destruction.

Time to save both universes.

If they could do it.

"You should be proud of your other self," he told Jack.

"I am," he said softly. "Frankly, I didn't know I had it in me. We all knew the risks. They gave their lives so we could have this chance."

"I know," Soren replied, his voice tight. "But that never makes it pleasant. If we accept losses without remorse, we're no better than our enemy." He shook his head, forcing his thoughts away from this dimension's FUP and its destructive intent to kill off his universe to supposedly save theirs. "We're out of immediate danger, but we still have our work cut out for us. Ethan, Lina, we have four weeks to complete all the upgrades and get that third reactor online. Can you do it?"

There was a pause, and Soren could almost hear the minds of his two lead engineers working through the calculations and resources. Finally, Ethan responded. "It'll be tight, Captain. Tighter than I'd like. We'll need to work around the clock, with continued help from Scorpion Squad to get it done."

"The Scorpions are yours until the work is completed," Soren said. "Keep me updated on your progress. If you need anything, anything at all, let me know immediately."

"Aye, Captain," Ethan replied.

Soren turned to Vic, who'd remained standing beside the command station. "Vic, you have the conn. Recall your team to the bridge. I need to check on our newest guests."

"Aye, Captain." Vic nodded, assuming the command station as Soren relinquished it.

"The rest of you have earned some downtime," Soren said, addressing his bridge crew. "As soon as you're relieved of duty, you're off for the next twelve hours. Hit the chow hall and then get some sleep. That goes for you, too, Jack."

"Aye, Captain. I can definitely use some rest."

Soren made his way off the bridge, the loudspeakers blaring as Vic assembled his rotation to take over bridge duties. Once the announcement ended, Soren activated his comm. "Liam, where did your Marines take Dana and Dr. Mitchell?"

"We put them in the officers' lounge on Deck Four, sir. It was the most comfortable space we could secure on short notice."

"Understood. I'm heading there now."

The trip to Deck Four was mercifully short, but it gave Soren enough time to steel himself for the confrontation he knew was coming. As the doors to the officers' lounge slid open, he was surprised to see Alex already there, standing nose-to-nose with his sister, the two of them engaged in what looked like a heated discussion.

Both turned as Soren entered, Dana's eyes flashing with relief and anger. "Captain," she said, her voice tight. "How could you do this? We belong—"

"You belong here," Soren interrupted, meeting Dana's gaze. "Both of you. I'd hoped a few minutes to cool off would have helped you see reason."

"I don't care about reason," Dana snapped back. "Galileo is my ship. My crew. I should have been there with them. Not trapped here. I don't even know if they made it out alive!"

"They did," Soren said quickly, holding up a hand to forestall another outburst. "The Galileo escaped. I made sure of it. They're on their way back to our dimension to report to Admiral Montoya."

Some of the tension drained out of Dana, but her eyes remained hard. "That doesn't change the fact that you had no right to keep us here against our will."

"I'll remind you a second time that as your superior officer I have every right to keep you here against your will."

"But not me," Lukas piped up, attempting to defend Dana before she could reply herself. "You had no authority to prevent me from returning to Omega Station. You aren't even from my universe."

"You can consider yourself a prisoner of war then if that makes your stay on Wraith more digestible," Soren said. "Omega Station is gone. Destroyed. And if I had let you go out there, you would be dead with it. Stopping the Convergence is much too important for me to have let that happen. Your knowledge and expertise is vital to that mission. I hope you can both come to accept that, but to be honest, I don't care if you do or don't. We have a job to do, and you're both here to help."

"Gone?" Lukas' shoulders had slumped at the mention of Omega Station's destruction. "You mean... everybody...?"

"I'm sorry," Soren said. "I doubt there were any survivors from the station, though it's possible some of your team may have made it onto Galileo before it departed."

Lukas nodded. "I'll hope for the best," he replied softly. "They were good people. Some of the smartest in the galaxy."

Dana's dogmatic expression had drained quickly away, turning to one of chagrin and embarrassment. "I'm sorry for questioning your orders, Captain. And I didn't mean to imply that we wouldn't help with the Convergence. That's why we were all on the station to begin with."

Soren let his face relax, offering them both a satisfied smile. "I knew you would be more reasonable once you calmed down and thought it through. You're not usually so stubborn."

"Unlike my father," she joked.

"I can be reasonable," Soren answered.

"As long as by being reasonable, you get your way," Alex said.

"Now you're ganging up on me."

"It's the only way to outmaneuver you, Dad," Dana added.

The three Stricklands shared a laugh. Soren relaxed fully, embracing his daughter. "I'm glad to have you here with me. Both of you. If you'd been on the station…"

"It's scary to think this may be the safest place in two universes right now," Alex said.

"Captain," Lukas said. "I want to help. I do. But my research…I lost so much. I don't even have a lab anymore."

"Right," Soren agreed, regaining his commanding officer demeanor. "Your research can continue here. What resources do you need? If there's one thing we have more than enough of on this ship, it's empty space for you to use."

"As long as we don't need to take down any of our training courses," Alex said. "I doubt you'll have much use for Marines in the Eye, but depending on what happens afterward…"

"Alex, there's no way I'll infringe on the Marine training spaces. I know you'll do what you have to do to be ready for anything that comes down the pike. I wouldn't stand in the way of that."

Lukas scrubbed his hand down his face. "The most critical thing is computing power. We need to run complex simulations and process the massive amount of data we'll be collecting once we reach the Eye and launch the probes." He paused, a flicker of worry crossing his face. "This is all going to be significantly more challenging without the rest of our team, but we'll make do." He sighed, sadness creeping back into his features. "We have to solve this, for them."

"We will," Dana said, rubbing Lukas' shoulder. "We won't let their deaths be for nothing."

"Lina," Soren said through his comms. "I need you to set up a lab for Dana and Dr. Mitchell as soon as possible."

There was a brief pause before Lina's voice came back. His maintenance chief sounded strained. "Captain, I'd love to get right on that order, but we need to prioritize. We're on an incredibly tight schedule with the shield upgrades. We don't have the resources to handle both."

Soren frowned, considering the problem. "Can you spare Tashi and Wilf?"

"Honestly, I don't think so, sir. Not if you want these shields at full strength when we reach the Eye."

He hesitated, still working on the problem. His eyes turned to Alex. "What if I traded you two engineers for as many Marines as you need?"

"Do any of them have experience with electrical work?"

Soren raised his eyebrows at his son.

"Zoe does," Alex replied. "And Malik knows enough to be dangerous. They're not total neophytes."

"Can you train two other Marines in the Karuta armor to replace them with the heavy lifting?"

Alex nodded. "The armor only takes a few hours to get accustomed to, at least for picking up heavy objects. Becoming adept in combat is a different story. I have a couple of Marines in mind."

"Lina, I'm going to send you Zoe and Malik from Scorpion Squad to replace Tashi and Wilf. They might need a little training but they have some experience. Let's see if we can balance things out this way."

"Aye, Captain," Lina replied. "I'll brief them on what needs to be done."

"Have Tashi and Wilf report to the officers' lounge immediately. They're to take direction from Lukas and Dana until I say otherwise."

"Aye, Captain. They'll be on their way momentarily."

"Thank you, Lina." Soren closed the channel and turned back to Dana and Lukas. "We'll have your lab set up as quickly as possible. Consider Tashi and Wilf part of your new research team. Tashi is especially good at equations, so he should fit right in. Wilf is a jack-of-all-trades, and I'm sure you'll find him useful, even if it's only to make coffee runs."

As Dana and Lukas nodded their agreement, Soren felt a small spark of hope ignite in his chest. They had suffered losses, but they were still in the fight. And with his daughter and the brilliant Dr. Mitchell on board, their chances of success were as good as ever.

But as he left the officers' lounge, that spark of hope was tempered by the weight of responsibility pressing down more firmly on him with each passing moment. They were on their way to the Eye, rushing headlong into a confrontation with cosmic forces beyond their understanding in hopes of ending the Convergence of their two universes.

The fate of not one but both hung in the balance.

CHAPTER 2

Soren made his way through the corridors toward the conference room. Two weeks had passed since their narrow escape from Omega Station, and the ship had settled into a rhythm of constant work and preparation. But tonight, Soren had arranged for a brief respite, a moment of normalcy amidst the looming chaos.

As he approached the conference room, he caught sight of Jack already waiting outside, a thoughtful expression on his weathered face.

"Evening, Jack," Soren greeted, coming to a stop beside his old friend.

Jack's lips split into a small smile. "Soren. I have to admit, I'm looking forward to this. It's been too long since we've had a chance to just sit and talk like normal folks."

Soren nodded, understanding the sentiment all too well. "Agreed. With everything that's happened, I think we all need that every once in a while."

The door slid open, revealing the transformed conference room. The large table that dominated the space had been given a makeover. A flat white bed sheet covered it and an assortment of colored plates, knives and forks, and glassware were set out on it. Soft lighting cast a warm glow over the room, and the large display on the wall had been set to the relaxing woodland scene Soren often used in his own quarters.

Dana and Alex were already sitting at the table, engaged in an animated conversation. They looked up and rose as Soren and Jack entered, their faces brightening.

"Dad," Dana said, moving to embrace him, Alex stepping up right behind her. "I was starting to think you'd forgotten about our dinner plans."

Soren returned her hug, savoring the moment. "Not a chance. I wouldn't miss this for anything."

Alex grinned, clapping his father on the shoulder. "We were just placing bets on whether you'd manage to tear yourself away from work long enough to eat with us."

"Your old man's not that predictable, is he?" Soren asked, feigning offense.

Jack chuckled. "I seem to recall a certain captain who once went three days without leaving the bridge during a particularly tense standoff with the Coalition."

"That was different," Soren protested, even as a smile tugged at his lips. "For one thing, I was a lot younger back then, and we were in pretty dire straits. The crew needed to see their captain standing strong with them."

"And I'm sure it had nothing to do with your stubborn refusal to admit you needed sleep," Dana teased, her eyes twinkling with mirth.

"Come on, sis," Alex said. "We all know wraiths don't need to sleep."

Before Soren could formulate a retort, the door slid open once more. Harry entered, pushing a cart laden with covered dishes, the tantalizing aroma quickly filling the air.

"Evening, folks," Harry said, his usual business-like demeanor softened by a hint of warmth. "Thought you might appreciate a proper meal for once, compliments of the chef."

Soren raised an eyebrow, pleasantly surprised. "Harry, I requested trays brought up from the chow line. You didn't have to go to all this trouble."

Harry waved off the comment as he began setting the serving dishes out on the table. "Nonsense, Captain. You've always been a good friend to me, and you're fortunate enough to have an opportunity to dine with your children. I'd give anything for that, if I had any of my own. Seeing that I don't, I intend to live vicariously through you. So I canceled that order of yours and whipped up something a bit more appealing. Now, eat up."

"You're a good friend, Harry," Soren replied. "You dropped everything to come on this crazy ride, and I'm forever grateful to you and everyone else."

"Which you make sure to tell us often," Harry said with a grin.

As he unveiled each dish, the group's eyes widened in appreciation. There was a golden-brown roast chicken, its skin crisp and glistening. Beside it sat a bowl of fluffy mashed potatoes flecked with herbs and steaming invitingly. Vibrant green vegetables, perfectly sautéed, added a splash of color to the spread. And at the center of it all, a bottle of red wine.

"Harry," Jack said, his voice filled with awe, "where in the world did you get all this?"

The quartermaster's eyes twinkled with mischief. "Let's just say I made some connections back at Omega Station before everything went sideways. Figured we might need a morale boost sooner or later. Don't tell the rest of the crew, but there's more where this came from. Saving it for a special occasion, yeah?"

As Harry finished laying out the meal, Soren placed a

hand on his shoulder. "Thank you again, Harry. This means more than you know."

Harry nodded, a rare smile crossing his face. "Just doing my job, Captain. Now, if you'll excuse me, I've got inventories to run. Can't have us running out of essentials on our way to save the universes, can we?"

Harry took his leave with a final nod to the group, the door sliding shut behind him.

"Well," Alex said, eyeing the spread with barely contained enthusiasm, "shall we dig in before it gets cold?"

They settled around the table, the familiar routine of passing dishes and filling plates providing a comforting sense of normalcy. For a few moments, the only sounds were the clink of cutlery and appreciative murmurs as they savored the first bites of their meal.

"Did Harry make this himself?" Dana asked, blissfully closing her eyes as she savored a forkful of the roast chicken.

"He keeps telling me he's a passable cook," Soren said.

"If this is passable, I want to try gourmet," Alex replied.

Jack nodded in agreement, his plate already half-empty. "Harry's truly outdone himself."

As they continued to eat, the conversation flowed easily, touching on lighter topics at first. They swapped stories of their time apart, filling in the gaps of the past few months. Alex regaled them with tales of the Scorpions' training exercises, while Dana shared some of the more amusing mishaps from her early days on Omega Station.

"You should have seen Lukas' face," she said, her eyes dancing with laughter as she recounted one particular incident. "He was so focused on his equations that he didn't even notice he'd wandered into the wrong place. Ended up lecturing a group of very confused technicians about temporal distortions for a good ten minutes before anyone worked up the courage to tell him they had no idea what he was blathering on about."

The others laughed, the image of the brilliant and intense scientist easily coming to mind.

"Speaking of Lukas," Soren said, his tone carefully neutral, "how are things going with the new lab setup?"

Dana's expression sobered slightly. "It's coming along. Tashi and Wilf have been incredibly helpful. We're not at the level we were on Omega Station, of course, but we're making progress."

"Have you started running any new simulations yet?" Alex asked.

"We just got everything up and running a few days ago. We're really putting the ship's mainframe through its paces. If you've noticed any slow down in data delivery to your terminals, that's probably why."

"Thankfully, there isn't much data to review right now outside of engineering updates," Soren said with a chuckle.

"Any breakthroughs?" Jack asked, leaning forward with interest.

Dana shook her head, a flicker of frustration crossing her face. "Nothing concrete yet. We're still trying to fill in some of the blanks that were left by the loss of the station. What happened has been pretty hard on Lukas. He blames himself for pretty much everything."

"I hate to say it, but it is pretty much his fault," Alex said.

"It's easy to point your finger at him," Dana replied, shaking her empty fork punitively. "But someone would have figured out what was happening with the rifts sooner or later."

"Would they, though?" Alex pressed. "Because our side certainly didn't. If not for him, we'd all be sitting around our table on Earth, and Mom would be there with us."

"That's not fair," Dana scowled. "You know this

universe isn't identical to ours. You can't assume things would have progressed in the same way, whether Lukas was involved or not."

"I'll accept that, but it's also not fair to say he has no blame."

"Lukas has accepted his part in what happened," Soren said. "He's trying to make it right. You can't fault him for that."

"No. I respect that he wants to fix what he broke," Alex agreed. "I just prefer that he hadn't broken it to begin with."

"Hindsight is always twenty-twenty," Jack pointed out. "In hindsight, I would have saved the potatoes for last." He grinned, trying to lighten the mood.

"I second that revelation," Soren agreed.

"I will say, we've come up with a new theory on the Convergence," Dana said.

"Do tell," Jack said.

Dana paused, gathering her thoughts. "It's like...imagine two soap bubbles slowly merging. At first, they're separate. Distinct. But as they come together, there's a point where it becomes impossible to tell where one ends and the other begins. We think the Convergence might work in a similar way, but on a cosmic scale."

"You mean our dimensions won't collapse together all at once?" Soren asked. "That they'll, for back of a better expression, sink slowly into one another?"

"It's just a theory," Dana said, "But it does help solve a couple of the equations that were leaving Lukas stumped. It also means that we may have more time than we think, because the Convergence won't happen all at once."

"That's good news," Jack said.

"I hope so."

"And what happens when the bubbles fully merge?"

Soren asked. "Does the outcome change, or only the timeline?"

"That's the part we're still trying to figure out. What has us most concerned is what might happen if the combined soap bubble pops."

A heavy silence fell over the table as they contemplated the implications of Dana's words.

It was Soren who finally broke it, raising his wine glass. "A toast," he said. "To family, to friendship, and to facing the impossible together."

They clinked glasses, the rich red wine a welcome distraction from the weight of their mission. As they sipped, Soren felt some of the tension drain from his shoulders. Here, at this moment, surrounded by the people he cared for most, he could almost forget the monumental task that lay ahead.

"You know," Alex said, setting down his glass, "all this talk of parallel universes and cosmic disasters reminds me of those old science fiction stories you used to read to us when we were kids, Dad. Remember those?"

Soren smiled, memories of quiet evenings spent reading to his children flooding back. "How could I forget? You two would beg for just one more chapter every night."

"The Adventures of Captain Quark and the Quasars," Dana said, her eyes misting slightly with nostalgia. "I used to dream about having adventures like that someday."

"Be careful what you wish for," Jack quipped, though his tone was gentle. "I'd say our current situation gives Captain Quark a run for his money."

Alex laughed. "True. Though I don't remember Captain Quark ever having to deal with evil doppelgängers or universe-ending convergences."

"No," Soren agreed, "but there was that one story about the mirror dimension. Remember? Where everything was backwards, and Quark had to figure out how to get his crew back to their own reality?"

Dana nodded enthusiastically. "Oh yes! That was one of my favorites. Didn't it turn out that the key to getting home was in seeing past their own reflections or something like that?"

"That's right," Soren said, impressed by her recall. "They had to recognize the fundamental similarities between the two worlds, rather than focusing on the differences."

Jack's expression turned thoughtful. "You know, there might be a lesson in that for us. We've been so focused on the differences between our universe and this one, on the threat of the Convergence... maybe we need to look at the similarities instead. Find common ground."

"It's not a bad idea," Alex mused. "We've seen how this universe's FUP operates, how they think. If we can understand them better, maybe we can find a way to communicate, to make them see reason."

Soren nodded slowly, turning the idea over in his mind. "It's worth considering. Though with any luck, we'll stop this whole mess before we need to communicate with anyone else from this dimension."

"What if we do stop it?" Alex asked. "Does that mean we end up here, stuck in this dimension like Captain Quark in the mirror universe?"

"No," Dana answered. "If the soap bubble theory is right, as long as we aren't too integrated, we'll slide apart again. It'll just take time."

"Time this dimension can use attacking our dimension."

"Which brings us back to diplomacy, after the fact," Soren said. "If it means we stopped the Convergence, I'll gladly accept the challenge."

The conversation lulled for a moment as they contemplated the possibilities and drank their wine.

"You know," Soren said softly, breaking the silence by waxing philosophical. "Everything we've been through...it makes me think about how we got here. Not just to this moment, but to who we are as people."

Alex tilted his head, curious. "What do you mean, Dad?"

"I'm thinking about choices. The paths we take, the decisions that shape us. In this other universe, things turned out so differently. Their Soren, their Jack...they made choices that led them down much different paths."

"You mean nature versus nurture," Jack mused. "How much of who we are is innate, and how much is shaped by our experiences?"

Dana leaned forward. "It's a fascinating question, especially in light of the Convergence. Are we fundamentally the same as our counterparts, just shaped by different circumstances? Or are there core differences that make us truly distinct individuals?"

"I'd like to think we're more than just the sum of our experiences," Alex said. "That there's something essential about who we are that transcends circumstance. That our souls are unique, no matter how many dimensions or duplicates of us there may be."

Soren nodded, understanding his son's perspective. "I'd like to believe that, too. But if not, I have to wonder...what made the difference? What crucial moment shaped their paths so differently from ours?"

"Maybe it wasn't one moment," Jack suggested. "Maybe it was a series of small choices, each one nudging them further and further from the people we know ourselves to be."

Dana's eyes lit up with a sudden thought. "You know, there's a theory in quantum mechanics about that. The idea of quantum superposition—that a particle can exist in multiple states simultaneously until it's observed. Some philosophers have applied that concept to decision-making, suggesting that every choice we make creates a new branch of reality."

"So you're saying there could be infinite versions of us out there?" Alex asked, his eyebrows raised in surprise.

"Theoretically, yes," Dana replied. "Each one shaped by the countless decisions we make every day."

Soren leaned back in his chair, trying to wrap his mind around the concept. "It's a bit overwhelming to think about, isn't it? All those potential versions of ourselves, spread across countless realities."

"I think two realities is about one more than I can handle," Jack said. "Any more than that, and I might go insane." That drew a laugh from the others. "In any case," he continued, "I'm glad we have this time to spend together. And that we're all here together regardless of the reality we're in."

"I'll drink to that," Dana said.

A comfortable silence fell over the table. Soren felt a surge of gratitude wash over him as he looked at the faces of those he held dear. Whatever challenges lay ahead, whatever impossible odds they faced, he knew he wouldn't want to face them with anyone else.

"Taking things a step further," Alex said after a moment, a mischievous glint in his eye, "with all this talk of alternate realities. In how many of them do you think Dad actually managed to beat me at tennis?"

Soren's eyebrows shot up in mock indignation. "I'll have you know, young man, that I let you win most of those games."

Dana burst out laughing. "Oh please, Dad. We all know Alex wiped the floor with you every time."

"I seem to recall a few close matches," Soren protested, though he couldn't keep the smile from his face.

Jack chuckled, shaking his head. "Face it, Soren. Your

son inherited your competitive streak and your athletic ability. It was a lethal combination."

As they continued to reminisce, trading stories and gentle barbs, Soren felt a warmth spreading through his chest that had nothing to do with the wine. These moments, these connections, were what made life worth living. What made their mission, impossible as it seemed, worth fighting for.

The conversation flowed easily, touching on memories, both old and new. They spoke of childhood adventures, of Academy mishaps, of the small, everyday moments that had shaped them into the people they were today.

"Remember that trip we took to Montana?" Dana asked, her eyes sparkling with the memory. "The one where Dad insisted he knew the perfect spot for stargazing?"

Alex groaned, though a smile played at the corners of his mouth. "How could I forget? We ended up hiking for hours, completely lost, only to set up camp right back where we started."

"In my defense," Soren said, holding up his hands, "the terrain looked very different in the dark."

Jack laughed, shaking his head. "I remember Jane telling me about that when you got back. She said she'd never seen you so sunburned and sheepish."

"Mom has always had a way of keeping Dad's ego in check," Dana said, a hint of wistfulness in her voice.

Soren felt a pang in his chest at the mention of Jane. "She certainly does. I can only imagine what she'd say if she could see us now."

"She'd probably tell us to stop reminiscing and get on with saving the universes," Alex answered.

"You're probably right," Soren agreed, raising his glass. "To Jane, and to all those we're fighting to protect."

They toasted once more.

The conversation continued late into the night, touching

on hopes, fears, memories, and dreams. They spoke of the future they hoped to secure, of the things they still wanted to accomplish once their mission was complete. As the hour grew late, Soren found himself wishing they could stay in this moment forever, suspended in time, safe from the dangers that awaited them.

But he knew they couldn't. The Eye loomed before them, a cosmic mystery that held the fate of two universes in its swirling depths. And beyond that, the battle for their very existence. They would need every ounce of strength, every moment of preparation, to face what lay ahead.

As the evening finally wound down, and they began to clear away the remnants of their meal, Soren felt a renewed sense of purpose. This gathering, this moment of connection and shared history, had rejuvenated him in a way he hadn't realized he needed.

"Thank you all for this," he said as they prepared to depart. "I think we needed this more than we knew."

Dana embraced him tightly. "We did, Dad. It was perfect."

Alex nodded in agreement. "It's good to remember what we're fighting for."

As they said their goodnights and went their separate ways, Soren lingered for a moment, taking in the now-empty conference room. The remnants of their meal, the lingering warmth of conversation and laughter, seemed to hang in the air like a tangible presence.

Jack, noticing his hesitation, paused at the door. "Everything alright, Soren?"

Soren nodded, a small smile playing at his lips. "Just savoring the moment, I suppose. Storing it away for the challenges ahead."

Jack's expression softened with understanding. "It was a good night. One to remember."

"That it was, old friend," Soren agreed. "That it was."

"Soren," Jack said, his voice carrying a weight of emotion, "whatever happens when we reach the Eye, I want you to know it's been an honor. Serving with you, being your friend. I wouldn't trade it for anything."

Soren felt a lump form in his throat, emotion threatening to overwhelm him. "The honor has been mine, Jack. I couldn't ask for a better friend or a more trusted advisor."

They clasped hands, the gesture carrying years of shared experiences and unspoken understanding. Then, with a final nod, they parted ways, heading to their respective quarters for some much-needed rest.

It was a night Soren would remember for the rest of his life. He could only hope that life would last more than the next few weeks.

He would do anything to ensure that it would.

CHAPTER 3

Soren stood on the bridge, hands clasped behind his back, eyes fixed on the viewscreen. Lukas and Dana stood beside him, their anticipation palpable. The pitch black void of folded space was about to give way to their destination: the Eye. The mysterious anomaly they believed to be the destructive source of the Convergence.

As he waited for the transition, Soren found his thoughts drifting back to the dinner he had shared with Jack, Dana, and Alex at the halfway point of their long journey to this point. The warmth of that evening, the laughter and shared memories, had rejuvenated him in a way he hadn't realized he needed. It wasn't just the break from the constant pressure of the mission, but the reminder of what they were fighting for. Family, friendship, the countless small moments that made life worth living.

Even as he steeled himself for whatever challenges lay ahead, the memory brought a small smile to his face. They were about to face the unknown, to confront forces beyond their comprehension. But he felt absolutely ready.

"Thirty seconds to exit, Captain," Bobby announced from the nav station, his voice taking on an anticipatory quiver. He was nervous, fearful, and eager, just like the rest of the bridge crew.

Just like Soren, himself.

Soren nodded, straightening his posture. "All hands to ready stations," he ordered over the ship-wide comms. "I repeat. All hands to ready stations." Then, to his bridge crew, "We don't know what we're about to encounter, so stay alert and be ready for anything."

They responded with a chorus of acknowledgments, each member focused intently on their stations, the tension hanging thick and heavy across the bridge.

"Ten seconds," Bobby called out.

Soren glanced at Dana, who met his gaze and nodded in silent support. Whatever lay on the other side of this fold, they would face it together.

"Three... two... one..."

With a familiar flash, the Wraith completed its fold. The darkness of the viewscreen gave way.

Soren blinked, momentarily stunned by what he saw. Lukas had claimed that the Eye was barely visible to the human eye, little more than a slight distortion of the surrounding stars, perhaps a subtle shimmer. But this...

"Stars above," Jack breathed from beside him. "Would you look at that?"

Before them loomed a massive, swirling vortex of energy, a colossal hurricane of galactic chaos suspended in the black. Ribbons of light in shades of blue, purple, and green twisted and writhed, forming intricate patterns that seemed to defy the laws of physics. Flashes of what looked like lightning arced through impossibly dark gaseous clouds, each bolt easily the size of a planet. The electric tendrils danced and twisted, leaving ghostly afterimages in their wake. The scale of it was breathtaking, stretching farther than the eye could see.

Soren struggled to find words. "It's incredible," he managed at last.

"And terrifying," Keira added from her station, her voice barely above a whisper.

As Soren studied the phenomenon, a frown creased his brow. Something about this didn't quite add up.

"This isn't right," Lukas said, moving closer to the viewscreen before Soren could pose the question on the tip of his tongue. "The Eye should have only been detectable through specialized sensors and software filters."

"The energy patterns are far more intense than we anticipated," Dana added. "It's as if the Eye has evolved somehow."

"Evolved?" Soren asked, a note of concern in his voice. "Or destabilized?"

Before Dana could answer, Mark's voice cut through the conversation. "Captain, sensor sweep complete. No sign of enemy vessels in the immediate vicinity. However..." He paused to glance back at Soren, his expression dark. "I am detecting a debris field near the outer boundary of the Eye. It appears to be the remnants of a ship. Based on the pattern of the debris, I'd say they attempted to enter the Eye and...well, they didn't make it far."

Soren's jaw tightened as he contemplated the implications. Whatever forces were at work here, they were clearly even more dangerous than they had anticipated.

"Lukas," Soren said, turning to the scientist, "you mentioned specialized sensors. Do we have anything that can give us a clearer picture of what we're dealing with?"

Lukas nodded. "Yes, we developed some custom software filters based on our earlier observations. They should help us see beyond the visible spectrum. Tashi helped us add the filter option to the feed selection menu."

"Mark, put the filtered view up on the primary viewscreen," Soren ordered.

"Aye, Captain," he replied. A moment later, the image on the main viewscreen began to shift. The swirling vortex of energy took on new dimensions, revealing layers of complexity that had been invisible before. Ghostly dark energy patterns intertwined with streams of exotic particles, forming a cosmic tapestry of unimaginable intricacy.

"It's beautiful," Dana whispered, her scientific curiosity momentarily overriding her apprehension.

Soren had to agree, even as his tactical mind worked to assess the potential dangers. The Eye was like nothing he had ever seen, a perfect example of the universe's raw power and mystery and a stark reminder of how much they had yet to understand.

But they didn't have the luxury of standing in awe. They had a mission to complete. "Ethan, Lina, how are we looking with the upgraded systems? Are your preparations complete?"

Ethan answered first from the engineering station. "The new reactor is online and stable, Captain. We're generating more power than ever before. But I'll be honest, I'm not sure how it will hold up under the stresses we're likely to encounter in there."

"Understood," Soren replied. "And the shields, Lina?"

"As good as we can make them, sir," Lina answered from her station. "We've reinforced every emitter and power conduit. Theoretically, we should be able to withstand energy surges several orders of magnitude greater than anything we've been hit with already. But..."

"But we're in uncharted territory," Soren finished for her.

"Exactly, sir."

Soren nodded, appreciating their honesty. "And the sensors?"

"We've integrated the upgrades Lukas and Dana designed," Ethan reported. "As you can see with the filter, the increased sensitivity and processing gives us a much deeper look into that monster."

"Good work, both of you," Soren said. "Keep a close eye on your systems. We can't afford any unexpected instability, especially once we forge ahead."

"Aye, Captain," Ethan replied. "The systems are as robust as ever. They'll hold up just fine."

With the status updates complete, Soren turned his attention back to the Eye. "Sang," he ordered, "take us closer to the outer boundary. But not too close. We don't want to end up like that other ship."

"Aye, Captain," Sang replied, adding a small amount of thrust to get the Wraith back underway.

"Lukas, is the debris from any of your initial research vessels?"

"No, Captain," he replied. "It can't be. We never lost any ships. Only probes. Our ships didn't even try to get this close."

"FUP, then?" Jack said. "But why would they try to just fly right into that thing like it's some harmless nebula?"

"Maybe at the time they entered, it looked like a harmless nebula," Dana answered. "To answer your earlier question, Captain, I believe what we're seeing is a sign of destabilization. The storm preceding the apocalypse."

"Let's hope not," Soren replied. "Or we may already be too late."

The Wraith edged forward, the Eye growing larger in the viewscreen. As they drew closer, the true violence of the phenomenon became more apparent. What seemed like lightning bolts from a distance revealed themselves to be massive tendrils of energy, each capable of engulfing a small moon. These tendrils writhed and twisted, occasionally intertwining before violently repelling each other in spectacular bursts of light and color.

"I'm detecting intense gravitational distortions," Mark

reported, his voice tight with concentration. "And the energy readings are off the charts, sir."

Jack stepped closer to Soren, his voice low. "Soren, are you sure about this? The odds of surviving in there..." He trailed off, leaving the somber implication hanging in the air.

Soren met his old friend's gaze, understanding the concern he saw there. "I know, Jack. But we don't have a choice. If we don't stop the Convergence, there won't be anything left to survive for."

Jack nodded slowly, a rueful smile tugging at his lips. "You're right, of course. I just want to make sure we're as prepared as we can be. We'll only get one shot at this."

"Agreed," Soren said. He turned to Lukas. "How many upgraded probes do we have?"

"Four," Lukas replied. "With their extra shielding and upgraded comms, I thought they might survive three or four minutes in there. But that was before we arrived. No, I think we'll be lucky if they make it one minute before they're knocked offline."

"That's not ideal, but there's only one way we're going to know for ourselves what we're up against," Soren said, opening a channel to his aerospace boss. "Phoebe, prepare the first drone for launch."

"Aye, Captain. Standby."

Unlike some of the smaller drones, the ones they had prepared to send into the Eye were too large to rack and automate. They needed to be manually unloaded and placed in the hangar bay for launch. While Soren waited for the task to be completed, he turned back to the viewscreen, once more fixing his gaze on the swirling chaos of the Eye. They stood on the precipice of the unknown, about to plunge into forces beyond their comprehension. The drone was their first step into the abyss. What it discovered could mean the difference between salvation and annihilation.

"Well," he said. "Let's see what we can find out."

CHAPTER 4

"Drone ready for launch, Captain," Phoebe's voice came over the comm.

"Bastian, launch the drone," Soren ordered, his voice carrying across the bridge. "Phoebe, once the first drone is away, prepare the next."

"Aye, Captain," both crew members replied.

"Drone is away," Bastian added a few seconds later. Soren quickly found the probe on both the sensor grid and the viewscreen, tracking its progress as it accelerated toward the Eye, a mote of technology compared to the cosmic maelstrom before it. As the drone approached the outer boundary, a few of the tendrils of energy seemed to reach out, as if the Eye itself was alive and aware of their presence.

"Receiving drone telemetry, Captain," Mark reported, his voice taut with concentration. "Entering the outer layer in three... two... one..."

The bridge crew watched in tense silence as the drone pierced the swirling outermost gaseous barrier of the Eye. For a heart-stopping moment, nothing happened. Then Mark's terminal screen exploded with incoming data.

"Geez," Mark breathed, his professional demeanor slipping for a moment as he struggled to make sense of the incoming information.

Lukas had already moved forward to lean over his shoulder, eyeing the streaming data with intense focus and interest as it came in. "The gravitational distortions are much greater than we anticipated," he said. "And the energy readings are fluctuating wildly. I can't really tell from this data what's causing those energy spikes."

"Captain," Bastian said. "The drone's holding together, but just barely. The shielding is already stressed to its limits."

"How far in has it penetrated?" Soren asked, his eyes fixed on the viewscreen where he could still see the faint signal of the drone amidst the swirling chaos.

"Approximately five thousand kilometers," Bastian replied.

"Distance measurements may be unreliable," Lukas warned. "The space inside the Eye doesn't follow expected rules."

Dana stared at the viewscreen beside Soren. "Do you see those orange ribbons?" she said. "Those are visual representations of anomalous temporal readings."

"What does it mean?" Soren asked.

"It's as if the very fabric of spacetime is being warped and twisted, but not in any kind of logical or identifiable pattern."

As they watched, the drone's signal began to falter, its telemetry becoming erratic. "We're losing it," Mark announced, a note of frustration in his voice. "The interference is too strong."

A moment later, the data stopped flowing from the probe. It vanished from the sensor grid, and Bastian's terminal went dark. "She's gone, Captain," the drone pilot said.

Soren's jaw tightened. They needed more information, but he wouldn't risk sending in another drone too quickly. "Lukas, Dana, what can you tell me based on what we've seen so far?"

The two scientists exchanged a glance. It was Dana who spoke first. "It's everything we expected. Temporal distortions. Energy spikes. Gravitational irregularities."

"It's also incredibly dangerous," Lukas added. "More dangerous than I anticipated, due to the increasing instability. The forces at work in there could tear this ship apart in seconds if we're not careful, even with the added protection."

"So we wasted our time adding it?" Jack asked.

"Not necessarily. It would likely take a direct hit from one of those lightning tendrils to punch through the shields in a single strike. But it's not impossible."

Soren nodded, absorbing the information. "Can we navigate it? Find a path to the center?"

Lukas hesitated, his fingers tapping nervously on the console. "Theoretically, yes. But it won't be easy. The currents of energy seem to shift and change unpredictably. We'd need to be constantly adjusting our course, reacting to the fluctuations in real time."

"Can you model it?"

"Given enough time. But Captain, I'm not sure we have enough time."

"Neither am I," Soren agreed, weighing their options. They couldn't turn back, not when they were so close. But charging in blindly would be suicide. They needed a plan to navigate the chaos without being torn apart.

"At the very least, we need to come up with a way to get one of our drones to the center of the Eye," Lukas added. "We can't even begin to counter something we've never measured."

"Except we don't know where the center is," Jack said.

"How far would we need to penetrate? Would it be possible for us to get that far, never mind a probe?"

"All good questions," Lukas said. "I can't answer any of them without more data."

"We need a means to model a path, regardless of the time it may take," Soren said. "The goal is to get to the center of the Eye as soon as possible, and we have three drones left. That's our problem. Now, someone come up with a solution."

The bridge fell silent, the entire crew suddenly plunged into hurried thought.

"What if we used the remaining drones to map out a path?" Jack suggested after a few minutes. "Send them in at different vectors, use their data to plot a course through the least turbulent areas."

Dana's eyes lit up at the suggestion. "That could work. We could program them to focus on specific types of data, give us a more comprehensive picture of what we're dealing with."

"The problem is that we only have three," Lukas said. "We can only get so much information from them."

"We have more than three probes," Soren replied. "The others might not be upgraded and shielded, but they can map the outermost portion of the Eye. That will allow us to push our limited supply of protected drones deeper in."

"Good thinking," Jack agreed. "We can use the basic drones to help us position the Wraith further into the Eye without risk of damage."

"Those drones will need some modifications," Lukas said. "And we might only get twenty seconds out of each one we launch. But I think it could work."

Soren nodded, a plan beginning to take shape. "Lukas, Dana, work with Phoebe to recalibrate the basic probes so they can send back the same types of data as the larger drones. Mark, coordinate with them to set up a real-time mapping system. We need to be able to plot the safest route ahead as we go. Sang, once we have our initial course plotted, I want you ready to take us in. This is going to require the best flying of your life. You'll need to do more than thread the needle. You'll have to drive a bus through it."

Sang nodded, focused and determined. "I'm ready, Captain. I'll get it done. Whatever it takes."

"We'll need to update the software on the other probes," Lukas said. "We can handle that directly from the hangar, but we'll have to manually install the package on each drone. It'll go faster with help."

"Then you'll have it. Wilf, Tashi, report to Lukas and Dana in the hangar immediately," he ordered over the comms. "They'll explain when you get there."

"Aye, Captain, on our way," Wilf replied.

"How long will it take the four of you to do the installs?" he asked Lukas.

"We have close to fifty drones. Probably about five minutes each."

"I'll go with them," Jack said. "We can have the updates done in less than an hour."

"Somehow, that still feels like an eternity," Soren said. "Get it done."

Jack, Lukas and Dana hurried from the bridge. Soren finally sat at the command station, watching the Eye with continuing, cautious awe.

"Sang, be ready to maneuver," he said. "Just in case that thing decides to get frisky."

"You talk about it like it's a living entity, sir," Sang replied.

"Because I feel as though it's acting like one," he said. He kept his attention on the anomaly and spoke to it as if it could understand him. Bargaining with it, as he had his children plenty of times before. "Now, be a good little Eye and sit still for another hour or two, and I'll buy you an ice cream."

Keira overheard him and laughed softly. "I hope it likes ice cream, Captain."

There was no mirth in Soren's response. Only concern. "Me, too."

CHAPTER 5

Soren remained at the command station, his eyes never leaving the swirling chaos of the Eye displayed on the main viewscreen. There was nothing else he could do right now except wait. Forty minutes had passed since Jack, Dana, and Lukas had left the bridge to reprogram the drones in the hangar bay.

Their time to complete the task was almost up.

Soren knew they were almost done when Jack returned to the bridge, taking his usual position in the seat beside the command station.

"The last set of drones are running firmware updates now," Jack announced. "How's the Eye?"

"Apparently, it likes ice cream," Keira commented, drawing a confused look.

Before Soren could explain, Dana's voice came through his personal comms. "Captain, we've finished updating the drones. They're all ready to go."

Soren straightened in his seat. "Good work. You and Lukas get back up here to the bridge. We're going to need your expertise."

"On our way," Dana replied.

A few minutes later, they stepped onto the bridge, both looking slightly disheveled but with a glimmer of hope in their eyes.

"Let's see what these updated drones can do," Soren said as they moved to stand nearby. "Bastian, prepare to launch the first one."

"Aye, Captain," Bastian replied. "Drone is prepped and ready for launch."

Soren took a deep breath. "Launch."

The viewscreen showed the small probe shooting out from the Wraith, barely visible against the vast, roiling expanse of the Eye. It streaked towards the anomaly's outer boundary, its sensors already transmitting data back to the ship.

"Drone has entered the Eye," Mark announced. "Receiving telemetry...wait, energy spike detected!"

Before anyone could react, a tendril of crackling energy lashed out from the Eye, engulfing the drone. For a brief moment, the probe's tiny shape was visible within the energy, its form distorting and twisting. Then, in a flash, it was gone.

"Drone destroyed," Bastian reported, his voice flat.

"How far did it get?" Soren asked.

"Not very," Mark replied. "It was only in motion for nine seconds."

A heavy silence fell over the bridge, the glimmer of hope fading fast. Soren turned to Lukas and Dana. "Well?"

Lukas was already poring over the data over Mark's shoulder. "We got something, at least. The drone managed to transmit valuable information before it was destroyed. But..." He trailed off, already lost in his next thought.

"But what?" Soren prompted.

"We need more data," Dana finished for him. "From different angles, different entry vectors. One sample isn't enough to establish any kind of pattern."

Soren nodded, understanding the implications. "Sang, reposition us. We'll launch the next drone from a different approach vector."

"Aye, Captain," Sang replied.

The Wraith glided through space, arcing around to a new position relative to the Eye. Once they were in place, Soren gave the order to launch again.

The process repeated itself four more times. Each drone lasted slightly longer than the last, but none survived more than twenty seconds within the Eye. With each launch, Lukas and Dana grew more animated, excitedly discussing the incoming data in hushed tones.

After the fifth drone was destroyed, Lukas turned to Soren. "Captain, we need to process this data more thoroughly. There's too much information to analyze effectively here on the bridge."

At his Operations Station, Mark nodded in agreement. "I'm sending all the collected data to your lab now, Doctor Mitchell."

Soren frowned, acutely aware of the passage of time. "How long will this analysis take?"

Lukas hesitated, glancing at Dana. "It's hard to say. We're dealing with phenomena that defies our current understanding of physics. It could take hours, maybe even days to—"

"We may not have days," Soren interrupted, his voice sharp.

Dana stepped toward him, her voice soothing. "Captain, I know time is critical. But if we're going to do this, we need to do it right. Rushing in without a proper understanding could be disastrous."

Soren met his daughter's gaze, seeing the determination there. He knew she was right, but sitting patiently by had never been his strong suit. After a long moment, he nodded. "Understood. Go. But work as quickly as you can."

Lukas and Dana hurried off the bridge. Soren, growing restless, got to his feet and began pacing the bridge. The rest of the bridge crew relaxed into their seats as best they could, and the waiting game resumed.

The minutes stretched into an hour, each passing minute like a stab in Soren's gut. His eyes barely ever left the Eye, searching it for signs it was about to complete its apocalyptic mission and set the collapse of two dimensions into motion.

Just as Soren was about to contact the lab for an update, Lukas's voice came over the comms. "Captain, I think we've got something."

Soren's heart leaped. "What have you found?"

"We've identified the beginnings of a potential pattern," Lukas replied, his voice tight with excitement. "I've put together a framework for a guidance algorithm. It's not perfect, but I think it might help us navigate the Eye."

"How sure are you?" Soren asked, not ready to yet again get his hopes up.

There was a pause before Lukas answered. "Honestly? Not very. The only way to truly test it is to try it out."

"Send the algorithm to Bastian. We'll load it into the next drone and see what happens."

"Aye, Captain. Transmitting now."

A few minutes later, Bastian looked up from his console. "Algorithm received and loaded, sir. The drone is ready for launch."

Soren took a deep breath. "Launch."

The drone shot out from the Wraith, streaking towards the Eye. As it penetrated the outer boundary, Soren squinted intently at the viewscreen, his fingers digging into his chair's armrest.

The drone weaved its way through the swirling chaos

and vanished from sight, turning Soren to Bastian's station and a low-resolution first-person view from the probe's camera feed as it ran through the visual filter. Bastian's hands remained off the controls, allowing Lukas' algorithm to do the flying. He watched intensely as the drone dodged tendrils of energy and pockets of intense gravitation. It penetrated deeper into the Eye than any of its predecessors, sending back a steady stream of data.

"It's working," Mark breathed, his voice filled with awe.

But just as hope began to blossom on the bridge, a massive tendril of energy lashed out, the flash bright on Bastian's feed, catching the drone in its crackling embrace. The probe's signal winked out.

"Drone destroyed," Bastian reported. "But it lasted nearly two minutes and penetrated over fifty thousand kilometers into the Eye."

A ripple of excitement passed through the bridge crew. Soren allowed himself a small smile. "It's a start. Lukas, Dana, did you get all that?"

"We did," Dana replied. "The algorithm worked better than we hoped. We're refining it now based on the new data."

"Good," Soren said. "Keep at it. We'll launch another drone when you're ready."

The process repeated itself over the next few hours. With each launch, the algorithm improved, allowing the drones to penetrate deeper into the Eye and survive longer. But none of them made it to the center, and soon they had exhausted their supply of basic drones.

"Time to use the upgraded drones," Soren announced. "Bastian, load up the first one with the latest version of the algorithm."

"Aye, Captain," Bastian replied.

Phoebe moved the larger drone into position in the hangar. Soon after, the upgraded drone launched, its enhanced shielding glowing faintly as it entered the Eye. It pushed past the point where the basic drones had failed, delving deeper into the swirling chaos.

But then, without warning, it vanished from their sensors.

"What happened?" Soren demanded.

Mark shook his head, bewildered. "I'm not sure, sir. It just... disappeared. No energy spike, no sign of destruction. It's as if it ceased to exist."

Lukas's voice came over the comms, tight with frustration. "The Eye is still unpredictable by nature. No algorithm can account for everything."

Soren's jaw clenched. They had reduced the danger but not eliminated it. And now they were down to their last two upgraded drones.

What he wanted more than anything was for one of them to reach the center of the Eye and collect data on what he hoped would be the source and cause of the Convergence.

"That last drone showed a shift in some of the markers we're tracking," Dana said. "I think we're close to the center."

"We need to try again," Soren said.

The penultimate drone streaked into the Eye, pushing even deeper than its predecessor. It transmitted data for several minutes before its signal abruptly cut out. Soren waited, nerves fraying silently, for Lukas and Dana's next report.

"Captain," Lukas finally said. "Based on the changes in telemetry, I think we reached the center of the Eye, but we need more data to confirm."

"We only have one probe left," Soren replied.

"Then let's make it count."

Soren exhaled sharply. "Bastian, launch the final drone."

"Aye, Captain. Drone away."

The final drone launched, plunging into the depths of the Eye. It surpassed all previous records, penetrating further than they had dared hope. But then, just like the others, its signal vanished.

Again, Soren had to wait for Lukas' feedback, his entire body tense with anticipation.

"Confirmed, Captain," Lukas said. "We believe the probes reached the center of the Eye."

A cheer went up from the bridge crew, though it faded quickly when Soren didn't join in.

"Can you determine the source?" he asked.

Lukas was slow to respond. "No, Captain. The data cut off abruptly. What we have suggests a sudden absence of any of the anomalies and disturbances we encountered on the way in, but that's the extent of it."

"So there could be anything in there," Soren said.

"Yes, Captain. Without any more drones, there's only one way to find out what's behind the chaotic curtain."

"And what if that turns out to be some kind of singularity?" Jack asked. "Or a previously undiscovered type of star? We could be flying straight to our doom."

"We can't rule it out," Lukas admitted. "But I'm still convinced that something unnatural is causing the Convergence. The patterns we've observed, the way the energy flows...it's chaotic, but it's also organized enough that we created a system to navigate it within a few hours. There has to be something there. Something we can affect."

"I agree," Dana added. "Whatever's at the center of the Eye, it's the key to stopping the Convergence. I'm sure of it."

Soren leaned back in his chair, the weight of command settling heavily on his shoulders. They had come so far and risked so much. But now, faced with the terrifying unknown of the Eye's depths, doubt crept in.

What if they were wrong? What if the Convergence

couldn't be stopped? What if sending the Wraith into the Eye meant certain death for his crew? For his children?

But even as these thoughts swirled through his mind, Soren knew only one choice existed. They couldn't turn back, not when they were so close. Not with so much hanging in the balance.

He straightened in his seat, his voice steady as he gave the order.

"Sang, take us in."

CHAPTER 6

A palpable tension settled over the bridge. Sang's hands hovered over the helm controls, her face stiff in concentration as she prepared to guide the Wraith into the cosmic hurricane.

"Lukas," Soren called out, his voice steady despite the gravity of the moment, "is the algorithm ready?"

"Yes, Captain," Lukas replied from the science lab. "I've uploaded it to the helm as a guidance package. It will provide real time visual cues for navigation, but Sang will need to make her own adjustments as we go. Our experience with the drones suggested the Eye is too unpredictable for full automation."

Soren nodded, his eyes never leaving the viewscreen as he straightened in his seat. "I agree with your assessment, Doctor. Sang, we're ready when you are. Take us in."

"Aye, Captain," Sang responded.

The Wraith slowly edged forward, main thrusters at single digit power on the approach to the outer boundary of the Eye. As they crossed the threshold, the ship shuddered slightly, the shields flaring a brilliant blue as they encountered the first waves of energy.

"Keira?" Soren asked, concerned about the immediate effect.

"Shields holding at ninety-eight percent," Keira reported from her station. "Minor fluctuations, but nothing we can't handle."

"These energy flares are expected, Captain," Dana said. "It's those larger spikes that we need to worry about."

Sang's right hand lightly gripped the control stick, her left on the control surface, handling thrust and other helm operations. The Wraith accelerated slowly, sinking carefully into the Eye. Lukas' algorithm provided a constantly updating path on her display, a series of green markers indicating the safest route through the chaos. But even as she followed its guidance, her eyes darted across the viewscreen, watching for the telltale sparks of light that preceded the massive energy tendrils.

When Sang spotted one, she reacted instantly, nudging the Wraith to port. A massive tendril of crackling energy lashed out, missing the ship by mere meters. The bridge crew collectively held their breath, only exhaling when the danger had passed.

"Shields at ninety-five percent," Keira updated.

"Nice flying, Sang," Jack commented, his knuckles white as he gripped the arms of his chair.

As they pressed deeper into the Eye, the challenges only intensified. The Wraith weaved through a maze of swirling energy patterns, each more complex and unpredictable than the last. Sang's reactions were put to the test as she constantly adjusted their course, sometimes deviating from the algorithm's suggested path based on her own instincts and observations. More than once, a tendril of energy speared right through the center of the proposed route in what would have been a direct hit, if not for her veering off course.

"Captain," Lukas said over the comms, "Sensor data

suggests an increasingly dense field of temporal distortions ahead."

Looking at the sensors, Soren could see them in the filtered view of the primary viewscreen, roiling and crashing like waves in a storm smashing against a rocky shore.

Soren frowned, leaning forward in his chair. "How do we avoid that?"

"We don't," Lukas replied, shaking his head. "They're too widespread. We'll have to pass through them."

"Understood," Soren said. "Should we expect turbulence?"

"Not in the way you might think. No physical shaking, but dizziness, nausea, and confusion are possible."

Soren's jaw clenched at the idea. If Sang became disoriented… "Bastian, be prepared to take over the helm if needed."

"Aye, Captain," Bastian replied, switching his station over to backup helm control.

The order had barely left his lips when the Wraith entered the first temporal distortion. A strange sensation washed over the bridge crew, as if reality itself stretched and contracted around them. Soren felt a moment of disorientation that quickly passed.

"What was that?" Jack asked, his voice sounding oddly distorted, even to his own ears.

"Temporal dilation," Lukas explained, his words seeming to come out faster than normal. "From our perspective, time hasn't changed. But to an outside observer, we would have appeared to speed up."

"By how much?" Soren asked.

Before Lukas could answer, they plunged into another distortion. Soren's stomach lurched, and he turned his attention from the sensor projection to Sang, watching her closely for signs of the distortion's effects on her. She appeared wholly unbothered, though Soren had known her long enough to know she could fight through all but the worst distractions.

As they continued their journey through the Eye, the Wraith encountered more pockets of dilation and distortion. The constant shifts made it impossible to gauge how long they had been traveling accurately. What felt like hours might have been mere minutes, or vice versa. The only constant was Sang's impeccably unwavering focus as she guided them through the chaos. Her reactions became almost precognitive as she anticipated and avoided dangers before they fully manifested.

Despite their best efforts, the Wraith couldn't escape every threat. Occasionally, a tendril of energy would graze the shields, causing the ship to shudder and alarms to blare across the bridge.

"Shields down to seventy-percent," Keira reported after the third glancing blow. "Still holding, but we can't absorb this punishment forever."

"Understood," Soren replied. "Sang, how much further?"

"Hard to say, Captain," she replied, her voice strained with concentration. "The algorithm suggests we're nearing the center, but with these temporal distortions..."

Her voice trailed off as another wave of temporal dilation washed over them. When it passed, Soren realized that the chaotic energy patterns around them had begun to change. The violent swirls and lashes of energy were becoming less frequent, the space between them growing calmer.

"Captain," Mark called out, excitement creeping into his voice, "I think we're approaching the eye of the Eye."

As if in response to his words, the Wraith suddenly burst through a final curtain of swirling energy. The viewscreen cleared, revealing a sight that left the entire bridge crew speechless.

Not because they had reached the center of the Eye. But because they found...nothing, instead of the source of cosmic destruction they had expected to find. The center of the Eye was a model of calm, almost eerily peaceful compared to the chaos surrounding it. No energy distortions, no gravitational anomalies—just an expanse of quiet, empty space.

"This can't be right," Lukas complained. "How can there be nothing here? No energy source, no unusual particles, nothing at all that could explain the Convergence."

"Maybe our instruments aren't sensitive enough?" Jack suggested. "Or perhaps the source is cloaked somehow?"

Soren leaned back in his chair, doing his best to process this unexpected development. They had come so far, risked so much, only to find emptiness.

"Sang, hold position here," he ordered. "Lukas, Dana, I want you to run every scan, every test you can think of. If there's anything to find here, I want it found."

"Aye, Captain," they responded in unison, already diving into their work.

Hours passed as the scientists pored over the data, running increasingly complex scans and analyses. The rest of the crew remained at their stations, the tension slowly giving way to confusion and disappointment.

Finally, Lukas reported from the lab, his voice tight with his confusion and frustration. "Captain, I don't understand it. By all accounts, there's nothing here that could be causing the Convergence. We've run every scan I can think of. Hunted for every particle we have sensors to search for. There's nothing here. Literally, nothing." He sounded ready to slam his head against his desk.

Soren stood, pacing the length of the bridge as he considered their options. They had come too far to simply give up, but without a clear target or objective, what were they supposed to do?

"Captain," Keira said. "What if the source of the Eye is cloaked, using the same nano-crystals as Wraith? We know this FUP has them. They had them on the Basilisk. Our sensors wouldn't be able to detect them."

Soren stopped pacing to point at her. "Excellent thought. Begin charging the cannon. Sang, bring us to the back edge of the center so we can cover as much of the empty space as possible. Ethan, we need the vortex cannon reconfigured to spread mode. If there is something in here with us, that'll find it."

"Aye, Captain," Ethan replied. "Give us five minutes."

Soren resumed pacing while Sang moved the Wraith into position. She had just brought the ship to a full stop when Tashi's voice came over the comms. "Vortex cannon is reconfigured, Captain."

He paused again, turning to face the viewscreen. "Keira, fire."

The cannon released its energy, rippling spacetime in a cone away from the bow. Mark switched the sensor filters to match, and they waited.

"No hits," Mark announced, the sensors remaining clear as the cannon's blast reached across to the far side of the Eye.

"What the hell?" Jack muttered, his eyes locked on the viewscreen instead of the projection.

Soren's head whipped toward the viewscreen just in time to see what Jack saw. The inner edge of the chaotic space at the center of the Eye appeared to be on fire, the interaction with the vortex cannon creating an unexpected reaction.

"I hope we didn't just finish destabilizing this thing," Keira said.

Soren stared stone-faced at the massive reaction, which,

through the filters, looked like a humongous fireball. He waited tensely as it reached its climax and diminished once more, returning the view to its prior state.

"I suggest not doing that again," Jack said.

"Lukas, did you get that?" Soren asked.

"Yes, Captain," he replied. "My initial guess is that your ship's weapon shares similar properties to the composition of the Eye. It triggered a reaction, but didn't have enough overall energy to further destabilize the phenomenon."

Soren breathed a sigh of relief. "Mark, anything?"

"Still nothing, Captain," he replied. "If there's something cloaked in here, it's maneuvering to stick tight to us to avoid detection."

"Possible, but unlikely," Soren said. "But just in case, Keira, fire the railguns in a sweeping defensive pattern. I assume the flechettes won't react with the Eye."

"Correct, Captain." Lukas confirmed.

"Pattern engaged, Captain," Keira reported. The railguns on all sides of the ship fired quick bursts, covering a wide swath of space immediately surrounding Wraith.

"Still nothing," Mark reported.

Soren exhaled in frustration. After a long moment, he turned to face his crew. "We've done all we can here," he said, his voice heavy with the weight of the decision. "Whatever is causing the Convergence, it's not something we can detect or interact with directly."

"So what now?" Jack asked, voicing the question on everyone's mind.

"We need to make contact with this dimension's FUP," he answered. "We need to try to negotiate. To see if we can get them to work with us on a mutually beneficial approach to dealing with the aftermath, instead of letting them kill everyone in our galaxy."

A murmur of surprise rippled through the bridge crew.

"Are you sure that's wise?" Jack asked, his voice low. "After everything that's happened...they don't seem like—"

"The only other choice is all-out war," Soren said, the words bitter in his mouth. "And from what I've seen of the enemy, it's a fight we can't win." He turned to Sang. "Take us out of here. Same route we came in, if you can manage it."

"Aye, Captain," Sang replied, immediately setting to work on bringing the Wraith about.

Soon enough, they were again facing the swirling chaos surrounding their peaceful emptiness. As they re-entered the maelstrom, the ship shuddered, the already weakened shields straining under the renewed assault.

"Shields down to fifty percent," Keira reported, her voice tight.

"Maintain course," Soren ordered, gripping the arms of his chair as the ship bucked and weaved through the energy storms.

Their journey out of the Eye was no less harrowing than their entry. Temporal distortions threw off their perception of time while massive tendrils of energy lashed out at them from all sides. Sang's piloting skills were again tested as she navigated the chaos, relying as much on instinct as on the algorithm's guidance.

By the time they finally burst free of the Eye's outer boundary, the Wraith's heavily upgraded and bolstered shields were down to a mere twenty percent, and the entire crew was exhausted from the constant tension and disorientation.

But as relief began to wash over them, Mark's voice cut through the moment of respite. "Captain! Multiple contacts detected!"

CHAPTER 7

Soren's attention snapped to the primary viewscreen. His eyes widened as he took in the sight before them. Dead ahead loomed a massive ship, its sleek lines reminiscent of a Komodo-class vessel, but noticeably larger and laden with what appeared to be additional railgun batteries. It was an impressive and formidable sight, but what truly caught Soren's attention was the fleet surrounding it. Nearly three dozen ships of varying sizes were positioned near the Eye, creating a protective net around the cosmic anomaly.

"Captain, should we cloak?" Keira asked.

Soren held up a hand, his eyes never leaving the screen. "Not yet, but be ready. Power up the vortex cannon."

"Captain," Ethan's concerned voice came over the comms, "we're still in the wrong configuration. The cannon's set for wide dispersal, not focused fire. At this distance, the best we can hope for is to disrupt them "

"I know," Soren replied, his jaw clenching. "There's not much we can do about it now. Let's hope these ships are friendly, whoever they are."

The bridge fell silent, the tension palpable as they waited to see how the situation would unfold. Soren's mind reeled as he tried to understand what they were seeing. How had such a sizable fleet assembled here without their knowledge? And more importantly, why?

Samira's voice broke the silence. "Captain, we're being hailed."

Soren took a deep breath, straightening in his seat. "Put it through."

"Unidentified vessel," the man began, his voice carrying the weight of authority, "you are inside of restricted space. Identify yourself immediately and explain how you came to be here."

As Soren opened his mouth to respond, Jack leaned in close, his voice low and urgent. "Soren, look at their hull markings. That's a Navy-style identifier, but it doesn't start with FUPN. It's SFN. What does SF stand for?"

Soren's eyes narrowed as he found the identification markings near the opposite ship's bow, confirming Jack's observation. But what did it mean?

He didn't have time to consider the question. The other captain awaited his answer.

"This is Captain Soren Strickland of the Federation of United Planets starship Wraith," he began, his voice steady despite the confusion roiling within him. "We entered the Eye from this exact position..." He trailed off, sudden realization hitting him like a physical blow. The temporal distortions they had experienced inside the Eye—how long had they truly been in there? Minutes? Hours? Or... His mind reeled at the possibility. What if hundreds of years had passed outside the Eye while they navigated its chaotic interior?

Before he could voice these concerns, Mark's urgent whisper cut through his thoughts. "Captain, they've locked weapons on us, and the rest of the fleet is moving in our direction."

Soren's mind immediately set to work planning their

escape. Every outside indication suggested these new ships might not be friendly after all. Still, he didn't want to be too hasty. Not when he was so unsure of what was really going on.

The man on the screen narrowed his eyes, studying Soren with increased scrutiny. "You're with the Federation, then?" he asked. "In that case, I'm sure you know what kind of trouble you're in right now. So don't waste my time playing games. What is your real name? And why and how did you navigate the disturbance?"

Soren's confusion deepened. "What do you mean, my real name? I told you, I'm Captain Soren Strickland." He stopped abruptly, the words dying in his throat. Something was definitely wrong here.

The other captain's voice hardened. "Stand down and prepare to be boarded. This is your only warning."

Whatever was happening, allowing themselves to be boarded was not an option. They needed answers, yes, but not at the cost of their freedom—or worse.

He reached forward, using the command surface to disconnect the comms. The other captains would react to the abrupt end of the conversation.

They needed to react faster.

"Keira," he snapped urgently. "Fire."

Keira responded by first tapping the fire control and then acknowledging the order. "Cannon fired."

The vortex cannon discharged, its energy rippling through space in a wide cone. Disruptions in spacetime crashed into the enemy ship, bypassing its shields and impacting the hull. The oversized Komodo shook like a sailing ship in a storm as the wave passed, the impact enough to buy them precious seconds.

"Sang, get us out of here," Soren commanded. "Keira, prepare to cloak."

The Wraith surged forward, Sang shifting its vector to

put them on a new course. They couldn't afford to cloak just yet. Not with the enemy ship's first volley incoming.

Railgun rounds peppered their shields, digging in on their starboard side as missiles spewed from launchers, following the target lock.

"Evasive maneuvers!" Soren cried as Sang tried to avoid the oncoming projectiles, hoping to limit direct impacts on the shields. The combined firepower pounded the Wraith, leaving the ship shuddering.

"Shields at ten percent," Keira reported.

Soren eyed the sensor projection. The other enemy ships were closing faster now and would be in firing range within seconds. "Activate the cloak. Sang, get us clear."

It was risky with the Komodo's guns rotating to track them, but they had no choice.

"Engaged," Keira replied.

At the same time, Sang fired full retro-thrusters and port vectoring thrusters, pushing the ship in a hard right turn that would minimize its profile relative to the Komodo. Railgun rounds split space around them, the enemy ship's firing solution losing them as they vanished from sensors.

They continued rotating, and at first, Soren thought Sang might plan to guide them back into the Eye. He opened his mouth to be more specific about direction, closing it again when she angled the ship toward the bulk of the incoming fleet.

They were cloaked. Invisible. She was going to fly right through them in a maneuver they were unlikely to expect.

Sang pushed the mains to max power, which pressed Soren back in his seat. The Wraith lunged ahead, a second enemy warship, similar to a Valkyrie, directly in front of them.

"Sang?" Soren questioned as they quickly approached the incoming ships. Behind them, the Komodo had stopped firing, likely trying to hunt them with sensors.

"Trust me, Captain," Sang replied, eyes narrowed in concentration, hand steady on the control stick.

The Valkyrie loomed ever larger ahead of them, slowing now that it had lost them on its sensors. Sang adjusted their vector at what seemed like the last second, the warship shifting from dead ahead to overhead while they streaked beneath as if they were a starfighter, not a battleship.

They cleared the converging enemy, continuing out toward open space. As they put distance between themselves and the mysterious fleet, the questions that had been pushed aside in the heat of the moment came flooding back.

"What the hell is going on?" Jack voiced the thought on everyone's mind. "Those ships...that captain...what did he mean when he accused you of playing games?"

Soren shook his head. "I don't know. I'm concerned about those temporal distortions we experienced." He activated his comms. "Lukas, is it possible that far more time has passed outside the Eye than we experienced within it? Could years, even centuries have gone by?"

Lukas' reply came slowly, and when it did, his voice was tinged with uncertainty. "I don't think we can rule it out, Captain. The nature of the temporal anomalies suggests the possibility. But I'm not sure that fully explains what we just witnessed. We need time to analyze the data to come to a solid conclusion. It's dangerous to make assumptions right now."

"Agreed. Sang, get us well clear of the Eye and that fleet. Bobby, prepare for a jump to the Wolf system. Once we're at a safe distance, execute the fold."

"Aye, Captain," both officers responded in unison.

As the Wraith continued to distance itself from the mysterious fleet, Soren leaned back in his chair, his mind churning with possibilities. The encounter had left them with far more questions than answers. Who were these people claiming to be the Federation, yet not recognizing one of its decorated captains? What did the "SF" in their ship designations stand for? And perhaps most pressingly, what had happened to the universe they knew while inside the Eye?

The minutes ticked by in tense silence as they maneuvered away.

"Captain," Mark's voice broke through the quiet. "We may have a problem. The ships we encountered are on the move. They're headed in our direction."

"What?" Soren replied, sitting up straighter in his seat. "Can they see us?"

"It's unclear, Captain. It may be a coincidence."

"Possible, but unlikely," Soren replied. Their FUP could see through the cloak thanks to a specific transmitter frequency. Could these other ships do the same? He wanted to have Sang change course, but from the distances and velocities, he knew they wouldn't have time to stop and fold when he did. They would have to tackle this new possibility another time. "Sang, full stop."

"Aye, Captain."

"Bobby, prepare to fold."

"Ready on your order, Captain."

Once they left the Eye, there would be no going back—at least not immediately. But they needed answers, and Soren's instincts told him the Wolf system might be the safest place to regroup and begin gathering them.

"Execute the fold," he ordered.

The Wraith vanished into folded space. They entered the Eye to solve a mystery and stop the Convergence. They had exited with the Convergence still a threat and, unexpectedly, an even greater mystery to solve.

One that threatened to unravel everything they thought they knew about their mission, their identities, and the very fabric of reality itself.

CHAPTER 8

Soren sat back in his seat, silently processing all that had just occurred. The rest of the bridge remained equally quiet and tense, every member of the crew confused and alarmed by the experience.

The good news was that they had entered and left the Eye intact, and that they had encountered a hostile force and escaped alive. He wasn't about to take that for granted.

The bad news…he didn't have a full grip on that just yet, but he was certain there would be bad news to discover, and it was better to get it over with as soon as possible.

"Samira, open ship-wide comms," he ordered.

"Comms open, sir," she replied.

Soren leaned forward. "Lukas, Dana, Tashi, Wilf, report to the primary conference room immediately. Vic, to the bridge. I repeat. Lukas, Dana, Tashi, and Wilf to the conference room. Vic to the bridge." He nodded to Samira to close the comms. "Ethan, Lina, Jack, you're with me," he said. "Keira, you have the conn until Vic arrives."

"Aye, Captain," she replied, getting up from her tactical

station so she could take Soren's place. "I have the conn." The other officers joined him as he headed for the exit.

"Well, this is a wrinkle, isn't it?" Jack asked as the group made its way down the corridor to the conference room.

"That's an understatement," Ethan replied. "Is it just me, or have things somehow found a way to go from bad to worse?"

"I hope it's just you," Soren said as they arrived at the conference room, taking their seats to wait for the others.

Wilf was first to arrive, an alarmed look on his face. "What's going on, Captain?" he asked, fingers twitching nervously. "It felt like we were taking fire."

"We were," Soren confirmed.

"If you don't mind me asking, sir, from who?"

"That's what we're trying to figure out."

Tashi arrived next, a similarly confused expression on his face, though he remained silent as he took his seat. Lukas and Dana entered last, having come from further astern. Both wore concerned looks.

"Thank you all for coming so quickly," he said. "I called you here because we've encountered a situation none of us anticipated, and we need to assess our position and determine our next steps." He turned to Ethan first. "Let's start with the ship. What's our status after traversing the Eye?"

"We could have done without the missiles pounding our shields," Ethan replied. "But thanks to the upgrades, they held during both trips through the Eye, and remained stable throughout the confrontation with...well, whoever that was."

"We'll get to that," Soren said.

"Right. We didn't take any direct hits, which is good. The fold time will allow us to make repairs and get our systems back to full strength, which is also good. And the new reactor held up like a champ, as did the upgraded shielding. In that respect, it's wins all around, sir."

"I'm eager for any wins we can get right now," Soren agreed. "At least we know the Wraith is hardened and ready for whatever comes next. There's another related matter we need to address. There's a possibility that the forces we encountered outside the Eye were able to lock onto us despite our cloak. It appeared to take them a minute to get a bead, but they did appear to capture our position."

"That's not good," Wilf said.

"No," Soren agreed. "It's possible these forces found a way to defeat the nano-crystals on the hull. It's also possible they're aware of the transmitter the FUP used to track us down and surround us earlier. We can't do anything about the first, but I'm hoping we can eliminate the second possibility. Lina, I want you and Tashi to look into it."

"We'll get right on it, Captain," she replied. "Tashi and I can begin a thorough sweep of the ship's systems immediately."

"Make it a priority," Soren replied. "Keep me updated on your progress."

With the immediate concerns about the ship addressed, Soren turned his attention to the larger mystery at hand. "Now, let's discuss what just happened out there. I'm concerned that the temporal distortions we experienced inside the Eye may have carried us much further into the future than we realized. It also occurred to me that the Convergence may have already happened. Thoughts?"

Lukas spoke up first, which didn't surprise Soren. "I don't think that's the case, Captain. If the Convergence had occurred, the Eye should be gone. It's the focal point of the event, after all."

"Should be," Soren emphasized. "But can we be sure?"

Lukas hesitated. "No, we can't be absolutely certain. The nature of the Convergence is still largely theoretical.

But based on our current understanding, it seems highly unlikely. Congruent to that, the size and position of the Eye suggests that we didn't lose more than a few hours to a few days to the temporal flux. This is based on preliminary data, mind you, so I can't prove anything one way or another, at least not yet."

"Understood," Soren replied. "I hope you're right. Does anyone else have a theory on what may have happened?"

Dana cleared her throat. "I do," she said. "I don't think we can rule out that we've entered a third dimension by passing through the Eye. One distinct from the other two."

A murmur of surprise rippled through the room. Jack leaned forward. "A third dimension? How is that possible?"

"Like Lukas, I can't prove it yet," Dana admitted. "And I'm not sure how possible it even is, but I think we need to consider the prospect."

"It would explain the different ship configurations we saw, and the SF identifier," Soren said. "But if there are three dimensions, could they all be caught in the Convergence? Could there be more? An infinite number, like the branching timelines you mentioned at dinner?"

"I hope there aren't that many," Dana replied. "We know so little, but we need to consider all possibilities at this point."

The group fell silent, trying to absorb the idea of infinite universes collapsing in on each other. To Soren, it was an impossible task.

"Right now, we need to deal with what we have in front of us, not on speculation. Whether there are three dimensions or three billion, our goal doesn't change." He looked at Lukas. "One more question. How do we know the Convergence hasn't started? Or that it won't while we're en route to the Wolf system?"

"We don't, Captain," Lukas replied. "We can't know,

unfortunately. We're at the whim of whatever processes are driving it."

"Fair enough," Soren agreed. "There's a lot we don't know, so let's focus on what we do know. What facts can we be certain of?"

Lina spoke up. "We know that the SF isn't the FUP. It appears the FUP is their enemy, and the SF is aware of the Eye and has control over it."

"And the SF captain accused you of playing games," Jack added. "But how? What did he mean by that?"

"The only information I gave him was my name, rank, and affiliation. I can't imagine why he thought I was being deceitful."

"What if it's because of your name?" Dana asked. "If we're in a third dimension, there could be another Soren Strickland here—one who's significant to them in some way."

Soren considered it. "You're suggesting that in this reality, I might be associated with the SF rather than the FUP? How and why would that happen, and what does it have to do with the Convergence?"

"Those are excellent questions," Lukas said. "But again, without more data, we're just speculating."

Soren nodded. "You're right. We need proof of where and when we are. Here's what I want: Lukas, Dana, Wilf, I need you to continue studying the data we captured. Focus on getting a deeper understanding of the Eye and the Convergence, but also try to determine our position in spacetime. Did we lose years of time in the Eye, or were we transported to another dimension? I want a definitive answer."

"Aye, Captain," Wilf replied.

"Lina and Tashi," Soren continued, "your priority is finding and disabling that transmitter. We can't afford to lose our cloaking advantage. Not here. Not now."

"Understood, Captain," Lina replied, with Tashi nodding in agreement. "I'm sure we can figure it out."

"Ethan, you'll oversee the repairs and ensure we're at full strength as quickly as possible. I also want you to work with Keira to review the sensor data and enemy ship configurations. We need to better understand their capabilities in case we encounter them again."

"Of course, Captain," Ethan answered.

"I want full reports by the time we arrive at the Wolf system," Soren concluded. "We need to be prepared for anything when we drop out of fold space. Dismissed."

As the others stood to leave, Jack leaned in close to Soren. "What if we've made a terrible mistake by abandoning the Eye?"

Soren met his friend's gaze. "We can't afford to think that way, Jack. We made the best decision we could with the information we had. Now we need to focus on moving forward and finding answers."

The team began to file out of the conference room, each heading to perform their assigned tasks. Soren remained seated. They were venturing into unknown territory, facing challenges they couldn't have imagined when they first set out on this mission.

Dana approached him as she was leaving. "Dad, there's something else," she said, clearly speaking to him as his daughter. "If we truly are in a third dimension, do you think we can ever get home?"

Her voice quivered, eyes misting. It was the question of a nervous child, not an officer and scientist. It hit Soren hard, forcing him to confront a fear he'd been trying to ignore himself.

What if they couldn't find their way back? What if, in trying to save their universe, they had inadvertently locked themselves out of it?

"I don't know, Dana," he replied. Like her, he wondered

if he'd ever see Jane again. "But we'll figure it out. We have to."

CHAPTER 9

Two weeks into their journey to the Wolf System, Soren was in his ready room, poring over the daily reports. He scrolled through Ethan's latest update, nodding with satisfaction as he read that repairs were completed and the shields were back to full strength.

A soft chime at the door interrupted his thoughts. "Enter," Soren called out, looking up from his terminal.

Tashi stepped inside, his usual nervous energy seemingly amplified. "Captain, do you have a moment?"

Soren set the datapad aside, gesturing to the chair across from him. "Of course, Tashi. What's on your mind?"

The young engineer settled into the seat, his fingers tapping an erratic rhythm on the armrests. "It's about the transmitter, sir. Lina and I have been working on it nonstop, but we've hit a bit of a wall."

"Go on," Soren encouraged, leaning forward slightly.

"Well, the thing is, there's no mention of it anywhere in the manual. Not a single line of code, no schematics, nothing." Tashi's words tumbled out in a rush. "At first, we thought it might be a software based transmission going through our regular comms array. A locator signal, you know? Something simple and easy to turn off. But now we're thinking it's something else entirely."

Soren frowned. "What's your current theory?"

"We believe it's a much shorter range beacon, completely self-contained," Tashi explained. "And probably attached to the hull somewhere. Much harder to remove."

"We'd need to send a team out in EV suits to find it," Soren said.

"Yeah. And even then, it's bound to be pretty small. On a ship this big, it would be like trying to find a pimple on a whale."

"That's not ideal," Soren agreed. "Do you have any ideas on how we might narrow down the search area?"

Tashi shook his head. "It would help if we knew exactly how the enemy—or our own FUP for that matter—tracked us with it. If the enemy tracked us with it. I guess we're still not sure that's the case, but the odds are pretty good. Anyway, if we could do the same thing from our side, that might give us a clue about its location. We could lock onto it like they did."

"That makes sense. Do you think you can devise a tracker like that?"

"We'll definitely give it a shot, Captain," Tashi replied, a determined glint in his eye.

"Good man," Soren said. Then, curiosity getting the better of him, he added, "I appreciate you coming to me with this, but why didn't you just include it in the daily status report?"

Tashi shifted in his seat, suddenly looking uncomfortable. "Well, sir, I...I wanted to talk to you on a more personal level, if that's alright. I hope you don't mind, but you're the closest thing I've ever had to a father, and your opinions mean a lot to me."

Soren leaned back, his expression softening. When he had lifted Tashi out of the Dregs, he never expected to become a father figure to the young man. But he wasn't about to complain. Tashi had proven his worth multiple times over. "Of course. What's on your mind?"

The young engineer took a deep breath before speaking. "I've been thinking a lot about what happens after our mission is complete. I've gotten used to being on the Wraith, sir. The thought of going back to the Dregs. I'm sure you understand. It doesn't sit well with me anymore."

Soren nodded. "You're worried about your life returning to the way it was before."

"Exactly," Tashi admitted, his shoulders sagging slightly. "I know we have bigger problems right now, but I can't help thinking about it."

Soren leaned forward, meeting Tashi's gaze. "Listen, Tashi. If we manage to stop the Convergence and get back home, I'll make damn sure your spacefaring license is reinstated. You've more than proven yourself on this mission. Hell, you could join the Navy if you wanted to."

Tashi's eyes widened, a mix of surprise and excitement washing over his face. "Really? You think I could?"

"Without a doubt," Soren affirmed. "You've got the skills and the dedication. Any ship would be lucky to have you as part of their engineering team."

A grin spread across Tashi's face, but it faltered after a moment. "But... do you think we'll actually make it back to our dimension, Captain?"

Soren sighed. "I wish I had a clear answer for you, Tashi. We're in uncharted territory here."

Tashi nodded, his expression growing more serious. "I've been thinking about that a lot, sir. What if we're stuck here, wherever *here* is? Win or lose, what if we can never go home?"

"That's a fear we all share," Soren admitted, his voice low. "But we can't let it paralyze us. We have to keep pushing forward, keep looking for answers and solutions."

"How do you deal with it, sir?" Tashi asked, his eyes searching Soren's face. "The uncertainty, I mean."

Soren was quiet for a moment, considering his response. "I focus on the mission, on the next step we need to take. But I'd be lying if I said I didn't have moments of doubt and fear."

"What scares you the most about it?" Tashi pressed, seeming to draw comfort from Soren's honesty.

"The thought of never seeing my wife again," Soren answered softly, his gaze drifting to the image on his desk he had brought with him from his office back on Earth. "Jane and I have been through so much together. The idea of her waiting for me, not knowing what happened...she had to do that once before. She understands how these things are. But I hate the thought of not coming back to her this time."

"Alex told me you were held prisoner by the Coalition. That must have been really hard."

Soren nodded, refusing to let his mind go back to the time he spent in their custody. "It was. And then there's the kids," he continued, gesturing to Dana and Alex in the image. "I'm lucky enough to have them here with me, but the thought of her never seeing them again breaks my heart."

"Do you talk to them about it?" Tashi asked.

Soren shook his head. "Not as much as I probably should. We're all trying to stay focused on the mission, on finding a way to stop the Convergence and get home. But maybe we need to address these fears more openly."

"It might help," Tashi agreed. "Knowing we're not alone in feeling this way. It helps me to hear you talk about it, sir. I really appreciate that about you."

"I'm glad I can help ease your mind. You're a valuable part of this crew, and I want you to feel at home here."

"Oh, I do, Captain. Your advice with Wilf helped a lot,

too. He kept trying to push me, and I kept pushing back with kindness. Now me and him and all his fingers are good buds." He laughed, wiggling his fingers the way Wilf did.

That got Soren to laugh, too. He was still chuckling when the door chimed again. "Enter," Soren called out.

Dana and Lukas stepped into the ready room, wearing expressions suggesting they had news to share.

"What's so funny?" Dana asked, smiling herself after seeing Soren grinning. "Captain," she added belatedly.

Tashi turned to them, wiggling his fingers. "Who am I?" he asked.

Dana laughed softly. Lukas remained serious enough to extinguish their mirth.

"Captain, we have an update on our assignment," he said.

Soren gestured for them to join the conversation. "Go ahead."

"Should I leave, Captain?" Tashi asked.

"Only if you want to," Soren replied.

Tashi planted himself in his seat, interested in what the two scientists had to say.

Lukas stepped forward, his eyes brightening with the excitement of discovery. "I've been analyzing the data we captured before, during, and after entering the Eye. I can say with a high degree of certainty that we didn't lose years to temporal dilation."

"How much time did pass, then?" Soren asked.

"By my calculations, we actually gained about an hour."

Soren wasn't sure whether to be relieved or more concerned by this news. "So, if we didn't travel through time, then..."

"The third dimension scenario seems much more likely," Dana finished for him.

"Does that mean we're dealing with infinite dimensions?" Soren asked, growing more concerned. "Because if they're all set to collapse into a single universe, I can't help but feel like all of this is as futile as futile can be."

"It would be," Dana agreed. "And I suppose it's possible. But I don't buy into the infinite timeline branching theory."

Tashi, who had been listening intently, spoke up. "How many dimensions do you think there could be, then?"

"My gut feeling is that we're dealing with a finite number of dimensions. Maybe three, maybe a dozen. But not an infinite multiverse."

"What makes you say that?" Soren asked, curious about his daughter's reasoning.

Dana paced as she explained, her hands moving animatedly. "Well, if we consider the Convergence as a natural phenomenon—albeit a catastrophic one—it makes more sense for it to involve a limited number of dimensions. Especially if it was triggered from one dimension and is only affecting the dimensions surrounding it, as it were."

"Like an explosion," Soren said.

"Precisely. Not every universe can be caught in the blast radius."

"If we look at the data from the Eye," Lukas added, "the patterns we observed seem to suggest a finite, though complex, structure. It's more like a cosmic highway interchange than an endless sprawl of parallel roads. It's also feasible that my dimension and yours are not first and second in a triumvirate, but rather first and third, straddling this center dimension."

"If that's the case, how would we have crossed over from one to three without passing to two?" Tashi asked.

"Because the composition isn't flat like a pancake," Lukas replied. "The dimensions may be intersecting at different places, which causes the rifts. But the largest interaction is in the middle of it all. The Eye."

Soren nodded, processing the information. "If that's the case, then the true source of the Convergence likely originates here. Correct?"

"Yes, Captain," Lukas answered. "Considering our outcome when we reached the center of the Eye, that's the most likely scenario."

"If so, then at least we're in the right place. Now, our priority needs to be determining who the good guys and the bad guys are. And more importantly, whether either side has anything to do with the Convergence."

"Agreed," Lukas said. "They're clearly aware of the disturbance, but they may have no idea what it actually is. We also need more data on this 'SF' organization and how they relate to the FUP in this dimension."

"And we need to be careful about making assumptions based on our own experiences," Dana added. "Just because they have an FUP here, that doesn't mean they're the good guys in this dimension."

"Good point," Soren agreed. "I may have gotten us off on the wrong foot because I didn't know any better, not because the SF is truly hostile." Soren stood, pacing behind his desk as he thought aloud. "But we also need to consider the possibility that neither side is entirely good or bad. This could be a complex political situation that we've stumbled into, rather than something cut and dried."

"What if the Convergence is a result of conflict between these two sides?" Tashi suggested, his earlier conversation with Soren giving him the confidence to speak up. "Maybe it's not a natural phenomenon at all, but the result of their war? Like radiation from an atom bomb."

The room fell silent for a moment as they considered this possibility.

"That's actually not a bad theory," Lukas said. "Certainly not outside the realm of possibility."

"But that raises even more questions," Dana pointed

out. "If it is a weapon, who created it? And why risk destroying multiple dimensions, including potentially their own?"

Soren held up a hand, sensing the conversation could spiral into endless speculation. "These are all good questions, but right now, we need to focus on gathering concrete information."

"What if we encounter versions of ourselves again?" Dana asked. "Or people we know?"

Soren considered the situation between the two Jack Harpers. Each had known when the other was nearby. Even if they tried to be stealthy, they couldn't completely hide from themselves. Still… "We avoid contact at all costs, at least until we have a solid understanding of this dimension's organization." He paused momentarily, recollecting his thoughts. "Lukas, I want you to prepare a detailed briefing for the crew. Everyone needs to understand the situation and the possibilities before we enter occupied space."

"Of course, Captain," Lukas replied. "I'll get right on it."

"Thank you. You're all dismissed."

As they began to file out, Soren called out, "Dana, a moment please."

His daughter hung back, a questioning look on her face.

Once they were alone, Soren's official demeanor softened. "How are you holding up, sweetheart? Really?"

Dana's composure wavered for a moment. "I'm…managing. It's a lot to process, Dad. The science is fascinating, but the implications…" She trailed off, her eyes glistening.

Soren stepped around the desk, pulling her into a hug. "I know. I've been thinking about your mother a lot lately. About home."

Dana nodded against his shoulder. "Me, too. Do you think we'll ever see her again?"

Soren pulled back, meeting his daughter's gaze. "I promise you, Dana, we will find a way home. No matter what it takes. We're Stricklands. We don't give up."

A small smile tugged at Dana's lips. "No, we don't."

"Now," Soren said, his tone lightening slightly, "what do you say to another family dinner tonight? You, me, and Alex. I think we could all use it. Though we'll have to settle for chow line fare this time."

"That sounds perfect, Dad," Dana replied, her smile growing. "I'll let Alex know."

"Actually," Soren said, reconsidering. "Invite Tashi, Wilf, and Asha as well, will you? And Lukas, if you'd like."

"Okay," she answered with a smile. "Thank you for including him."

As Dana left the ready room, Soren returned to his seat. They were venturing into unknown territory, facing challenges they couldn't have imagined when they first set out on this mission. It was his job to ensure that they were ready for anything.

The answers they sought, and their way home, were out there.

They just had to find them.

CHAPTER 10

The Wraith exited the fold near Wolf 1061c. Soren stood on the bridge, hands clasped behind his back as he studied the viewscreen intently. The familiar reddish-orange orb of the exoplanet hung before them, its surface a swirling mix of clouds and dust storms.

"Keira, activate the cloak as soon as possible," Soren ordered.

"Aye, Captain," she replied.

"Sensors are clear, Captain," Mark reported from his station. "No signs of any ships in the immediate vicinity."

Soren nodded, grateful they had made the journey without landing right in the lap of another confrontation.

"Cloak engaged, sir," Keira followed up.

"Well, we're here," Jack said. "Now what?"

"I'm not sure yet," Soren admitted. "For lack of a better immediate destination, this seemed like the best, safest place to start. We may only stay long enough for the engineering team to find and remove the locator beacon."

"It does appear to be safe, for the moment at least," Jack agreed.

Soren opened his mouth to contact Tashi. The young

engineer, Lina, and Wilf had cooked up a device they believed would help them narrow down the search area for the FUP's beacon, and he was eager to be rid of the potential tracker in their cloaking system.

"Captain," Samira said before he could speak. "I'm picking up transmissions from Wolf 1061C. Multiple encrypted radio signals."

"Encrypted?" Soren replied. "Are there any unencrypted channels, or an Internet hub?"

It was a long shot, but if the Wolf system was settled in this dimension, gaining access to the Internet would be a massive help in understanding the situation here, just like it was for Dana when she entered the second dimension.

"Negative, Captain," Samira came back. "Encrypted signals only. Could be a milNet. I am picking up a tranSat link as well."

"Mark, can we get the planet's surface up on screen?" Soren asked.

Mark used his console to check the camera feeds. Picking out the best one, he put it on the main viewscreen, zooming in on a section of the planet's surface. Soren's eyebrows rose in surprise as he saw what looked like a series of large domes clustered together, spread out over several kilometers.

"It's definitely occupied," Jack said. "But by who?"

"And how long have they been here?" Soren added.

Jack frowned, stroking his chin thoughtfully. "This has all the hallmarks of a military installation. The encryption. The lack of civilian broadcasts. The concentrated settlement pattern."

"Agreed," Soren said. "But whose military? SF or FUP?"

"Or neither," Keira added from her station. "We shouldn't rule out the possibility of other factions in this dimension."

"Good point," Soren agreed, considering their options.

Part of him wanted to make contact, to try and gather more information about this new reality they found themselves in. After the disastrous first encounter with the SF ships near the Eye, he felt he might handle things better given a second chance. But was it worth the risk?

"Jack," he said, turning to his old friend. "What do you think? Should we try to make contact?"

Jack's brow sank as he weighed the pros and cons. "It's dangerous, Soren. We don't know who's down there or how they might react. And just because we don't see any ships now doesn't mean they're not nearby. We could find ourselves in another firefight before we know it."

Soren nodded, seeing the wisdom in Jack's caution. Still, the need for answers gnawed at him. "I don't see any harm in getting a closer look. Sang, bring us into orbit."

"Aye, Captain," Sang replied.

The Wraith glided through space, drawing nearer to Wolf 1061c. Soren's eyes remained fixed on the viewscreen, hoping to determine who the settlement belonged to. He wouldn't have moved in closer without the cloak. His desire for information made it worth the minimal risk with it.

They had closed about half the distance to the planet when Mark's voice cut through the tense silence. "Captain! New contact!"

Soren's head snapped to the sensor projection. "Where?"

Before Mark could answer, a massive ship materialized in a brilliant flash of light less than fifty thousand kilometers from their position. Soren's eyes widened as he recognized the familiar lines of a Komodo-class vessel.

"It's marked as FUP, sir," Mark reported within seconds, already primed to check the designation immediately.

The bridge crew watched in stunned silence as the Komodo accelerated towards Wolf 1061c, paying them no attention. If they could ping the locator beacon, they didn't seem to be doing so now. As the warship neared the planet, several midsized craft launched from its hangar bay.

"They're launching dropships," Jack observed. "This looks like an invasion."

Soren considered this new development. If the FUP was attacking, then did the settlement below belong to the SF? But why were they here? Why was the FUP attacking now? What were the odds of this happening at almost the exact moment of their arrival at Wolf 1061c?

And what was so important about this installation?

Before he could give further thought to any of the questions, another flash of light lit up Mark's monitor. "Second contact, Captain!"

This one was similar to the craft they encountered outside the Eye. It loosely resembled a Valkyrie-class vessel but was noticeably larger and bristled with additional weapon emplacements. The newcomer immediately set an intercept course for the Komodo.

"Looks like we're about to see how these two stack up against each other," Jack said. "We couldn't have timed it any better if we'd tried."

Suddenly, both ships opened fire. The space between them erupted in a storm of finned railgun projectiles and missiles streaking across the void. The missiles left criss-crossing ionized gas trails as they homed in on their targets. Shields flared brilliantly as both ships absorbed the impacts, creating a dazzling light show against the black backdrop of space.

"Sang," Soren barked. "Get us clear of the engagement zone. Now."

With practiced ease, the helmsman maneuvered the Wraith away from the expanding battlefield, giving them a perfect vantage point to observe the conflict.

Smaller craft began pouring from both vessels. The SF

fighters made a beeline toward the FUP dropships, clearly intent on preventing them from reaching the surface. The Komodo's escorts moved to intercept, resulting in a frenzied melee of streaking missiles, deadly railgun fire and fighters weaving through the space surrounding the capital ships. Soren watched, eager to absorb the strategies and tactics of both sides, as starfighter pilots showcased their skills and the two capital ships maneuvered for dominance over each other.

One SF fighter pulled off a particularly daring maneuver, cutting its main engines and rotating on its axis to fire a spread of missiles at a pursuing FUP craft. The FUP pilot barely had time to react, jinking hard to port and releasing countermeasures. Two missiles streaked harmlessly past, but the third found its mark, turning the FUP fighter into a brief, brilliant fireball.

Not to be outdone, a wing of FUP fighters executed a perfectly coordinated pincer movement, catching a pair of SF craft in a devastating crossfire. Their combined railgun fire shredded the two ships in seconds.

Meanwhile, the capital ships continued their duel. The Valkyrie's superior firepower was evident, each salvo of its oversized railguns hammering the Komodo's shields with devastating force. Swarms of missiles streaked between the two ships, deflected by shields in brilliant explosions.

The FUP vessel was far from outmatched. Its movements were crisp and precise, enabling it to avoid the worst of the incoming fire while landing solid hits of its own. The skill of the Komodo's gunners more than made up for its lighter armament with their uncanny ability to find weak points in the Valkyrie's defenses.

"That Komodo pilot is good," Soren said, admiration creeping into his voice. "They're outgunned, but they're making the most of their maneuverability."

Jack nodded in agreement. "Makes me wonder who the underdog is in this one, much less who's in the right."

The battle raged on, minutes stretching into what felt like hours. Soren found himself leaning forward, completely engrossed in the tactical display. The Komodo was taking a beating, its hull scarred and blackened from multiple impacts, but it was giving as good as it got.

In a particularly bold move, the Komodo's pilot used the ship's superior agility to duck under the Valkyrie's guard, bringing them dangerously close to the larger vessel. The SF ship's heavy weapons were less effective at this range, while the Komodo captain could bring its full broadside to bear. A punishing salvo of railgun fire and short-range missiles slammed into the Valkyrie's shields, overloading them and scoring direct hits to the hull.

In the fighter engagement, things were more evenly matched. Both sides had lost several craft, their wreckage creating a deadly obstacle course for the surviving pilots.

"Looks like we have a winner," Jack announced, dragging Soren's attention to a pair of FUP dropships that had managed to slip through the chaos, leaving the SF vessel behind, its weapons and thrusters dark.

"Damn, I missed that. What happened?"

"That Komodo snuck a missile through a gap in the Valkyrie's stern," Jack answered.

"It must have hit a reactor coupling to kill the power," Ethan added from his engineering station. "As surgical a hit as I've ever seen. But, haven't we done that a few times ourselves?"

"A long time ago," Soren replied. "I'm surprised these ships haven't been modified to minimize that attack vector."

"We have no idea how old those ships might be," Jack pointed out. "They look bigger and meaner, but they might be old news."

Soren returned his attention to the starfighters. Like the SF's Valkyrie, they were no match for the superior skills of the FUP pilots. With nowhere to run, they gave it all they had, but it wasn't enough. Within minutes, the field was clear, the battle won by the FUP.

"Well," Jack said, a note of surprise in his voice. "I guess that settles that."

"Wait, what are they doing?" Keira asked, confusion evident in her voice as the Komodo began to close the distance to where the SF's Valkyrie was desperately trying to limp away.

"I'm not sure," Soren replied. Just as confused as Kiera, he watched with interest and concern.

When the Komodo was close enough, several small drones launched from its hangar bay, streaking towards the Valkyrie to attach themselves to the SF vessel's hull. The backside of the drones began pulsing. Sections of the Valkyrie's hull pulsed back in sync. Meanwhile, the Komodo's starfighters were pouring back into the hangar, their mission complete.

"What the hell?" Ethan drawled.

"Whatever they're doing, the Valkyrie is slowing down," Mark said, reading the sensor data. "And the Komodo is getting closer to it. Almost too close."

Indeed, Soren stared in amazement as the Komodo moved between the Wraith and the stricken warship, making it impossible for them to see whatever it did next.

A couple of minutes later, both ships vanished in a simultaneous flash of light, jumping away to an unknown destination.

"Ha!" Jack laughed. "They took her whole for salvage."

"Interesting," Soren replied. The sight led him to wonder if this entire attack was part of a strategy on the FUP's part, to not only capture the installation on the planet below, but to pick up the valuable remains of a relatively intact warship.

"So," Keira said, her voice a mix of awe and confusion, "Does this mean the FUP are the good guys here after all?"

Soren frowned, not quite willing to jump to that conclusion just yet. "They certainly seem to have the tactical advantage, despite their ships appearing less advanced."

"Maybe that's exactly why they're the good guys," Jack mused. "They're the underdog, fighting against a technologically superior force."

"Or maybe they're just better trained," Soren countered. "We can't make assumptions based on a single engagement, impressive as it was."

"At least we know there isn't a third group," Jack said.

"At least, not here," Soren agreed.

He returned his gaze to the viewscreen, where the zoomed-in view of the settlement showed the dropships had reached the surface and the ground forces—tiny dark specs on the Wraith's display—had already breached the interior. Small flashes indicated rifle fire in two of the domes, which died out quickly. Within minutes, the attackers had moved on to the inner domes, where they met even less resistance.

By the time they advanced to the center, it appeared the installation's defenders had surrendered.

"They made that look easy," Jack said.

"They sure did," Soren agreed.

"What now, do you suppose?"

Soren considered. They had come here seeking answers, but this brief, violent encounter had only raised more questions. Who was the SF, really? What was the nature of their conflict with the FUP? And what was so important about this settlement on Wolf 1061c that it warranted such a brazen attack?

As he saw it, there was only one way to find out.

"The invaders should have access to the CIC by now," Soren said.

"Are you sure you want to make contact?" Jack asked.

The cautious part of him urged restraint, to remain cloaked and simply observe. But his instincts, honed by years of command, told him that this event had provided them a window of opportunity. One that wouldn't stay open for long.

"Keira, deactivate the cloak," Soren ordered. "Samira, open comms across all hailing frequencies. Also, monitor for outgoing tranSat communications. Let's see if we can introduce ourselves to whoever's in control down there."

"Aye, Captain," both officers replied.

Soren returned his attention to the zoomed-in view of the settlement as the Wraith became visible to their sensors. There was no immediate reaction from the installation or the dropships.

They waited for a couple of minutes. "No response, Captain," Samira said.

"I have a feeling that they don't know what to make of us," Jack said. "They aren't sure how to respond."

Soren nodded, tapping on his command surface to send a message through the hailing frequencies, rather than a basic request.

"This is the starship Wraith, contacting the forces currently in control of the installation on Wolf 1061c. We're in need of assistance. Please respond."

Another thirty seconds of silence followed. Soren opened his mouth, ready to repeat the message.

"Wraith," a deep voice replied. "Is this a joke? Because if it is, nobody's laughing. Who are you, really?"

Soren glanced at Jack. First, the SF had thought he was playing games. Now the FUP believed he was joking. What the hell was going on here?

"This is Captain Soren Strickland of the Federation of

United Planets starship Wraith," he said, repeating his original response. "Really," he tacked on.

There was no reply. "Comms disconnected, Captain."

"This dimension isn't exactly rolling out the red carpet," Jack quipped.

"For whatever reason, they don't believe we are who we say we are," Soren replied. "They must think we're two-bit smugglers or a pleasure boat in the wrong place at the wrong time. A nuisance, instead of a threat."

"To be fair, they may have never seen a ship like Wraith before," Jack said. "They obviously haven't connected us to their enemy, and if piracy is non-existent in this dimension there would be no reason for them to feel threatened. Even if they were afraid of us, they probably don't think we want to bombard them from orbit, in which case the best option is to focus on shoring up defenses on the ground."

"Or talking to us," Soren countered. "This is a stupid misunderstanding that could be cleared up in five seconds if they would just listen." He exhaled his frustration. "I get the feeling telling them we came through a rift from another dimension won't be treated seriously, either." He paused, considering their options. "But we need to make contact with someone if we're going to have any hope of figuring all this out. My instincts brought us here. They haven't let me down before." Decision made, he activated his comms. "Minh, prepare your squadron for launch."

"Copy that, Captain," Minh replied.

"Liam," he said next.

"How can I help you, sir?" Liam answered.

"Prep the Scorpions. I have a mission for them."

CHAPTER 11

Alex stood in the armory, the familiar weight of his Karuta power armor settling around him as he stepped into it from behind and pressed his chest into the cushioning foam. The sensors sealed it shut at his back, and the sleek exoskeleton hummed to life. He flexed his fingers, feeling the suit's enhanced strength and responsiveness. "Finally, some real action," Jackson said, his voice tinged with excitement as he secured his helmet. "I was starting to think we'd spend this whole mission cooped up on the ship, running drills and playing foosball."

Malik, already fully suited up, shook his head. "Be careful what you wish for, man. I'd rather spend the rest of my life playing foosball than wind up stuck in another Jungle."

"You don't have to worry too much about that," Sarah said. "Where we're headed, there's only rocks."

"Malik's right," Alex agreed, his tone serious as he picked up his non-lethal "freezer" pistol. The gun seemed kind of pitiful in his hand, compared to the protective armor surrounding him or the rifle he had stowed on his back. "The last time we wished for more action, we got more than we bargained for."

Sarah nodded. "Copy that, One. Though I have to admit, Jackson isn't completely wrong. I could use a little more excitement."

"Trust me," Alex said, memories of their harrowing experiences on Jungle flashing through his mind, "boring is good. Boring means we all come back in one piece. I'd rather have a dull mission than lose any of you."

"So, what's the plan exactly?" Zoe asked. "We just walk in and say 'hello, we come in peace'? Should I bring a white flag?"

Alex chuckled. "Something like that. The Captain wants us to locate whoever's in charge and persuade them to open a dialogue. How we do that is up to us, as long as we don't kill anyone. And no, Zoe, no white flags. We're not surrendering; we're negotiating."

"Sounds simple enough," Jackson said, a hint of sarcasm in his voice. "What could possibly go wrong? It's not like we're dropping into potentially hostile territory with non-lethal weapons or anything."

"We're the Scorpions," Malik barked. "This is our bread and butter right here. This is how we earn our keep."

"Oorah!" the others snapped.

"Alright, Scorpions," Alex said. "Let's move out. And remember, we're professionals. Let's act like it."

The squad made their way through the Wraith's corridors, the heavy footfalls of their powered armor echoing off the deck. Crew members they passed stepped aside, some offering nods of encouragement. The squad's reputation preceded them, and there was a palpable sense of anticipation in the air.

As they entered the hangar bay, Alex saw the Stinger prepped and ready, its sleek design a stark contrast to the utilitarian surroundings. Around the Stinger, the Hooligan squadron's Pilum fighters were arrayed in a protective formation. Captain Pham offered Alex a thumbs-up from the lead Pilum, which Alex returned with a wave.

Soren waited near the Stinger, deep in conversation with Lieutenant Moffit. As the Scorpions approached, both men turned to face them.

"Scorpions reporting as ordered, sir," Alex said, snapping to attention.

Soren nodded, his eyes scanning the squad. "At ease. I want to go over the mission parameters one last time before you deploy. We can't afford any misunderstandings."

The squad gathered around, listening intently as Soren spoke, his voice carrying clearly over the background noise of the hangar.

"The situation is this: we've attempted to make contact with the forces that have taken control of the installation, but they've chosen not to take us seriously and ignored any of our further efforts to communicate. As I'm sure you can imagine, I'm running out of patience, and I'm tired of being ignored." Soren's jaw tightened slightly, a telltale sign of his frustration that Alex recognized all too well. "Your objective is to reach the Command and Information Center, locate whoever's in charge, and compel them to communicate with us. I want answers, and I want them now. Any questions?"

"What are our rules of engagement, sir?" Sarah asked, her hand resting on her freezer.

"As Alex has no doubt already told you, lethal force is off the table unless your lives are in immediate danger. We're here to gather information, not start a war." Soren's gaze swept over the squad, his eyes meeting each of theirs in turn through their faceplates. "That said, if they insist on remaining stubborn, you have my permission to...persuade them as necessary. Just make sure any injuries you inflict are within our medical squad's ability to treat to a full recovery."

Alex cleared his throat, the sound slightly distorted by his helmet. "With all due respect, sir, we may want to reconsider that red line. Asha's an incredibly skilled doctor. There's not much she can't fix. We might accidentally go too far if we can't take time for caution."

The ghost of a smile crossed Soren's face. "Point taken, Gunny. We trust you to use your best judgment. The goal is to open a dialogue, not create more enemies. Remember, we're in unknown territory here. Every action could have far-reaching consequences. The only reason I'm even willing to take this risk is because we ran out of time weeks ago. Every second counts."

"Understood, sir," Alex replied, nodding. "We'll be as mindful as possible."

"Any more questions?" Soren looked at each squad member in turn, his expression grave. When no one spoke up, he nodded. "Very well. Good luck, Scorpions. Bring us back some answers." His gaze lingered on Alex for a moment, expression softening. Then he looked away, turning to leave.

"This is what you were born to do, Marines," Liam added. "Give 'em hell. Oorah!"

"Oorah!" they snapped back.

Liam nodded to them, and Alex led his squad towards the Stinger. Sang greeted them with a nod over the back of the pilot's seat as they boarded, her voice coming through their helmet comms.

"Welcome aboard, ladies and gentlemen," she said, her tone light despite the moment's tension. "Please keep your arms and legs inside the vehicle at all times, and remember that the nearest exit may be behind you. In the event of a water landing...well, if we end up in a water landing on a planet with no surface water supply, we're in so much trouble it probably doesn't matter what you do."

Jackson chuckled as he strapped himself in, the harness automatically adjusting to his armor. "You should take that act on the road, ma'am."

"Maybe during my second retirement," Sang replied dryly.

Alex felt the familiar lurch in his stomach as Sang activated counter-mass and the Stinger lifted from the hangar deck, maneuvering closer to the bay doors and lining up directly behind Minh's lead Pilum.

"Stinger, you are clear for launch," Phoebe's voice came over the comms, as crisp and professional as always. "Good hunting, Scorpions."

With a smooth acceleration, the transport shot out of the hangar bay behind Minh's fighter and began their descent, with the rest of the flight surrounding it and the bulk of Wolf 1061c looming in their view. Alex could make out the domed installation as they approached the planet.

They entered the upper atmosphere, the Stinger shuddering slightly, the familiar rattle vibrating through their suits. Alex looked through the viewscreen beside him, watching the Pilums adjust their formation, spreading out to provide better coverage against potential threats.

The invaders had to know they were coming by now. The lack of opposition was a good sign.

He hoped.

"Alright, Scorpions," Alex said, his voice steady despite the turbulence. "Let's keep up the tradition. Who's got a good mom joke?"

"Since when is this a tradition?" Sarah asked.

"Since Malik started it on our last drop," Alex answered. "Which means he's responsible for the first joke."

Malik groaned. "Really, man? Now?"

"Come on, it's tradition. We always do this before a mission, remember?"

"I need to remember to think more often before I speak," Malik said. "Okay, I've got one, but you may have heard it before. Your mom is so fat, she has two watches… one for each time zone she's in."

The others laughed. "That's harsh," Jackson said. "But hilarious."

"What about you, Gunny?" Zoe said. "You've never made a joke in your life."

"I have so," Alex replied.

"If you have, I've never heard it," Sarah said.

"Me, either," Malik added. "Come on, Gunny. You must have one in there somewhere."

"I'm not the one who started this tradition. There's a reason for that."

"Your homework for next time, Gunny," Jackson said. "One joke. Any joke."

They all laughed.

"Okay, I've got one," Jackson said. "To cover for you, Gunny. Your mom is so lazy…she woke up from a coma and went to sleep."

A round of groans filled the transport, punctuated by a chuckle from Sang in the cockpit.

"Everyone's a critic," Jackson complained.

"If you're quite finished with the comedy routine back there," Sang called out, her voice tinged with amusement. We're beginning our final approach to the drop point. You might want to check your gear one last time. And maybe come up with better jokes for the next mission."

"Any response to our approach from the target?" Alex asked.

"Negative. They appear to be hunkering down, probably hoping to wait us out until that Komodo returns."

"Copy that," Alex said. It appeared the occupiers didn't plan to make it easy for us to contact them.

The mood in the transport sobered as the squad ran through their final equipment checks. Alex could feel the familiar mix of tension and anticipation building in his gut.

"Remember," he said to the Scorpions, his voice low and serious, "we're here to talk first. Fight only if we have to. Watch each other's sixes, and let's all make it back in one piece. We don't know what we're walking into down there, so stay sharp."

A chorus of affirmatives sounded from the Scorpions.

"Thirty seconds to drop," Sang announced, her voice all business now.

"Scorpions, prepare to disembark," Alex ordered, unstrapping himself from his seat and moving toward the Stinger's hatch. They couldn't jump from the transport at altitude like they could from a dropship, so they had to settle for a touch-and-go.

"Ten seconds," Sang announced while the other Scorpions lined up behind Alex. He tapped the door control, the hatch moving inward and sliding aside. Air rushed into the transport, creating a soft howl quickly dulled by the sound dampening in Alex's helmet.

Alex led the charge, jumping out of the Stinger as it came within a few meters of the ground. He fired his jump jets, landing smoothly, Sarah right behind him. Zoe leaped out last, just before the Stinger's landers skimmed the dirt and immediately lifted off. The Pilums soared overhead, splitting into two criss-crossed formations before falling in around the Stinger. Together, the formation raced across the rocky terrain and over the installation before ascending toward space.

"Captain, Lieutenant," Alex said, activating his helmet camera. "We're boots on the ground, en route to the first checkpoint."

"Copy that, Gunny," Liam replied. "We have visuals. The Hooligans will be standing by up here if you need air support. Good hunting, Scorpions."

"Thank you, sir. Scorpions, let's move out!"

CHAPTER 12

"So, Gunny," Sarah said as the Scorpions jogged across the rocky terrain of Wolf 1061c. "How many bad guys do you think we need to get through to reach the CIC?"

"Rough estimate?" Alex replied. "Two hundred."

"You do know there's only five of us, right, Gunny," Malik said.

"I might not know any jokes, but I do know how to count," Alex answered.

"So how exactly are we going to crack this nut? Those are pretty long odds, even for us."

"They can't cover all of the domes at the same time," Alex answered, having already reviewed the details with Liam and his father. A lot of this mission would be improvised, but the approach had some pre-planning to it. "They likely tracked us on the way in, and are repositioning the bulk of their units to the domes on this side of the installation. So we're going to take the scenic route, circle the long way around, and hope they haven't guessed our intent. Defenders will still be there, but the resistance will be lighter, making it an easier infil."

"Hope isn't a strategy, Gunny," Zoe reminded him.

"Everything we've done since we left Jungle has been grounded in hope," he replied. "But you're right. We'll split up when we reach the ridge near the base. I'll go for the far side dome with Two, while the rest of you take the middle road. Whichever team hits the least resistance will plow through to the CIC. The others will harass the defenders and keep them occupied. When the time comes, we'll throw in the Hooligans for a little more shock and awe. Clear?"

"I'm thinking maybe we should have brought more Marines," Jackson said.

"More Marines would only slow us down. We've run missions like this in training. We spent a month on Balboa, remember?"

"I remember it well," Malik said. "The nightlife, the rocks. The female Marines, the rocks. Waking up early to finish PT before sunrise, the rocks."

Alex chuckled. "Okay, tighten up Scorpions. We're closing on the ridge. Overwatch, how do we look?"

"Still clear, Gunny," Liam replied. "These buggers don't want to come out and play."

Once the Scorpions crested the ridge, Alex knew their armored forms would be silhouetted against the alien sky behind them, making them visible from the domes below. He signaled his squad to get low and take cover behind the rocky outcroppings dotting the top of the ridge. From there, they could view the circle of seven interconnected domes, the largest in the center. The clear bubbles took on a very light rose hue in the reddish light, but it wasn't enough color to inhibit their view into the domes.

"Alright, Scorpions. Two, you're with me. Three, Four, and Five, spread out and find good vantage points into your first dome. Report what you see."

As the team fanned out along the ridge, Alex and Sarah moved to a position that offered an unobstructed view of the central dome. Alex zoomed in with his helmet's optics, methodically scanning the area beneath the dome.

"Gunny," Sarah said. "Check out the flagpole in the center."

Alex shifted his gaze, focusing on the tall metal pole jutting from the top of the building in the middle of the dome. As he watched, a group of figures emerged onto the rooftop and surrounded the pole. They began to lower a flag—navy blue with what looked like a closed black fist in the center.

"That must be the SF flag," Alex murmured.

The SF banner disappeared, replaced moments later by a familiar sight.

"Looks like the new management is making themselves at home," Sarah commented, the white and gold of the Federation of United Planets now flying over the CIC.

Alex grunted in agreement, a strange mix of emotions at the sight swirling through his chest and gut. On one hand, it was comforting to see something familiar in this alien landscape. On the other, he knew this wasn't his FUP. This one was something else entirely.

Alex continued to survey the domes. He could make out barracks, admin buildings, and what looked like parade grounds and training courses.

"That big dome in the middle," Alex said. "Reminds me of the simulator complex back on Jungle."

"Yeah," Sarah agreed. "The whole place has that same feel. Military through and through. No sign of anything like Hut here. No civilians at all."

"Maybe the SF doesn't believe in R and R."

As they continued their observations, Jackson's voice came over the comm. "Gunny, we've got a count on tangos. Looks like Marines, but the good news is, we haven't seen any with power armor. We've counted about sixty tangos in our dome."

Alex felt a surge of relief at the news. No power armor meant their job just got a whole lot easier. "Copy that, Three. Good work. Time to lower the setting on your freezers. We don't want to risk permanent damage if we can avoid it."

A chorus of acknowledgments came back as the team adjusted their weapons.

"Alright, Two," Alex said, turning to Sarah. "Let's move. The rest of you, hold position and keep eyes on the target. We'll signal when we're in place."

With that, Alex and Sarah began cautiously descending the ridge, using the terrain for cover as they circled around to approach the installation from the far side. As they moved, Alex checked in with Liam again.

"Overwatch, Scorpion One. We're on the move. Any changes up there?"

"Negative, Gunny," Liam replied.

"Copy."

Alex and Sarah continued their approach, slowing as they neared the installation's outer perimeter at the base of the ridge. Alex hand-directed Sarah to move more to his left to get a different perspective on their entry point to the first dome they intended to take.

Sarah nodded, moving until her helmet optics could zoom in for a clear view of the first structure. "I count maybe forty SF tangos, Gunny. No fortifications to speak of. Looks like they're still scrambling to set up a proper defense."

Alex studied the scene, noting the positions of the SF Marines they could see. Most were clustered around the main entrance, with a few patrolling the perimeter. It was a hasty defense at best, clearly thrown together in the aftermath of the FUP's attack.

"Looks like the SF never expected to be hit here," Alex

mused. "Makes our job easier. Scorpions, this is One. We're in position. Status report."

"Three here. We're good to go, Gunny. Clear line of sight to our target dome."

Alex took a deep breath, running through the plan one last time in his head. "Here's how this is going down. We've got the lighter load, so Two and I will hit our dome hard and fast. You're the diversion. Hit your dome, make a lot of noise, then work your way towards the center dome. Keep them busy and confused." He paused, making sure everyone was clear on their roles. "Remember, we're here to talk. Use those freezers, but don't hesitate to switch to lethal if things go sideways. Questions?"

When no one spoke up, Alex glanced at Sarah, who nodded. She was ready. "On my mark...three...two...one...mark!"

Alex and Sarah burst from cover, their power armor's jump jets flaring to life, propelling them forward at incredible speed. As they closed the distance to the first of the smaller domes, Alex could see its defenders reacting, shouting and scrambling for their weapons.

The entry gates were still offline from the FUP's attack, allowing the two Scorpions to power right through the force field in the dome's atmosphere. As they landed inside the perimeter, the air around them erupted with weapons fire. Most of it pinged harmlessly off their armor, but Alex felt a few impacts that hit a bit too hard for comfort.

"Push through!" he shouted, charging towards the nearest group of defenders.

Sarah was right beside him, her freezer already out and firing. The non-lethal weapon sent arcs of electricity dancing over the Marines, dropping them to the ground in convulsing heaps.

Alex barreled into another group, using his armor's enhanced strength to bowl them over. He fired his freezer quickly, taking down three more defenders before they could even raise their weapons.

"Gunny!" Sarah's voice cut through the chaos. "On your six!"

Alex spun just in time to see a Marine leveling a heavy weapon at him. He activated his jump jets without thinking, launching himself into the air. The Marine's shot went low, and Alex came down hard on top of him, the impact of his armored form knocking the man unconscious.

As they fought their way through the defenders, Alex could hear the sounds of battle erupting from the other side of the installation. The rest of the Scorpions were doing their job, drawing attention and resources away from Alex and Sarah's advance.

"Gunny," Jackson's voice came over the comm, punctuated by the sound of weapons fire. "We're encountering heavy resistance here. These guys aren't going down without a fight."

"Good," Alex replied, freezing another Marine as he spoke. "Keep them busy. Give us a few more minutes. I'm willing to bet they'll let up as soon as they hear us hit the central dome."

Its disorganized defenders in disarray, Alex and Sarah cleared the first dome with next to no opposition. They paused briefly to assess the situation. Unprepared for such a swift and decisive attack, this dome's defenders may have been easy takedowns, but Alex knew he and his Scorpions couldn't afford to get cocky.

"Overwatch," he called. "We've cleared the first dome. What's the situation ahead?"

"Be advised, Scorpion One," Liam's voice came back, tense but controlled. "The SF forces in the next dome are setting up railgun emplacements. Recommend extreme caution."

"Copy that," Alex replied. He turned to Sarah. "Looks

like they're finally getting their act together. We'll need to split up, hit those railguns from the flanks."

Sarah nodded, her posture tense but ready. "Just like the sims, eh, Gunny?"

"Let's hope it stays as easy as the sims," Alex answered. "You go left, I'll go right. Use the buildings inside for cover and hit them from above if you can."

With a quick nod, Sarah took off, her armor's jump jets carrying her down the connecting corridor to the next dome and onto the roof of what looked like a barracks. Alex followed, turning the other way as he raced out of the connector. He zigzagged between buildings to avoid presenting an easy target.

As he rounded a corner, he saw the first railgun emplacement. The massive weapon was just being lowered into firing position, its operators too focused on their task to notice him.

Alex didn't hesitate. He fired his jump jets, launching himself high into the air, holstering his freezer and unslinging his rifle as he climbed, opening fire as he descended in an arc. The armor-piercing rounds tore into the railgun's exposed mechanisms. The weapon sparked and sputtered, rendered useless before it could fire a single shot.

Alex hit the ground rolling, coming up fast and swapping his rifle for the freezer. A few small caliber rounds pinged off his armor before he dropped the stunned operators with two quick shots. "Railgun one down," he reported, already moving towards his next target.

"Same here," Sarah added. "Railgun two down. Operators neutralized. These SF guys really weren't expecting anything like us."

"Gunny, we could use a little of that shock and awe," Jackson said as the sounds of much heavier fighting echoed from his position.

"Copy that, Three, " he replied. "Hooligan One, requesting shock and awe, cleared hot."

"Hooligan One, shock and awe incoming, ten seconds."

"Scorpion One copies."

As they worked their way through the defenses, Alex counted down the seconds. As he hit zero the sound of explosions joined the cacophony of weapons fire. Multiple fireballs appeared around the domes, the concussive force of the warheads enough to rattle the ground beneath Alex's feet, not to mention the defenders' teeth.

Sure enough, the display sent the remaining fighters into disarray, easing up the resistance on both fronts. As Alex and Sarah approached the umbilical connecting to the central dome, they encountered a final pocket of resistance. A group of Marines had set up a hasty barricade, laying down suppressing fire that forced the two Scorpions to back out of the umbilical and hunker down behind the edge of the dome's rosy bubble.

"Two, you thinking what I'm thinking?" Alex asked, a plan already forming in his mind.

"If you're thinking we should stop hiding and start flying, then yeah, I am," Sarah replied, a grin evident in her voice.

"On three," Alex said. "One...two...three!"

They burst from cover, jump jets flaring as they took off down the umbilical, the defenders struggling to track them. Only a few of their rounds pinged off their armor as both Alex and Sarah rained down freezer fire from above. Electricity arced between the tightly grouped Marines, taking them all down in a matter of seconds.

Landing among the unconscious Marines, Alex took a moment to catch his breath. "Overwatch, this is Scorpion One. We're about to enter the central dome. Three, status report."

"We're good, Gunny," Jackson replied, his voice strained

but determined. "These guys in our dome one are tough, but we've got them dazed and confused. They won't be bothering you anytime soon."

"Good work," Alex said. "Keep the pressure on. Two and I are going for the CIC."

With a nod to Sarah to follow, Alex entered the umbilical leading to the central building. Devoid of defenders, the main doors had been sealed, but the control panel beside them was still active. Alex retrieved his pad and put it against the panel, letting it work its magic. With a groan of protesting metal, the doors began to slide apart.

"Here we go," Alex muttered, bringing his freezer up to a ready position. They moved cautiously into the dome, scanning for threats. The interior was so like the central structure on Jungle that they had no trouble navigating their way through the corridors toward the CIC.

They encountered only sporadic small arms resistance along the way. Small groups of Marines would appear, laying down fire before retreating toward the command center. Alex and Sarah worked in perfect sync, covering each other and steadily advancing despite the opposition.

Finally, they reached the entrance to the CIC. The blast doors were sealed shut, a clear indication that the remaining defenders were holed up inside.

"That's cute," Sarah said in response to the effort to keep them out.

"Hold this for me, will you?" Alex said, passing her his freezer. "You know what to do once I crack this egg open."

Once more, he placed his pad against the door's controls. It took longer for it to crack the security than the outer door, but it still successfully unlocked for them.

Handing Alex's freezer back to him, Sarah used her jump jets to leap through the doors as they slid apart. Alex rushed through the doors behind her, both of them already firing their freezers as consoles urgently beeped displaying a multitude of warning messages. The FUP Marines still on their feet scrambled for cover, their return small arms fire plinking off their armor. At the center of all the chaos stood a man who could only be the commander, trying desperately to rally his troops. His uniform identified him as a major.

Alex activated his helmet's external speakers, setting them to full volume. "That's enough," he shouted, his voice firm but not aggressive. "We just want to talk. Surrender now, and no one else has to get hurt."

The fighting stopped in an instant. The few Marines Sarah hadn't frozen cast down their sidearms and raised their hands in surrender.

"Too easy, Gunny," Sarah said over comms.

The Major stared at him, a mix of confusion and disbelief on his face. "Who the hell are you people? That's FUP armor you're wearing, but you can't be with us. You aren't with the Strickland Federation either, or you would have helped them defend this place. So what is it you want?"

Alex stared at the man, his mind suddenly reeling. SF stood for Strickland Federation? He couldn't understand it or accept it.

"He told you," Sarah said, covering for him while he stood frozen. "We want to talk. We're not with your side or their side, at least not yet. We came through the Eye."

"The Eye?" the Major repeated, his confusion deepening. "What are you talking about?"

"The disturbance in space," Alex explained, overcoming his immediate shock, though his subconscious continued reeling from the commander's words. "It...it brought us here from another dimension."

The Major's expression shifted from confusion to outright disbelief. "Another dimension? Do you really expect me to believe that?"

Alex sighed, realizing that words alone weren't going to

convince this man. But maybe there was something that would. Slowly, deliberately, he reached up and deactivated his helmet seal. With a soft hiss, the faceplate retracted, revealing his face.

For a moment, the Major's eyes registered confusion, and then they widened in shock, his mouth falling open. "You look like...but that's...that's impossible," he whispered.

"What's impossible?" Alex asked.

The Major swallowed hard, his voice shaky as he spoke. "You...you look like Alexander Strickland. But you can't be. He's..."

Alex felt a chill run down his spine. "He's what?"

"He's the son of that bastard Soren Strickland, and there's no way he would be here, standing in front of me, without immediately putting a bullet between my eyes or sliding a knife between my ribs. But here you are, all the same." He paused, shaking his head. "You want to talk? Fine. Let's talk."

"Not me," Alex said, his voice trembling in confusion. "My father, who's in command of the Wraith, the ship orbiting overhead. Captain Soren Strickland."

CHAPTER 13

Alex stared at the FUP Major, his mind struggling to process the implications of what he'd just heard. The idea that there was a version of his father out there, one who had become a tyrant, felt like a punch to the gut. But he couldn't afford to dwell on it now. They needed answers, and they needed them fast.

"Major," Alex said, his voice steady despite the turmoil in his mind, "I need you to contact all your units and tell them to stand down. We have a lot to talk about, and I'd rather do it without any more fighting."

The Major, still visibly shaken by Alex's appearance, nodded slowly. "Fine. But I want assurances that my people won't be harmed."

"You have my word," Alex replied. "We're not here to hurt anyone." He motioned to the Marines in the CIC, static on the floor. "We hit them with freezers. They'll recover fully in twenty minutes or so. We just want information."

The Major moved to a nearby console, his movements stiff and cautious. He pressed a few buttons before speaking. "All units, this is Major Gray. Stand down and hold your positions. I repeat, stand down and hold your positions."

Alex activated his comm. "Scorpions, stand down. Hold your positions and wait for further orders."

"Everything okay in there, Gunny?" Jackson asked.

"It's just fine. Standby."

"Copy that."

With the immediate threat of violence defused, Alex turned his attention back to Major Gray.

"Now," Alex said, "I know this is going to sound crazy, but I need you to listen carefully." He took a deep breath, trying to figure out how to explain the complex situation in simple terms. "We came here through what we call a rift—a tear between dimensions. In our dimension, we discovered that multiple universes are on a collision course. We call it the Convergence. If we can't stop it, it could mean the end of everything."

Gray shook his head in confusion. "Multiple universes? Convergence? That definitely sounds crazy."

"Yeah, that's pretty much what we originally thought, too, but it's the absolute truth," Alex said. "That we're standing here, having this conversation, is proof of that. I'm obviously not your Alexander Strickland."

"On that I'm pretty sure we can agree," Gray replied.

"We believe something in this dimension is causing the Convergence, but we don't know what. That's why we're here. We're trying to find answers, to find a way to stop it before it's too late for our dimension, and for yours."

Gray stared at Alex, clearly still struggling to wrap his mind around the concept. "Even if what you're saying is true, why come here? Why this installation?"

"Gunny, the Captain would like to take over from here," Liam said into Alex's comms, before he could answer Gray's question. "We're hailing the installation now."

A light on the nearby communications console began

blinking insistently. Startled, Gray's eyes darted to the flashing indicator.

"You should probably answer that," Alex said, pointing to the console.

Gray hesitated a moment, then moved to the station and established the connection. "This is Major Gray," he said, his voice tense.

"Major Gray," Soren's voice came through, clear and authoritative. "My name is Captain Soren Strickland of the Federation of United Planets Navy."

Gray's face paled. "That's impossible," he whispered, despite what Alex had already told him.

"No games. No jokes," Soren continued, his tone level. "Obviously, I'm not your Soren Strickland. As my son has explained, we've come through a rift between dimensions in search of a means to stop the destruction of our universe and yours."

Gray's eyes darted to Alex, then back to the console, as if trying to reconcile the voice he was hearing with the man standing before him.

Soren went on, his words measured and careful. "We believe something in this dimension is causing it, though we don't know what. We encountered Strickland Federation ships as soon as we exited the rift, and they subsequently attacked us. We came here because this location was meaningful in our dimension, and to be honest, it appears more meaningful here. It wasn't my preference to resort to such drastic measures to have this conversation, but as I'm sure you can gather, our situation is dire, and our time is already up. I need information. Answers. And I need it now."

"I...I understand," Gray replied, still shaken by Soren's voice and Alex's face. "But I won't tell you anything that could put my FUP at risk."

"I wouldn't expect you to, and I don't need any sensitive details. My questions may seem basic to you, but we weren't able to locate an Internet portal on the tranSat relay nearby."

"That's because Strickland has a tight grip on the Internet," Gray said. "Just like he does everything else. Go ahead and ask your questions, but be quick. We have a thirty-six hour turnaround on this raid, and then we need to be in the wind before SF reinforcements arrive."

"And that's why you attacked this installation? For supplies?" Soren asked.

"Simple as that," Gray replied. "Most importantly, food. After that, ordnance, equipment, and spare parts. We'll take whatever we can organize and move in the given timeframe."

"Understood. Maybe I should back up a little. I want to know more about the SF—the Strickland Federation. I also want to know more about the Soren Strickland you know, the ideology of your FUP, and anything else you can tell me that might help us understand the situation we've found ourselves in. In other words, we need to know who the bad guys are."

Gray was silent for a long moment. When he finally spoke, his voice was heavy with a weariness that seemed to go beyond mere physical exhaustion.

"The Soren Strickland of this universe," he began, each word seeming to pain him, "was once considered a hero. A decorated officer, beloved by his crews and respected by his peers. I knew him personally. Served under him on one of his commands against the CIP. He was a great man." Gray paused, expression souring. "Until he wasn't. Something changed in him. Maybe it was always there, lying dormant, waiting for the right moment. Or maybe the power just went to his head. Whatever the reason, he betrayed his oath and his duty. He became a traitor to the FUP."

Alex listened, a cold feeling settling in his stomach as Gray continued.

"He used his influence, his charisma, to turn a significant portion of the military against the government. It started small—whispers of corruption, of incompetence in the civilian leadership. But it grew. Before anyone really understood what was happening, Strickland had launched a coup, with three-quarters of the Navy backing him. He positioned ships around our occupied worlds, ready to bombard at his command. The devastation would have killed millions. He overthrew the government in a matter of hours and established the Strickland Federation."

Gray's eyes met Alex's, his gaze fearful but defiant. "The flag you saw outside? That closed fist? It's not just a symbol. It's a promise. Strickland rules with an iron fist, crushing any opposition, any hint of dissent. The FUP...we're all that's left of the old order. A shrinking resistance, doing our best to counter the SF, but..." He trailed off, shaking his head.

"It didn't look like you were losing from what we saw," Jack's voice cut in over the comm. "That battle we witnessed? Your forces seemed more than capable."

A bitter laugh escaped Gray's lips. "You saw one battle. One victory. But for every installation we raid, every ship we take, Strickland has ten more waiting in the wings. We captured their ship, and we'll make off with a good amount of ordnance and equipment from this place. But do you know what that buys us? A few more days. Maybe a week if we're lucky."

He gestured around the command center, his movements sharp with frustration. "This? This is like throwing pebbles at a tank. But if that's all we can do, that's what we'll do. Until the last man falls, if that's what it takes."

The room fell silent as Gray's words sank in. Alex felt a complex mix of emotions swirling inside him—horror at the actions of this alternate version of his father, admiration for the determination of Gray and his fellow resistance fighters, and a growing sense of urgency about their mission here.

"There's one thing I don't understand," Alex said. "If Strickland has such overwhelming force at his disposal, why hasn't he already crushed the resistance? How are you still able to mount operations like this one? No offense, Major, but your Marines don't seem up to the task."

Gray's expression darkened. "They're good people, doing the best they can with what they have. But most of these Marines would never have made the cut before all of this. We can't afford to turn anyone away. In any case, the galaxy's a big place, and we've gotten good at staying mobile, striking fast, and disappearing before the SF can bring their full might to bear. Plus, not everyone under Strickland's thumb is happy about it. We have sympathizers, people who feed us information, help us stay one step ahead."

Alex nodded, processing this information. "What about Earth? What's happening there?"

Gray's face twisted into a grimace. "Earth is Strickland's seat of power. It's...it's not the Earth you'd remember. He's turned it into a fortress, the heart of his empire. It's so heavily fortified that we haven't been able to get anywhere near it in years. And forget about freedom. His Ghosts spy on everyone, and quell even the slightest hint of dissent."

"So it wouldn't go well for your sympathizers if they were caught," Jack said.

"That's an understatement."

"And the rest of the Federation planets?" Soren asked.

"Most fell in line pretty quickly after the coup," Gray explained. "Some out of fear, others because they actually bought into Strickland's rhetoric about strong leadership and security. A few tried to resist, but..." He trailed off, shaking his head.

"What about the Coalition?" Alex asked, thinking of their old enemies. "Do they still exist?"

"They do. But they're in a precarious position of their own. Strickland's been making noises about reunifying humanity, which is just a fancy way of saying he wants to conquer their territories, too. For now, there's an uneasy truce between them, but everyone knows it's just a matter of time before Strickland turns his full attention their way."

"Have they offered any support to your resistance?" Soren asked.

"Some," Gray admitted. "Mostly in the form of intelligence, occasionally some supplies. But they're walking a tightrope. They can't be seen openly supporting us, or Strickland would have the excuse he wants to move against them. Not that he needs an excuse. To be honest, I don't know what he's waiting for."

"Major, you mentioned earlier that Strickland turned against the government," Soren said. "What sparked that? Was there a specific event, or...?"

Gray's expression turned thoughtful. "That's a complicated question. There wasn't one single event, more a series of them. I don't know about you, but the Strickland I know was always a man of action, eager to seize the day and get results. He was always vocal about his disagreements with civilian leadership, especially when it came to military matters."

"That does sound familiar," Jack said.

"But things really started to heat up after the Proxima Incident."

"Proxima Incident?" Soren asked.

Gray nodded. "About seven years ago, there was a civilian uprising on Proxima B. The local government requested military assistance to quell the riots. Strickland was in command of the strike force sent to deal with the situation."

He paused, his face grim. "What happened next is controversial. The official story is that the rebels had gotten their hands on some heavy weaponry and were threatening to use it to destroy multiple domes. Strickland ordered an orbital bombardment that took out the entire habitation dome where the rebels were holed up."

Alex felt his stomach turn. The idea of his father—any version of his father—ordering such an attack was almost unthinkable.

"The casualties were significant," Gray continued. "When news got back to Earth, there was an uproar. The government tried to distance itself from the decision, claiming Strickland had exceeded his authority. There were calls for his court-martial."

"But it didn't happen," Alex guessed.

Gray shook his head. "No, it didn't. Strickland had too many supporters in the military, too much public goodwill from his previous accomplishments. The government backed down, but the damage was done. Strickland started speaking out more and more against what he called 'weak civilian leadership.' He claimed the government's hesitation and lack of support for the military was putting lives at risk."

"And people listened," Soren's voice came through, a note of understanding in his tone.

"They did," Gray confirmed. "Especially in the military. Strickland painted himself as the defender of the common fighter, the only one willing to make the hard choices necessary to keep humanity safe. It was all bullshit, of course, but it was effective bullshit."

"What about his family?" Alex found himself asking. "His wife? His children?"

"Alexander Strickland is the head of his father's elite

special forces unit, the Scarabs. He's the one they send when Strickland wants to make an example of someone. He's ruthless. Cold. With no hint of morality or decency."

Alex felt like he'd been punched in the gut. The idea of himself—any version of himself—as some kind of brutal enforcer was almost too much to bear.

"I'm sorry," Gray said, seeming to sense Alex's distress. "I know this must be difficult to hear."

"What about Dana?" Soren asked. "Strickland's daughter."

Gray shook his head. "Strickland doesn't have a daughter."

"What about his wife?"

"He and his wife divorced not long after Alexander was born."

"Do you know the circumstances?" Soren questioned, his tone changing, becoming more eager.

"Not really. We're going back a ways, but I think it had something to do with him being upset that his wife attained a higher rank than him."

"A higher rank?" Soren said. "He was married to Jane Yarborough, though, wasn't he?"

"He was."

"Where is she now?"

Gray laughed. "If I didn't believe you were from another dimension before, I do now, with the way you asked me that. Admiral Jane Yarborough is the leader of the resistance."

Alex stared at Gray in shock. Soren, apparently left speechless, didn't reply right away. When he did, his request was simple.

"I'd like to speak to her, right away."

CHAPTER 14

Alex watched as Major Gray's expression shifted. The FUP officer straightened his posture, his jaw set in a firm line as he addressed Soren's request.

"I'm sorry, Captain," he said, his voice steady despite the tension in the room. "But meeting with Admiral Yarborough isn't possible right now. We have no direct tranSat link back to our base, and even if we did, we have orders to maintain radio silence. If we're captured or defeated...well, we don't know jack shit about any of their plans."

Soren laughed, understanding those orders all too well. "I assume you won't divulge her physical location either. I'm willing to go to her if necessary."

"You know that would be just about the worst thing I could do," Gray replied. "I'm certain you understand."

"I do," Soren answered. "I'd like to meet with you face-to-face, and speak with one of the captured SF Marines, if that can be arranged."

Gray hesitated, his eyes darting between Alex and the comm panel. "I'm not sure that's wise, Captain. We're in a precarious situation as it is."

"Major," Soren replied, his tone firmer now. "I think

you're forgetting the current balance of power here. My Marines control your CIC. My ship is in orbit, with more than enough firepower to reduce this installation to dust. I'm making a sincere request, but I need you to understand the gravity of our situation. Speaking with one of your captured SF officers is of great importance to me."

"Do you mind if I ask why?" Gray said.

"Yes, I do mind. I also consider your resistance to such a meeting suspect."

The room fell silent as Gray considered Soren's words, which left Alex impressed by his reasoning. They still needed to be sure who the good guys and bad guys were in this dimension. Speaking to an untampered enemy would either confirm or counter Gray's story.

He glanced at the Major. He could almost see the wheels turning in Gray's mind, weighing his options. Finally, he nodded slowly as he answered.

"Very well, Captain. You've made your point. But I have one condition," he said, his voice resolute. "As I mentioned, we have limited time to complete our mission and get out of here. Thirty-six hours to be exact, including pick up, and we'd better not be a single second late or we'll be stuck in the middle of SF reinforcements. I need you to let my Marines get back to work prepping supplies for transport."

"As long as we can agree to an end to any hostilities between our two groups, I agree to those terms," Soren replied. "In fact, I'll do you one better. My Marines will assist your people in packing and loading the supplies. To ensure our security, you and the CIC will remain under our control for the duration of our stay. Does that sound fair?"

Gray considered for a moment. "I agree to those terms. But I warn you, Captain, if this is some kind of trick..."

"It's not," Alex interjected, stepping forward. "You have my word, Major."

Gray studied Alex for a long moment before sighing. "Very well. Let's get to work then."

As Soren began coordinating the logistics of his arrival and the deployment of additional Marines to assist with the supply gathering, Alex turned his attention to his team. He activated his comms.

"Scorpions, this is One. The fighting's over. Report to the CIC immediately."

A chorus of acknowledgments came back, and Alex could hear the relief in his team's voices. As he waited for them to arrive, he watched Major Gray contact his Marines, explaining the sudden cease-fire and instructing them to resume their supply-gathering efforts.

"And if any of you are still frozen," Gray added, a hint of dark humor in his voice, "resume your duties as soon as you've recovered. We don't have time to waste."

The rest of Scorpion Squad filed into the CIC, their armor bearing the scuffs and scorch marks from recent combat. Gray, hearing them enter, turned to face them. His eyes widened slightly as he took in their powered armor. "I have to admit, seeing you together brings back memories. All of our power armored units were wiped out three years ago."

Alex felt a pang of sympathy for the Major. He could only imagine their losses, fighting against overwhelming odds for so long. "I understand things have been hard for you and the other members of the FUP. This situation in this galaxy is...I'm not sure I even have the words. But I understand being the underdog. The galaxy we came here from is currently laying siege to our galaxy, invading our planets and gassing the populations."

"What?" Gray gasped. "Chemical warfare is illegal. Why would they do that?"

"They believe that when the Convergence happens, anyone who has a duplicate will either merge with that duplicate, one will be wiped out, or both will be wiped out. So they're trying to eliminate the duplicates."

"Which is going to be hard," Malik said. "Since y'all have third copies of everyone spread across the galaxy."

"Oh, damn," Jackson breathed. "I never even thought about that."

"Lukas' dimension is waging war on us and killing our people," Zoe whispered in shock. "And everything they're doing is completely futile."

"All the more reason to figure this out and get back home as soon as possible," Alex said. "Major, how can we help you make up for lost time?"

Gray's face had gone pale listening to them chatter about the Convergence. He struggled to recover. "We could use some extra hands in the armory, packing up guns and ammunition." He turned to Malik, Jackson, and Zoe. "If you three could report there, it would be a big help to have your strength loading heavy weaponry."

The three Scorpions looked to Alex, who nodded his approval. "You heard the Major. Get to it."

"The armory is—" Gray started.

"We know where it is, Major," Jackson said. "Your military bases look a lot like ours, and I spotted it on the way in. I figured we could direct the Hooligans to blast it if things got out of control, Gunny."

"I'm glad it didn't come to that," Alex replied.

The three Scorpions headed back out of the CIC. Alex and Sarah waited for Soren together while Gray returned to his duties. The paralysis from the freezers had begun to wear off on the other officers in the room, and a couple made it back to their stations, eyeing the two Marines warily as they settled into their seats.

Soren arrived shortly after, flanked by a squad of Marines led by Lieutenant Moffit. Alex noticed his father had his face hidden under a makeshift hood—a wise precaution, given the circumstances. As they entered the CIC, a hush fell over the room. All eyes were on the hooded figure at the center of the group.

Slowly, deliberately, Soren lowered the covering. Gasps and shocked murmurs rippled from the FUP officers present. Alex saw fear flicker across Major Gray's face before he seemed to remember that this wasn't the Soren Strickland he knew.

He stepped forward, his posture stiff. "Captain Strickland," he said, extending his hand. "Major Thomas Gray. Welcome to our... well, I suppose it's your installation now."

Soren clasped the offered hand firmly. "Thank you, Major. And please, there's no need for formality. Call me Soren."

Gray nodded, relaxing slightly. "Soren, then. I have to admit, even knowing you were coming, it's...unsettling to see you in person."

"I understand completely," Soren replied. "I hope we can move past that quickly. As you pointed out, time is of the essence." He gestured to the Marines behind him. "These Marines are here to assist with your supply gathering efforts. Lieutenant Moffit will coordinate with your team leaders to ensure everything runs smoothly."

Gray nodded, turning to Liam. "Thank you, Lieutenant." He pivoted to face one of his recovering officers. "Lieutenant Rashi can show you to the shuttle bay. That's where we're staging everything."

As Liam and the Marines filed out, Soren turned back to Gray. "Now, about that SF officer I requested to speak with..."

"Right. Follow me. I'll take you to the brig."

"Scorpion Two," Soren said. "Remain here and keep an eye on things. Scorpion One, you're with me."

"Copy that," Alex replied.

As they made their way through the corridors, Gray spoke in a low voice. "I have to admit, I'm still struggling to wrap my head around this whole convergence idea. Multiple universes colliding...it sounds crazy. And the consequences…" He trailed off, paling again. "How can the source of this instability be here?"

"I don't know," Soren replied. "That's what we're trying to figure out, as quickly as we can. But I assure you, the threat is very real."

"We only put the officers down here," Gray said as they reached the door to the brig. "The holding area isn't large enough for everyone we captured. The enlisted are being held in their barracks. Fortunately, they have a light deployment right now."

"You knew that ahead of time," Soren said. "You planned your attack around it."

"We did," Gray agreed. "We also sent out the distress signal that brought their battle cruiser running, with the timing pretty well coordinated."

"It would have been smoother if the dropships had landed before the SF warship arrived."

"I agree. We were off on our estimates by a few minutes. A few minutes are often the difference between life and death, so we got lucky."

They reached the brig, a stark, utilitarian space with a row of cells along one wall. Gray led them to the nearest occupied cell, where a female officer sat on a narrow bunk, her posture rigid.

Soren approached the cell, his hood still up. The officer's eyes snapped to him, her expression defiant. But when Soren walked up to her cell, her demeanor changed completely.

The color drained from her face, and she scrambled off the bunk, falling to her knees. "Grand Admiral!" she cried, her voice quavering. "Please, forgive me! I...I didn't know...I failed you. I'm so sorry. Please, spare my life!"

Alex felt a chill run down his spine as he watched the scene unfold. The sheer terror in the woman's voice, the way she prostrated herself, it drove home the reality of what Gray had told them about this universe's Soren Strickland.

His father seemed equally taken aback. For a moment, Soren just stared at the kneeling officer.

"Stand up, officer," he said, his voice firm but not unkind. "I'm not Grand Admiral Strickland. I'm with the FUP."

The woman's head snapped up, confusion replacing fear in her eyes. As the words sank in, her personality shifted once more. She climbed to her feet, stiffening as she glared at Soren.

"FUP," she spat, her voice dripping with contempt. "I should have known. Resorting to cheap impersonators to frighten us. So predictable."

Soren's gaze remained steady as he regarded the officer. "Tell me something," he said. "Why do you follow someone you're so afraid of? What kind of leader inspires that kind of terror in their own people?"

The officer's eyes flashed with anger. "You know nothing," she hissed. "Grand Admiral Strickland has brought strength and security to the galaxy. He's made tough choices, yes, but everything he does is for the greater good. I only cowered because I wish I hadn't failed him."

Gray stepped forward, placing a hand on Soren's shoulder. "Don't waste your breath trying to reason with her," he said. "Strickland's military is blindly loyal to him. He makes sure of that."

Soren turned away from the cell, facing Gray. "I've seen and heard enough. Thank you for allowing this, Major."

They reversed course, exiting the brig. As soon as they

were outside, Soren paused, stopping Alex and Major Gray with him.

"Major, I'd still very much like to speak with Admiral Yarborough. I understand your hesitation, and your reasons for it, but as you know, we need to identify the possible source of the Convergence as soon as possible, for all our sakes. I wouldn't expect Grand Admiral Strickland to be much help in that regard."

Gray exhaled, shaking his head. "Captain, I—"

"You don't need to divulge any coordinates. You've clearly modified your space fold envelopes to encompass a second ship. You can take us to speak to the Admiral at a meeting point completely under your control."

The Major considered his words more carefully. Seeming to sense an opening, Soren pushed through the man's hesitation. "We can make it worth your while. We need information. You need assistance. A high-value target you'd really like to hit, but don't have the resources, perhaps."

"I don't know…" Major Gray replied, remaining hesitant.

"Let me put one more question to you, Major," Soren said.

"Go ahead."

"What have you got to lose?"

CHAPTER 15

Soren waited as Major Gray considered his question. The FUP officer's face shifted with his conflicting emotions—caution warring with desperation, hope tempered by years of hard-learned skepticism. Gray's eyes darted between Soren and Alex, as if still struggling to reconcile their presence with everything he knew about the Stricklands in his universe. Finally, he took a deep breath and nodded, his decision made.

"Okay, Captain," he said, his voice low and gravelly. "I'll arrange a meeting with Admiral Yarborough, with your promise to help us accomplish a mission that might otherwise be beyond our reach. But in the meantime, I also want your continued assistance gathering supplies. Your powered Marines have already put us back on track."

Soren nodded without hesitation. "Of course." He paused, considering for a moment before adding, "I'll also send for our quartermaster, Harry. He's the best logistics man I've ever known. He'll make sure everything's packed and loaded with maximum efficiency."

Gray's eyebrows rose slightly, a flicker of interest crossing his face. "Your quartermaster? That good, is he?"

"Trust me, Major," Soren said with a hint of a smile. "Harry could organize a symphony with a pair of spoons if you gave him half a chance. He'll have your supplies sorted and loaded before you know it."

"Alright," Gray conceded, looking somewhat impressed. "I'll take your word for it." His expression sobered again as he added, "And one more thing. Some of our people were hit pretty hard by those stun weapons of yours. I'd feel better if one of your medical staff could look them over to make sure there are no lasting effects."

Soren's face grew serious at the mention of potential injuries. "Of course," he agreed immediately. "My apologies for any damage they might have caused."

"We dialed back the settings quite a bit when we saw your people weren't wearing armor," Alex added. "But I'm sorry, too. We didn't intend to hurt anyone."

"I'll have our chief medical officer come down as well," Soren said. "Your people will be in good hands."

Gray's posture relaxed slightly, some of the tension leaving his shoulders. "Thank you, Captain. I appreciate your cooperation. It's refreshing, to be honest."

"We're in this together now, Major," Soren said. "The sooner we can meet with Admiral Yarborough, the sooner we can start working on a solution to the Convergence threat. And that's something that affects all of us, regardless of which universe we call home."

Gray nodded slowly, his eyes distant for a moment as if contemplating the enormity of what Soren had just said. Then he shook his head slightly and refocused on the present. "Right. Well, let's get to it then. Time's wasting, and we've got a lot of work to do."

With the agreement in place, Soren activated his comms. "Sang, head back up to the Wraith. Tell Jack that I need Harry and Asha to report to the surface immediately. Tell Asha to come equipped with her little black bag."

"Copy that, Captain," Sang's voice came back. "I'm on my way."

"Oh, and Sang, I want Bastian to bring them down. You need a break."

"What do you think I've been doing in here while you're forging alliances, Captain? I'm good to go."

Soren chuckled. "Very well. But if you do need a breather, Bastion is ready to take over."

"Aye, Captain."

As they waited for the additional personnel to arrive, Soren turned to Alex. "Gunny, I want you to help Liam oversee our efforts here. Keep an eye out for any potential misunderstandings. We're guests here, so let's make sure we stay on good terms."

Alex nodded, his expression serious. "Copy that, sir."

Soren turned back to Gray. "Major, I'm at your disposal."

Gray nodded, gesturing towards the door. "This way, Captain. I'll give you a quick tour of what we're working with."

As they continued out of the central building, Soren was grateful things had worked out with the FUP. They were progressing, but every step forward revealed new complications. The image of that SF officer cowering before him in the brig still haunted him. What kind of man was this other Soren Strickland? How had he become that way?

He pushed those thoughts aside. They had supplies to load, a rendezvous to make, and an Admiral to meet. One step at a time, he reminded himself, one foot in front of the other.

An hour later, Soren stood in the shuttle hangar, watching a whirlwind of activity unfolding before him. FUP Marines and Scorpion Squad members worked side-by-side, hefting crates and equipment onto three waiting shuttles. The hangar echoed with the sound of boots on synthcrete, the soft hum of counter-mass sleds, and the constant chatter of coordinating voices.

At the center of it all stood Harry, directing the flow of supplies with the precision of a conductor. His voice carried across the hangar, somehow cutting through the din without ever raising to a shout.

"No, no, no," Harry called out, waving his arms at a group of Marines carrying a large crate. "That goes in shuttle two, not three. We need to keep the categories consistent and the containers organized to fill the available space with no gaps. Have none of you ever done this before?"

Soren grinned as the Marines quickly changed direction, following Harry's instructions without question. Most likely, none of them had ever done this before.

As he watched, Harry intercepted another group of Marines entering with a sled of crates. He stopped them and opened one of the crates, examining the contents closely. He picked out what Soren believed was a railgun ejector coupling and turned it over in his hands, looking closely at it.

"Hold up," he said, shaking his head. "These aren't going anywhere. Leave them aside."

The Marines looked confused, exchanging glances. One of them, a young corporal, spoke up hesitantly. "Sir? These parts were requested by our engineers. They said we needed them for—"

Harry cut him off with a wave of his hand. "Did you look at these before you started grabbing them? These parts aren't fit for salvage."

Before the Marines could protest further, Major Gray appeared at Soren's side, his face creased with concern.

"Is there a problem?" Gray asked, his eyes darting between Harry and the Marines.

"It seems there may be," Soren replied, guiding Gray over to Harry.

Harry turned to face them, his expression serious. He knew why they'd approached before they had to speak. "Major, with all due respect, some of this equipment is no good. Look here," he said, holding up one of the components. "This coupling is completely shot. See these microfractures along the housing? One good power surge and this thing would blow apart like a cheap firecracker. Considering it goes inside a railgun, that would be especially bad."

Gray frowned, stepping closer to examine the parts himself. "Are you sure?"

"I'm sure," Harry replied firmly, handing the coupling to Gray. "And this regulator? It's clearly defective. Look at the way the internal mechanism is misaligned. You load these on your ship, and you're asking for trouble."

Gray turned the parts over in his hands, his frown deepening as he saw what Harry pointed out. "I see what you mean, but...why would this base have faulty parts in surplus?"

Harry's voice dropped lower, his expression grave. "That's what worries me, Major. Some of this stuff looks like it was intentionally placed here. Sabotage, maybe. Your SF friends might have planted some nasty surprises for you to find."

"As though they knew we would raid this installation?" Gray asked doubtfully.

"Considering the information you've shared with me," Soren said, "I think that's very possible. How many targets might you have the resources to attack?"

Gray shook his head. "Unfortunately, not enough. Your man knows his stuff, Captain."

Soren nodded, pride evident in his voice. "That he does.

And if he says something's not right, you can bet your life on it."

Gray considered for a moment, then nodded decisively. "Harry, you have full authority over what goes on those shuttles. If you say it stays behind, it stays behind. No questions asked."

Harry nodded with a slight grin. "Thank you, Major."

As Harry returned to his work, barking out new orders to the waiting Marines, Gray turned to Soren. "I have to admit, Captain, I'm impressed. Your people work well together. And they certainly know their business."

"They're the best crew I could ask for," Soren replied, watching as the Scorpions entered, each carrying a large crate that would take four Marines to lift. "Speaking of which, how are your injured Marines doing? Has Asha had a chance to look them over?"

Gray's expression softened slightly. "She has, and I have to say, I'm impressed there as well. Dr. Nguyen told me that there shouldn't be any lasting effects. A couple bumped their heads when they went down, and some people need more recovery time than others. Thanks to your assistance, we'll make our timeline without the affected Marines."

Soren nodded, relief washing over him. "Good to hear. Asha's an excellent doctor. I'm glad she could put your mind at ease."

Gray shook his head, a rueful smile on his face. "You know, Captain, when you first showed up, I thought you might be the death of us all. Now I'm starting to think you might be the best thing that's happened to us in a long time."

"Let's hope that turns out to be true, Major. For all our sake."

CHAPTER 16

The next twenty-four hours passed in a blur of activity. Marines and Scorpions worked tirelessly, guided by Harry's expert direction. True to his word, the quartermaster ensured that every crate loaded onto the shuttles contained quality equipment and was strategically placed for efficient offloading.

Soren spent the time moving between different areas of the base, overseeing operations and lending a hand where needed. He worked alongside his crew, hefting crates and moving equipment, much to the surprise of the FUP Marines. At one point, he caught Major Gray watching him, a look of respect in his eyes.

"You know, you don't have to do this," Gray said, approaching Soren as he helped secure a heavy piece of machinery. "Most officers I know would be content to just give orders."

Soren wiped sweat from his brow, offering Gray a wry smile. "I've never been one for sitting on the sidelines, Major. Besides, it's good for morale."

Gray nodded slowly. "I can see that. Your people certainly seem motivated."

"I have a fantastic crew," Soren agreed. "But I have to say, your Marines are impressive too. They've been through hell, but they're still fighting. That takes real courage."

A shadow passed over Gray's face. "They've had to be tough. This war has taken so much from all of us."

"I can only imagine what you've been through. We'll do what we can to help."

As the last of the supplies were secured, Soren gathered his team near the Stinger. Everyone looked tired but satisfied with their work.

"Good job, everyone," Soren said as they boarded the transport. "We've made a difference here today." He turned to Gray. "We'll wait for your word before decloaking again. I don't want to cause an incident."

"Of course," Gray replied. "Thank you again for your assistance. You not only saved us time, but by rooting out those bad parts you also saved our lives."

As the Stinger lifted off, heading back to the Wraith, its occupants fell into an exhausted silence. It was Asha who finally broke the quiet, her voice subdued.

"I hope you don't mind me speaking up, Captain," she said, shaking her head. "I just still can't wrap my head around it. How could any version of you turn out like that? A tyrant willing to bombard his own people and overthrow the government? It just doesn't make sense."

Soren sighed heavily. "I wish I knew. The idea of it goes against everything I believe in, everything I've fought for. To think that there's a version of me out there capable of such cruelty..." He trailed off, unable to find the words to express the horror he felt.

"It's not you, sir," Alex said firmly. "No more than the Alex Strickland in this universe is me."

"No," Soren agreed. "They aren't us. But they still offer reflections of us. Who we might have become under different circumstances. That's what eats at me the most.

That beneath who I know I am, I have the ability to become this dimension's Soren Strickland."

"But you aren't," Asha said. "You're a good man, Captain. Don't let this shake that belief."

Malik nodded in agreement. "Yeah, sir. I mean, look at what we just did down there. You navigated a tough situation and turned it into an alliance."

Soren looked around at his crew. "I appreciate your support."

"So, Captain," Jackson said, "what's our next move?"

"We're going to meet with Admiral Jane Yarborough, who as luck would have it is this dimension's version of my wife. If anyone can give us the information we need about this universe, it's her. About their war with the SF, for one thing. But more importantly, I'm hoping she can give us some direction on what might be behind the Convergence. Or at least, maybe she'll know someone else who can provide that information."

"It'll be strange to have a meeting with this version of your wife, won't it?" Asha said. "How do you feel about that, sir, if you don't mind me asking?"

Soren was quiet for a moment, considering his response. "Honestly? I'm not sure how to feel. But we can't let personal feelings get in the way of the mission."

It wasn't long before the Stinger glided into the Wraith's hangar, met by Phoebe as it settled gently on the deck.

"I want all of you to get some rest," Soren said as they disembarked. "You've worked hard, and you've more than earned it."

After a few hours of much-needed sleep, Soren returned to the bridge, relieving Vic from his extended shift. He noticed Jack's absence; his old friend was likely still catching up on rest and would be along soon enough.

"Status report," Soren said as he settled into the command station.

"All systems nominal, Captain," Keira replied from her station.

"Ethan, any news on the transmitter?"

"We made our first EVA to locate it," Ethan answered. "No luck so far, but we eliminated some of the negative space."

"That's something, then," Soren replied. "Keira, activate the cloak. We'll remain hidden when the FUP ship arrives, until Major Gray gives the go-ahead to show ourselves."

"Aye, Captain," she responded. "Cloak engaged."

Soren leaned back in his seat, waiting patiently for the FUP ship to arrive. After so much chaos, he was thankful for the lull, no matter how slight or short it might be.

He didn't have to wait long. Within the hour, the familiar shape of the Komodo flashed into presence.

Soren watched the warship's approach on the main viewscreen.

"Komodo is entering synchronous orbit, Captain," Mark reported from his station. "They're maintaining position approximately twenty thousand kilometers off our port bow."

Soren's eyes never left the screen. "Thank you, Mark. Keep a close eye on them, just in case."

The minutes ticked by slowly, tension building on the bridge with each passing moment. Finally, Samira turned to him.

"Incoming transmission, Captain," she announced. "It's Major Gray."

"Put him through," Soren ordered.

Gray's voice echoed from the bridge speakers. "Wraith, this is Gray. I've explained the situation to Captain Ulysses. You can decloak when ready."

"Understood, Major," Soren replied. "Stand by." He turned to Keira. "Deactivate the cloak."

"Aye, Captain," she responded. "Decloaking now."

The Wraith shimmered into view, and almost immediately, a new hail came through.

"This is Captain Xin Ulysses of the FUP Navy vessel Ever Valiant," a deep, authoritative voice announced.

Soren took a deep breath, steeling himself for the reaction he knew was coming. "This is Captain Soren Strickland of the Wraith," he replied. "Thank you for your cooperation, Captain."

There was a long pause, and Soren could almost feel the shock radiating through the comm channel. When Ulysses spoke again, his voice was strained with disbelief.

"I...Major Gray explained the situation, but hearing your voice...it's uncanny, and honestly a little frightening."

"I understand, Captain Ulysses," Soren said. "I know it's a lot to take in, but I hope we can move past the initial shock quickly. Time is of the essence."

"You're right about that," Ulysses replied. "We have a closing window of opportunity to get the shuttles up and all of the supplies loaded. I understand Major Gray negotiated a meeting with Admiral Yarborough?"

"That's right, Captain," Soren replied. "I hope you intend to honor his agreement."

"It was beyond his purview to make promises like that, but from what I hear, you've been invaluable to our efforts on Wolf, and you helped prevent us from loading potentially sabotaged equipment. You've earned the meeting, as far as I'm concerned. And you're in luck, Captain. As it happens, the Admiral is set to meet us at our rendezvous coordinates."

Soren felt a surge of nervous excitement. He missed Jane more than he wanted to admit to himself. Even if it wasn't the same Jane, it would be good to see her face again, and sooner than he had expected.

"That is fortunate," he said, trying to keep his voice

neutral. "When do we leave, and how long will it take to get there?"

"As soon as we finish loading the supplies from the surface," Ulysses replied, "which should be within the hour, thanks to your team's assistance. We'll signal when we're ready to depart. As for how long it will take...well, I'm not about to let you draw a sphere around our current position. We'll get there when we get there. I'm sure you understand. Ever Valiant out."

True to Ulysses' word, the supply shuttles began round-tripping with the Ever Valiant less than an hour later. Soren watched the efficient operation with approval, noting how quickly the FUP crew worked to secure their newly acquired resources.

"They're good," Jack commented, having joined Soren on the bridge. He looked refreshed after his rest, but there was still a tension in his shoulders that spoke of the gravity of their situation. "Not as smooth as our people, but they've clearly had practice at this sort of thing."

Soren's gaze stayed on the viewscreen. "They've had to become experts at hit-and-run tactics. In their shoes, I'd make sure my crew could load and unload supplies faster than anyone in the galaxy."

As the last shuttle slipped into Ever Valiant' hangar, Ulysses' voice came over the comm once more. "Wraith, this is Ever Valiant. We've secured the last of the supplies and are preparing to depart. We'll need to use our tether drones to bring you into our fold envelope."

Soren frowned, exchanging a glance with Jack. "I'm afraid that won't be possible, Captain," he replied, his voice calm but firm. "The Wraith's hull is...unique. Your drones could damage it. We'll need to maneuver into the envelope ourselves."

There was a pause before Ulysses responded, his

concern evident. "Captain Strickland, with all due respect, that's extremely risky. We'd have to get dangerously close without colliding. And we don't have much time before SF reinforcements arrive."

"I understand your concern," Soren replied, his tone reassuring. "But I assure you, my helmsman is more than capable. We've done this type of precision maneuvering before."

Another pause, longer this time. Soren could almost picture Ulysses checking with his crew to confirm the maneuver was even possible in the short time they had left before they expected the SF ships to arrive. Finally, the FUP captain's voice came back, reluctance clear in every word. "Very well."

Soren turned to Sang, who was already poised at her station. "You heard the man. Think you can thread that needle for us?"

Sang's lips spread into a small, confident smile. "Aye, Captain. It'll be tight, but I can do it. It's no different than moving into position to mask external objects with the cloak."

"Ever Valiant," Soren said, turning his attention back to the comm, "we're beginning our approach."

"Understood, Wraith," Ulysses tensely replied. "But hurry. We need to be gone within the next ten mikes."

"We'll make it," Soren assured him.

As the Wraith began to move, Soren could feel the tension on the bridge ratchet up. Every crew member's eyes were glued to the viewscreen, monitoring the rapidly closing distance between the two ships as the invisible timer counted down.

"Five hundred meters," Mark called out, his voice steady despite the pressure.

"Three hundred meters."

"One hundred meters."

"Captain," Ulysses said. "We have less than a minute."

"We'll make it," Soren repeated. "Sang, a little faster."

Sang's hands moved with preternatural precision, making minute adjustments to their trajectory. The Ever Valiant loomed larger and larger on the viewscreen, filling it completely. Soren could make out individual hull plates, the glow of running lights, and the seams where the ship's missile launchers were tucked behind protective armor.

"Twenty meters," Mark announced, his voice tight with concentration.

"Steady," Soren said, his own heart racing despite his calm exterior. He trusted Sang implicitly, but even he had to admit this was cutting it close.

"Captain!" Ulysses barked. Time was almost up.

"Ten meters."

"Five meters."

Just when it seemed collision was inevitable, Sang made a final, delicate adjustment. The Wraith slid into position below the Ever Valiant with barely a meter to spare.

"We're in position, Captain," Sang reported, a hint of pride in her voice. "Fold envelope stable and holding."

Before anyone could respond, Mark's urgent voice cut through the moment of relief. "Captain! Multiple contacts detected!"

Soren's head snapped to the sensor display. A chill ran down his spine as he took in the number of enemy vessels. Not just a few ships, but an entire strike force.

"Ever Valiant," Soren called out, his voice sharp with urgency, "we're in position."

"Initiating fold," Ulysses' voice came back, tight with tension. "This is going to be close!"

Soren gripped the arms of his chair as the familiar sensation of folding space washed over him. Through the viewscreen, he caught a final glimpse of the SF strike force bearing down on them. The lead ships were already opening fire, streaks of projectiles reaching out towards them.

All of it disappeared in a flash.

CHAPTER 17

Two days after their narrow escape from the Wolf system, Soren sat in his ready room aboard the Wraith, his eyes fixed on the swirling nothingness of folded space visible through the compartment's screen. The familiar sight, once a comfort during long journeys, now felt suffocating. They had no idea when or where they would emerge, and the uncertainty and anticipation gnawed at him like a persistent itch he couldn't scratch.

A chime at the door pulled him from his brooding thoughts. "Enter," he called out, turning to face his visitors.

Lukas and Dana stepped inside, both looking tired but excited. Dark circles under their eyes spoke of long hours poring over data, searching for any clue that might help them understand their predicament. The smiles on their faces suggested they had found one.

"Captain," Lukas began. "We've been analyzing the data from our passage through the Eye, and we've made some interesting discoveries."

Soren gestured for them to take seats across from his desk. As they settled in, he noticed Dana fidgeting with a datapad, her fingers tapping an impatient rhythm on its surface.

"Go on," Soren encouraged, leaning forward slightly.

Dana took a deep breath before speaking. "We believe the Eye may not be as unstable as we initially thought. There's evidence to suggest that a specific event caused the initial disruption."

Lukas nodded eagerly, picking up the thread. "And not only that, but it seems this event, or perhaps a series of similar events, has been exacerbating the instability over time."

Soren frowned, considering their words. "So, you're saying this isn't something some unknown entity is controlling?" He looked at Lukas. "You'd theorized earlier that an intelligence of some sort was keeping the Convergence from beginning despite the instability reaching critical mass."

"Yes and no," Dana answered, her voice gaining confidence as she explained. "It's more like...well, imagine scratching an itch until it bleeds. If you let it scab over and leave it alone, it heals. But if you keep scratching it or even let it scab over before you scratch it open again..."

"...it never heals and can even get worse," Soren finished for her.

Lukas leaned forward, his eyes intense. "If we're right, then whatever triggers the instability needs to be triggered either at a higher frequency or larger amplitude, so to speak."

"So shooting a gun once every ten seconds versus shooting it ten times in one second?" Soren asked, trying to understand the explanation.

"Exactly," Dana said. "Or swapping out a pistol for a bazooka and firing once every ten seconds."

"Can it happen at any time?"

Lukas nodded grimly. "Yes, but it won't be random.

And one thing we still don't know, one thing the data can't even hint at, is whether or not the event is being intentionally triggered, or if whoever is doing it has no idea it's happening."

"So we're looking at three key factors," Soren said, ticking them off on his fingers. "The event causing the worsening instability, the source of that event, and whoever's triggering it."

"Exactly," Dana agreed. "And we need to determine if it's the FUP, the SF, or even something or someone else we haven't considered yet."

"We thought we were racing against time, but now it seems we're in a race against a complete unknown. Are we making progress, or falling behind?"

"If we're right about this, it means we might have more time than we initially thought," Lukas said optimistically.

"Or less," Soren countered. "We just don't know. But there's nothing we can do about that now. I'm hoping Jane can help us narrow down our search. Even if she doesn't have direct knowledge of a specific event or trigger, she might be able to point us in the right direction."

"Jane?" Lukas asked, confusion evident in his voice. "You mean Admiral Yarborough, Captain?"

"Yes," Soren agreed, realizing his slip. He took a breath to refocus. "Is there anything else?"

Dana shook her head. "Not at the moment, Captain. We'll keep analyzing the data and let you know if we find anything else."

"Thank you both," Soren said, genuine appreciation in his voice. "Keep up the good work. We're going to need every scrap of information we can get."

As Lukas and Dana left the ready room, Soren returned to the viewscreen, considering the new information. He didn't have long to dwell on these thoughts before the door chimed again. "Enter," he called out.

Jack stepped into the room, a concerned look on his face. "Got a minute, Soren?"

"Of course," Soren replied, gesturing to the chairs. "What's on your mind?"

As Jack settled into a seat, Soren filled him in on what Lukas and Dana had just shared. Jack listened intently, occasionally nodding as he absorbed the information.

"Well," Jack said when Soren finished, leaning back in his chair with a heavy sigh, "that's certainly a lot to process. But if they're right, it means we have something to focus on. Something out of the ordinary. Maybe something we don't have in our dimension."

"That's a good thought," Soren said. "I'm hoping Jane... Admiral Yarborough can shed some light on the situation when we meet her."

Jack's expression grew serious. "That's actually what I came here to talk to you about. Do you think we can trust the FUP?"

Soren raised an eyebrow. "You're having doubts?"

"I just think we need to be cautious," Jack replied. "I know you're excited about the prospect of seeing this Jane, even if she's not your Jane. I wouldn't mind seeing a friendly face like hers again, either. But we can't let that cloud our judgment."

"I appreciate your concern, old friend," Soren said. "But I assure you, I'm not going into this blindly. Yes, the FUP is run by this dimension's version of my wife, but that doesn't mean I trust them implicitly."

Jack held up his hands in a placating gesture. "I'm glad to hear that. There's too much at stake here to take anything for granted. If some event is the reason for the Eye, it's entirely possible the FUP holds the trigger."

"Whether they know it or not," Soren agreed.

"And if that event, that trigger, is somehow the only

thing keeping them from being consumed by the Strickland Federation?"

"I would assume this dimension continuing to exist is more important than retaking the galaxy, but if not…" Soren trailed off, shaking his head. "The last thing I wanted to do was go against the FUP. But I will if I have to."

"Would you be able to kill Admiral Yarborough, if it came to that, do you think?"

It was a tough question, but Soren was glad Jack had posed it. He needed to be ready to answer those kinds of questions ahead of time because he wouldn't have time to consider it in the moment. "Yes," he decided. "But it wouldn't be easy, and I wouldn't like it."

"I wouldn't expect you to," Jack said, visibly relaxing. He stood up, stretching slightly as if to shake off the weight of the conversation. "Now, how about we head to the chow hall and grab something to eat? I don't know about you, but all this heavy talk has me famished."

Soren chuckled, the sound breaking some of the lingering tension in the room. He realized he couldn't remember the last time he'd eaten, his stomach growling softly as if responding to Jack's suggestion. "You know what? That sounds like a great idea."

CHAPTER 18

Soren jolted awake at the sound of his quarter's comm unit chirping insistently. He blinked away the fog of sleep, quickly alert. Sliding out of bed, he tapped on the comm to open the channel. "Go."

"Captain," Vic said, "we've just emerged from the fold."

"I'll be there in five minutes," he replied, his voice rough with sleep.

As he ended the call, Soren cursed under his breath. He should have been on the bridge for their arrival. The anticipation of speaking with Jane—even if she wasn't his Jane—had kept him on edge for days. But without knowing when they would arrive, he had to be oblivious to the ETA and rest at normal intervals. It just figured they would arrive at the most inopportune moment for him.

He moved quickly through his quarters, shedding his t-shirt and pajama pants before stepping into the shower. The hot water helped chase away the last vestiges of sleep, but did nothing to quell the nervous energy building in his chest. By the time he finished dressing in his uniform, his heart pounded with nervous anxiety. He had to reign himself in, remind himself that this Jane he would soon meet with wasn't his wife. He had to see her as who she actually was. A woman who looked just like his wife. The leader of this dimension's FUP.

Hopefully, it wasn't easier said than done.

Soren strode purposefully through the corridors of the Wraith, nodding to the few crew members he passed. As he approached the bridge, he paused to steady himself. He couldn't afford to let his personal feelings cloud his judgment, not with so much at stake.

The bridge doors slid open. Soren's eyes immediately went to the main viewscreen, taking in the scene before them. Bastian had already maneuvered the Wraith away from Captain Ulysses' Ever Valiant, providing some breathing room between the two ships.

A dozen ships hung in the void around them, a ragtag fleet that spoke volumes about the FUP's current situation. Most were familiar designs, but a few stood out—clearly salvaged SF vessels—a stark contrast to the rest of the fleet. All of them bore the scars of prolonged conflict: scorched hull plating, obvious patches covering battle damage, and in some cases, entire sections that looked like they'd been salvaged from other ships and then grafted on to make repairs.

"Vic, I have the conn," Soren said as he approached the command station.

"Aye, Captain," Vic replied, abdicating the seat. "You have the conn."

"Status report," Soren requested as he sat.

"We've moved to a holding position about ten kilometers from the Ever Valiant," Vic answered. "The rest of the fleet is maintaining a loose formation around us."

Soren nodded, his eyes still on the viewscreen. "Any word from Admiral Yarborough?"

"Not yet, sir," Vic replied. "But Captain Ulysses asked to

be notified when you arrived on the bridge. He wants to speak with you."

"Very well," Soren said, settling into his chair. "Samira, hail the Ever Valiant."

A moment later, Captain Ulysses' voice came through the bridge speakers. "Captain Strickland. I trust you enjoyed the trip?"

Soren allowed himself a small smile. "If it helps me save my galaxy and my Jane, I loved every minute of it."

Ulysses nodded, a flicker of understanding passing across his features. "I'm afraid I have some news that you may not find as agreeable. Admiral Yarborough isn't here."

Soren felt his stomach drop, but he kept his expression neutral. "I see. May I ask why?"

"Security concerns," Ulysses replied. "The Admiral wants to mitigate risk. Especially with...well, with you here. No offense, Captain."

"None taken," Soren said, though he couldn't quite keep the edge out of his voice. "You promised me a meeting. Can we speak over tranSat?"

"Negative, Captain. We only use tranSat in emergencies to avoid potential eavesdropping or interception by SF spies."

"You have spies in your ranks?"

"It's happened before," Ulysses admitted.

"We had a deal, Captain," Soren pushed.

"We did, and Admiral Yarborough intends to honor it, if you're agreeable to her restrictions."

Soren bristled internally but kept a calm demeanor on the outside. The last thing he'd expected from this FUP was a bait and switch. His conversation with Jack replayed in his head. Had he made a mistake trusting the FUP this far?

"Go on."

"You and one other person of your choosing will be

transferred to a fold-capable shuttle. It will take you to the Admiral's location."

Before Soren could respond, the bridge doors slid open, and Jack strode in. He'd clearly overheard the last part of the conversation.

"Now wait just a damn minute," Jack said, moving to stand beside Soren. "That's not what we agreed to. You can't expect us to just hand over our captain without any guarantees."

"I understand your concerns," Ulysses replied, "but the decision isn't mine to make. The Admiral was quite clear on this point. You can either go along with it, or go without the meeting."

Jack opened his mouth to argue further, but Soren held up a hand, silencing him.

"We've been through too much to trust too easily," Ulysses continued. "And I'm sure you can appreciate how hard all of this is to believe from our perspective. If you have no ulterior motives, if you have nothing to hide, then you have nothing to fear. You have my word on that."

Soren didn't answer right away while he considered the ultimatum. They needed this meeting, needed information. The risk was substantial, but was it more risky to go alone than start over from square one, or worse, seek out his doppelgänger?

"Very well," Soren said finally. "We'll agree to the transfer. When can we expect the shuttle?"

"I'll send it over immediately," Ulysses replied. "You have ten minutes to decide who will accompany you and prepare for departure."

As the communication ended, Jack turned to Soren, his expression a mix of concern and frustration. "Are you sure about this? It could be a trap."

"It could be," Soren agreed. "But we don't have much choice. We need that meeting."

Soren stood, his mind already working through the possibilities of who to bring with him. Jack was the obvious choice. His decades of experience and tactical mind invaluable in any situation. But there was also Alex, whose combat skills might prove necessary if things went south. Dana's scientific knowledge could be crucial in discussions about the Convergence. And then there was Lukas, whose understanding of the phenomenon surpassed them all.

After a moment of internal debate, Soren made his decision. "I'm taking Lukas," he announced. "His expertise on the Convergence will be invaluable during the meeting."

Jack nodded, though Soren could see he wasn't entirely happy with the decision. "I hope you know what you're doing, old friend."

"So do I," Soren replied quietly.

He activated his comms. "Lukas, meet me in the hangar bay in twenty minutes. You're going with me for a meeting with Admiral Yarborough. Pack light, but bring any data you think might be relevant to our discussions with the Admiral."

"Understood, Captain," Lukas replied, a hint of nervousness in his voice.

Soren turned to Vic. "You have the conn. Keep the ship at ready stations." He pivoted to Keira. "Keira, keep the vortex cannon charged and ready. If things go south, you need to hit them fast and hard, and get the hell out of the area. Understood?"

"Aye, Captain," Keira replied.

As Soren made his way to the hangar bay, he ran through countless scenarios in his head. What would he say to this Jane? How much could he trust her? And most importantly, would she have the information they so desperately needed?

When he arrived at the hangar, not only was Lukas

waiting for him but also Alex and Dana. His children's faces were etched with concern.

"Dad," Dana said, stepping forward. "Are you sure about this? It seems incredibly risky."

Soren nodded, understanding their worry. "It is risky," he admitted. "But it's a risk we have to take. We need answers, and Admiral Yarborough is our best chance at getting them."

Alex's jaw clenched. "At least let me come with you. I can provide better protection than—"

"Than the scientist?" Lukas interjected, a hint of defensiveness in his tone.

"That's not what I meant," Alex said quickly. "I just...I don't like the idea of you going into an unknown situation without proper backup."

Soren placed a hand on Alex's shoulder. "I appreciate your concern, son. But Lukas' knowledge is what we need right now. And I need you here, ready to fight for the ship if something goes wrong."

Alex nodded reluctantly. "Yes, sir."

Dana stepped forward, hugging Soren tightly. "Be careful, Dad."

"I will." As they broke apart, Soren addressed both of his children. "No matter what happens, focus on the mission. the Convergence is the priority, not one old starship captain who happens to be your old man. Understood?"

"Understood," they replied in unison.

The sound of engines drew their attention to the hangar entrance, where a slightly beaten up, wedge-shaped shuttle was gliding in. It spun to face out into space before settling onto the deck.

Soren turned to Lukas. "Ready?"

The scientist nodded, though Soren could see the apprehension in his eyes. "As I'll ever be, Captain."

As they approached the shuttle, its hatch slid open. The interior was dimly lit, with no sign of a pilot or crew. An automated ship? Soren hesitated for a moment at the threshold, a flicker of doubt passing through his mind. What if they decided to blow the ship up to get rid of this strange man who looked and sounded just like their worst enemy?

But they'd come too far to turn back now.

"Let's go," he said to Lukas, stepping into the shuttle.

They settled into the seats, the hatch closing behind them with a soft hiss. As the shuttle lifted off, Soren caught a final glimpse of Alex and Dana's worried faces through a camera feed on the viewscreen beside him.

The shuttle launched out of the Wraith's hangar bay, the stars of unfamiliar space stretching out before them. Soren opened his mouth to ask Lukas a question, but before he could speak, a faint hiss emanated from the shuttle's ventilation system.

"What the—" Lukas began, his eyes widening in alarm.

"Relax," Soren said, memories of his trip from Mars springing immediately to mind. "We're just going to sleep for a while." After saying it, he realized the gas could be poisonous as well.

But he had seen the FUP's ships. Judging by their dilapidated state, the last thing these people needed was to make another enemy.

And if he didn't return to the Wraith, boy, would they ever.

Soren's limbs grew heavy, his vision blurring at the edges. Rather than fight, he relaxed into the encroaching darkness. The last thing he saw was Lukas slumping in his seat, already unconscious.

Then nothing.

CHAPTER 19

Soren's consciousness slowly rose to the surface, pulled from the depths of artificial slumber by a gentle shaking. As his eyelids fluttered open, a familiar face swam into focus above him. For a moment, reality blurred with memory, and his heart swelled with an overwhelming sense of relief and love.

"Jane," he murmured, his hand instinctively reaching up to cup her cheek. "I've missed you so much. I love you."

The words left his lips before his mind fully engaged, before he remembered where he was and who he was truly looking at. He saw the emotions play across her face—surprise, longing, a flicker of pain—and immediately regretted his lapse.

Admiral Jane Yarborough's eyes softened, a bittersweet smile tugging at her lips. "I remember when my Soren used to look at me like that," she said softly. "So loving, so gentle. It's been a long time since I've seen that expression on his face."

Soren lowered his hand, feeling a complex mix of emotions churning in his chest. "This Soren still is that man," he said quietly. "But I have my own Jane waiting for me back home. I'm sorry I—"

"It's alright. I understand."

He watched as she straightened, composing herself. But he couldn't miss the lingering desire in her eyes, the silent longing for the man she had once known and loved. It was disconcerting to see such raw emotion directed at him from a face so achingly familiar, yet belonging to a stranger.

Admiral Yarborough cleared her throat, her professional demeanor reasserting itself. "Let's wake up your companion," she said, moving to Lukas' side.

As she gently roused the scientist, Soren took a moment to gather himself. The shuttle's interior came into sharper focus, and he realized they had arrived at their destination while he was unconscious. He stood, stretching to work out the stiffness in his muscles.

"Huh?" he heard Lukas say across the aisle from him. "What? Where?"

"Relax. It's okay," Admiral Yarborough said. The softness in her voice brought Soren all the way back home, dragging up memories of raising Alex and Dana, setting them at ease when the nightmares came. His heart ached for his Jane. He would give anything to see her one more time.

"Ma'am?" Lukas said before glancing over at Soren. "Captain?"

"This is Admiral Jane Yarborough," Soren said. "We're here."

Lukas stiffened, looking at the Admiral. "My apologies, ma'am. I...it's the gas."

"Of course," she answered. "I understand completely. And you are?"

"Doctor Lukas Mitchell, ma'am," he replied.

"A medical doctor, or..."

"Astrophysics," he answered. "And mathematics."

"You have two doctorates?"

"Yes, ma'am."

"I'm impressed." She glanced at Soren. "If you two will follow me."

Admiral Yarborough led them out of the shuttle and into a bustling hangar bay. Soren's eyes darted around, taking in every detail. The ship seemed to be of similar design to the Ever Valiant. Another Komodo, most likely. Having seen the FUP's other ships, he doubted the exterior looked as spotless as the interior. The Admiral ran a tight ship.

"I'm sure you have a lot of questions," she said as they walked, her stride purposeful. "So do I. And since you requested this meeting, it seems proper that I should go first."

"That's more than fair," Soren agreed.

"Captain Ulysses passed on some of the information he gathered from Major Gray. I have to admit, the idea of alternate dimensions bleeding into one another is hard to accept. But as they say, seeing is believing." She stopped and turned to Soren. "The way you looked at me when I woke you..." That same deep longing Soren had noticed earlier flashed across her face. "I had considered that perhaps Strickland physically altered someone to play a part in his twisted games. But you can't fake love like that."

"I sure hope not," Soren agreed. "To be honest, it's difficult to look at you and not see my wife and hear her in your voice."

"I'm afflicted with the same suffering with you, Captain," she admitted. "Though perhaps circumstance has made the burden easier for me to bear." She turned away and resumed walking. "I want to hear more about this convergence and the Eye directly from the source."

Lukas, still shaking off the last vestiges of the sedative, launched into an explanation. "the Convergence is a phenomenon we believe is causing multiple dimensions to collapse into one another," he began, his words tumbling out rapidly as they navigated through the ship's corridors. "The Eye appears to be the focal point of this event, a sort of cosmic storm where the barriers between dimensions are weakest."

As they walked, Soren noticed the reactions of the crew they passed. Shock and fear flashed across many faces at the sight of him, followed by confusion when they saw him walking freely alongside their Admiral. But Yarborough's presence seemed to reassure them, and many visibly relaxed once they realized she was in control of the situation.

They reached what Soren assumed was the Admiral's ready room, and Yarborough ushered them inside. As the door slid shut behind them, she turned to face Lukas, her expression intense.

"Continue," she said. "I want to hear everything."

Lukas nodded, taking a deep breath before diving back in. "We've determined that the Convergence isn't a natural phenomenon, at least not entirely. Our latest analysis from within the Eye itself suggests that some event, or perhaps a series of events, triggered the initial instability. This trigger seems to have exacerbated the problem over time, pushing us closer and closer to a catastrophic collapse of multiple realities. Today, we're on the precipice of disaster, and one final, powerful enough shove will be enough to..." He trailed off.

"To what?" she prompted.

"We aren't really sure," he replied. "There's a belief that the dimensions will be merged into a single universe, and everyone in them will be combined with their counterparts. Another theory that anyone who has a duplicate will die. And a third postulation that the event will be cataclysmic. No survivors."

Admiral Yarborough stared at Lukas as she absorbed this information. "That's a lot to take in," she said slowly. "Like I said, it's very hard to believe. But I refuse to discount the possibility of anything. The universe has a way of surprising us."

"Admiral," Soren said, "our greatest need is to identify whatever might be triggering this destabilization."

"How can I help you with that?"

"Is there any new technology your dimension has developed?" Lukas asked. "A new power source, perhaps? Or research into manipulating atomic structures? Anything that might have had unforeseen consequences on a cosmic scale?"

Yarborough's eyes narrowed in thought. "Nothing springs immediately to mind," she said after a moment. "At least from our side of this equation. We've been so focused on survival that we haven't had an opportunity lately for groundbreaking research."

Lukas' face reddened. "Of course not. I didn't mean to imply…"

"I suppose it's possible the SF may have caused the trouble," the Admiral continued. "They have robust R&D programs, mostly military based, but also across a wide spectrum of technologies. We have spies among the enemy, but none of them with clearance to the most top secret projects. Still, assuming things go well here, I can reach out to them and see if they might have any ideas."

"That would be incredibly helpful," Soren said. "And of course, we want to be helpful to you in return. What can you tell me about your current situation? The state of your war effort?"

A shadow passed over Yarborough's face. She moved to sit behind her desk, gesturing for Soren and Lukas to take the seats across from her. "It's not good," she admitted. "We're down to the equivalent of three strike forces and have barely a thousand Marines in our ground forces. We lost our last power armored and mechanized units years ago, and advanced munitions are in critically short supply." She paused, her eyes distant. "We had to abandon our last planetside installation three months ago. It just became too dangerous for the population to maintain. Of course, it's now under the Strickland Federation flag and the people who live there live in fear. But at least they're alive. We survive by hit-and-run tactics, raiding SF installations for supplies. But even those opportunities are dwindling. The SF knows our most likely strike locations, and they've started leaving traps for us."

"Like the sabotaged parts at the Wolf installation," Soren said, recalling what Harry had discovered.

Yarborough nodded. "Exactly. Strickland could bolster the defenses at these locations, wipe us out quickly. But he's not doing that. He's toying with us. Dragging it out."

"Maybe part of him doesn't want to hurt you, specifically," Soren suggested.

The Admiral laughed bitterly. "Perhaps. Or more likely, he's prolonging our suffering for his own amusement. You have to understand, the man we're fighting isn't the man I married. I see that version of him in you, but I haven't seen it in him since Alex was a boy."

"If you don't mind me asking, what happened to him?"

"I don't know. After Proxima…well, even before then. Sometimes I think it was because I got promoted ahead of him, but I have such a hard time believing he would ever be so petty. In any case, I still don't understand it. It's like something inside of him just broke. He left for that tour as my husband and came back a stranger. Cruel. Power-hungry. By the time I realized how far he'd fallen, it was too late to save Alex. He had always idolized Soren and believed everything he said. He turned my own son against me."

Soren felt a chill run down his spine at her words. The idea that he could become such a monster in any reality was deeply unsettling. And seeing this Jane's eyes moist with tears broke his heart. "I'm sorry," he said softly. "As difficult as it is for me to know another version of me could be so cruel, I can't imagine how difficult this must be for you."

Yarborough's gaze met his, a complex mix of emotions swirling in their depths. "It's challenging," she admitted. "Fighting against overwhelming odds is one thing. But when the face of your enemy is the man you loved and your only child...it takes a toll." Her gaze softened slightly. "Do you and your Jane have children, Captain?"

Soren nodded. "We have an Alex of our own and a daughter, Dana. They're both here with me, on the Wraith. Alex is Marine Special Forces. Dana is a starship commander, and an accomplished scientist in her own right."

"Dana," Yarborough repeated, a wistful note in her voice. "A daughter. I wonder..." She trailed off, shaking her head. "Well, no use dwelling on what might have been." She paused, collecting herself. "We're getting a little off-track though, aren't we? You negotiated a deal with Major Gray. You promised to help us against a high-value target of our choosing."

"Within reason," Soren said. "None of us can afford to lose our chance to stop the Convergence while attempting to capture rations and ammunition."

"And to think, part of me was tempted to send you straight to Earth, to take out Strickland himself. With your cloaking technology, you might actually stand a chance." She chuckled as Soren stiffened. "I'm only joking, Captain. I wouldn't actually ask that of you. But I hope you can appreciate the temptation."

Soren nodded, relaxing slightly. "Of course. If our positions were reversed, I'm sure I'd feel the same way. Do you have anything a little more reasonable in mind?"

Yarborough leaned back in her chair. "I do. It's a target I've had my eye on for some time. One that we might be able to pull off alone, but between your ship's cloaking technology and your powered Marines, we can decrease the risk dramatically. The SF's largest forward operating base, a massive space station. If we could capture it intact, we'd gain access to ships, equipment, maybe even power armor of our own. It could be a game changer for us and would let us at least pause the SF's initiative. The risk would still be significant, but so would the potential reward."

"I'd need to see all the relevant intel you have on the operation and share it with my advisors before making any decisions."

Yarborough nodded. "Of course. I'll provide you with everything I have so far. Perhaps we can finalize plans together." She paused, studying Soren intently. "But before we go any further, I need to know something."

"I have nothing to hide from you," Soren replied. "What is it?"

"Why us? Why not approach the SF? They have far more resources, and far more power. From a purely strategic standpoint, they'd be the logical choice for an alliance against the Convergence."

Soren met her gaze steadily. "Because there are some lines I won't cross, even with the fate of multiple universes at stake. Working with a despot like Strickland...I couldn't stomach it."

"Are you sure it's not just because of me?" Yarborough asked, her voice soft.

Soren hesitated, weighing his words carefully. "I won't deny that your presence is a factor," he admitted. "But it's more than that. Wars are fought by people, Admiral. Human beings with emotions and convictions. Sometimes it's those very human elements that pull victory from the jaws of defeat."

"And sometimes, it's those emotions that pull the rug of victory out from under you," she countered.

"There's one other reason," Soren said. "We have no proof either way, but we can't be completely sure the SF is not only triggering the destabilizing events, they may be doing it intentionally."

Yarborough flinched at the idea. "Why would they do that? They'd need to have something to gain by it. But what would they stand to gain?"

"Good questions. Again, we have no proof of that. But the potential exists. Asking them for help to stop it doesn't seem like the most prudent course of action."

"Fair enough. I appreciate your honesty." She stood, signaling the end of their meeting. "I'll have the helm set course for the rendezvous point to return you to your ship. In the meantime, I'll provide you with a stateroom and all the intelligence we discussed for your review. Maybe we can meet later to discuss tactics. You're still a version of Soren Strickland, so I assume your strategic mind is a cut above most."

"According to Dana, he's a legend in his dimension, ma'am," Lukas said, smiling.

"As I'd hoped. What do you say, Captain?"

Soren nodded. "Give me at least two hours to review the details before you send for me."

"Of course. The fold back to your ship will take eight hours. We have plenty of time to reconnect." The door to her ready room opened. A pair of Marines were on the other side. "These men will show you to your quarters. If you need anything, ask them, and it will be provided."

"Thank you, Admiral," Soren said, rising to his feet. Lukas joined him, and together they exited the room. Soren glanced back just before the door closed, wanting to see Jane's face one more time.

He found her staring back at him, that same deep longing playing across her features. Seeing him looking at her, she turned her head away.

He had known interacting with her wouldn't be easy, but he hadn't expected it to be this hard.

CHAPTER 20

Soren sat in the officer's lounge, his eyes fixed on the datapad in his hands. The screen glowed softly, illuminating his face in the dimly lit room. Across from him, Lukas hunched over his own device, likely combing through the same data he'd reviewed hundreds of times already. Soren had been staring at his pad for nearly four hours now, poring over the intelligence Yarborough had provided. Other than the occasional soft beeps from their datapads, the lounge was quiet.

It amazed Soren how Lukas could remain so focused on discovering even the most minute new detail he may have overlooked. In fact, he was so engrossed in his work that he barely seemed to register Soren's presence.

"Any progress?" Soren asked him, breaking the silence, mostly to ensure Lukas wasn't in some sort of quiet distress.

Lukas looked up, blinking as if coming out of a trance. "Nothing conclusive yet, Captain."

"Keep at it," Soren encouraged. "Even the smallest detail could be crucial."

"Yes, sir."

Soren returned his attention to his datapad, studying the schematics of the SF space station. The information was extensive, but not as complete as he would have liked. Still, it was enough to start formulating a plan.

Before he could delve deeper into his analysis, a soft chime at the door interrupted them. Two Marines entered. "Captain Strickland," one of them said, "Admiral Yarborough requests your presence."

"Of course." Soren left his datapad on the end table beside him. "Lukas, I'll be back as soon as I can." Lukas merely looked up and nodded.

As Soren followed the Marines through the corridors of the ship, he did his best to ignore the strange looks from the crew who hadn't seen him earlier. Most looked confused, but a few stared daggers at him, their expressions taking on such violent hate at the very sight of him he was glad to have his Marine escort. He couldn't blame any of them for their hostility, considering the war crimes this dimension's version of himself had committed, but it still left him feeling uncomfortable.

He had expected to be led back to Yarborough's ready room, but as they continued past familiar landmarks, he realized they were heading somewhere else entirely.

The Marines came to a stop outside a nondescript door and tapped the control pad beside it. The door slid open, revealing what was obviously Admiral Yarborough's personal quarters. The room was spartanly furnished, with a small sitting area and a table set for two on his left. A desk sat against the wall to his right, a terminal and some personal effects set out on it. There were two closed doors in the back, obviously leading to a head and bedroom.

Standing near the table, the Admiral looked up from the datapad in her hands. "Captain," she greeted him, "I hope you don't mind the change of venue. I thought we could discuss our plans over dinner."

One of the Marines motioned Soren through the doorway. He hesitated, caught off guard by the casual nature of the meeting, not to mention the Admiral's choice of attire: wide leg black pants with a chiffon overlay and matching wraparound blouse. "Admiral…" It was exactly the same style of evening wear his Jane would choose for a special occasion dinner. "…I'm not sure this is appropriate."

"Please, Soren," she said, her voice softening. "It's a working dinner. Nothing more. We have a lot to discuss, and I find that good food often helps fuel good ideas. As for my civilian attire, I get tired of wearing a uniform day in and day out, and I didn't think entertaining you in my usual t-shirt and ratty sweatpants would be appropriate."

After a moment's consideration, Soren smiled, and then nodded. "I understand, Admiral. Thank you for your hospitality."

Soren entered and walked across the main room to the table. If it had been his wife waiting there for him, he would have seated her before taking his own seat. Instead, considering the circumstances, he took his seat as the Admiral laid her datapad beside her silverware and settled at the table, where a simple meal of roast meat and mixed tubers and vegetables had been served.

As they began to eat, Yarborough activated a holographic display above the center of the table, showing a detailed image of the SF station. "Forward Operating Base Alpha," she said, "what are your initial thoughts?"

Swallowing his first bite of the tender medium-rare meat that tasted a lot like venison, Soren regarded the hologram. "It's a formidable challenge, that's for certain. Multiple layers of security, both external and internal. The patrol ships are a primary concern; we'll need to neutralize them quickly."

"Agreed," Yarborough said, laying her fork down and manipulating the display to zoom in on the station's outer defenses. "The gun batteries are another significant obstacle. They've got enough firepower to dig hard into our ships before we can even get close. That's why the patrol ships need to go before they can soften us up."

"What about the shields?" Soren asked, leaning forward to get a better look.

"State of the art," Yarborough replied. "They can withstand sustained bombardment from multiple capital ships, not that they would ever need to. And even if we manage to get through all of that, there's an entire company of Marines inside to deal with."

"Powered or standard?" Soren asked.

"That's a problem, Captain. We don't know."

Soren sat back, considering the challenge before them. After a moment, he leaned forward again. "I have a plan for at least part of the attack."

"Oh?" Yarborough raised an eyebrow, intrigued. Her fork poised over her plate, she waited for him to elaborate.

"The Wraith's cloaking technology," Soren explained. "We've used it before to sneak our elite Marine unit, the Scorpions, onto heavily defended targets without detection. If we can get them inside, they can work to sabotage the defenses from within."

"That's intriguing," Yarborough said, her eyes widening slightly. "It's risky, but..." She stabbed a forkful of the mixed tubers and what looked like green beans in gravy. "...it could give us the edge we need. How would we get them in, though?"

Soren watched the food disappear into her mouth, the way her little finger curved away from the fork's handle catching his attention.

"Do I have something stuck in my teeth?" she asked, chuckling as she closed her mouth and chewed.

Soren blinked and looked up to meet her golden brown eyes, so like his wife's. And Dana's. "Uh...no. I'm sorry."

He could feel his face reddening, and then he smiled. "My apologies for staring. My wife..." He gestured to the fork she still held over her plate. "...she does the same thing you do with her little finger."

"Oh..." She looked at the finger in question, lifting it away from the fork's handle and waving it in the air. "I fell out of a swing and broke it when I was a little girl. It didn't heal quite right. It's pretty much stuck in this one position."

"The same with my wife, only she wrecked her brother's mini bike. She was a tomboy growing up, but you wouldn't know it now."

The Admiral's smile widened. "Amazing. I wonder how else we're the same, yet different. How old was she when she broke her finger?"

"Ten."

"I was eight when I broke mine. Still, the similarity is curious."

"That it is."

They merely stared at each other for a moment as they watched the reflection of memories and wishes cross each other's faces. Then Soren cleared his throat. "Back to this," he said, leaning forward and adjusting the holographic display to focus on a specific section of the station. He pointed to what appeared to be a maintenance airlock. "This airlock is small and likely not guarded on the inside. As long as we can get the Scorpions to it without being spotted, they can hack through any security locks and slip right in."

"Clever," Yarborough nodded. "But one misstep and we'd lose the element of surprise and possibly the entire squad."

"True," Soren agreed. "But I have faith in my team's abilities. They've pulled off similar maneuvers before."

As they continued to discuss the plan, Soren found himself impressed by Yarborough's sharp tactical mind. She quickly grasped the nuances of his suggestions, offering her own insights and refinements. They connected on a similar level as he and his Jane did, not a comfortable thought he wanted to dwell on.

"There's one more thing that might help," Soren said after they had hashed out the initial insertion plan. "The Wraith is equipped with a weapon called a vortex cannon. It's capable of—"

"Wait," Yarborough interrupted, her voice suddenly tense. "Did you say vortex cannon?"

Soren nodded, surprised by her reaction. "Yes. It's a powerful energy weapon capable of—"

"Tearing holes in spacetime," Yarborough finished for him. "We know about them. The SF has a few ships equipped with similar weapons."

Soren felt a surge of surprise and concern. "They do?"

Yarborough nodded. "Yes. They first appeared a few years ago. I assume out of their research and development programs."

"Omega Station," Soren said. "It has to be."

"I'm not familiar with that name."

"It's a skunkworks in the other dimensions I've been in. Probably the same here."

"Well, wherever they originated, they're incredibly powerful. Thankfully, they have limited range and can't be turret mounted. Still, we've lost several ships to them."

Soren hesitated, his mind sticking on the new information. "Have you noticed any strange effects when these weapons have been used?"

"Not that I can speak to," Yarborough replied. "Why do you ask?"

"It's just a hunch," he said. "But I'm starting to wonder if there might be something more to these weapons than just destroying starships with a single hit."

"I see," the Admiral replied. "Well, regardless of their

wider implications, they're a threat we need to be wary of in every operation."

"Agreed," Soren said. "But there is one advantage we might have. We've modified our cannon to be able to disrupt targets rather than destroy them. It's how we managed to escape from an SF fleet near the Eye."

"That could be incredibly useful. If we could use it to disable their ships without destroying them..." Yarborough's eyes lit up with what Soren took as the idea of potentially capturing so many ships fully intact.

"I was thinking more along the lines of using it to knock out the station's gun batteries," Soren said.

"Either way, it could give us a tactical advantage."

As they continued to eat, they pored over the station schematics, discussing potential entry points and strategies. Soren pointed out what he believed to be the best route for the Marines from the infiltration point, as well as key locations they would need to secure to take control of the station and how they could quickly do that.

"It's a solid plan," Yarborough nodded. "Risky, but I believe we have a good chance of success. You know, it's both wonderful and painful to have this discussion with you. You think just like I assumed you would. Like he used to..." Her vocalized thoughts trailed off as she looked down at her lap.

Soren felt a pang of sympathy. "I'm sorry. I can't imagine how difficult this must be for you."

She shook her head. "No, don't apologize." Sighing, she looked up. "It's nice, in a way, to be reminded of the man I fell in love with." She cleared her throat. "Tell me about your children. What were your Alex and Dana like growing up?"

Soren couldn't help but smile at the memories. "They were quite the pair. Always getting into mischief together, but fiercely protective of each other. There was this one time when Alex was about seven and Dana was five. We were visiting my parents on Earth, and they decided to go exploring in the woods behind the house..."

As Soren recounted the story of how his children had gotten lost, built a makeshift fort, and eventually were found covered in mud, proudly declaring they had "conquered the world," he watched Yarborough's expression soften.

"They sound wonderful," she said when he finished. "So different from my Alex. He never had a sibling, always had to fend more for himself. Growing up with both of us in the military, and then the divorce...he never really developed that protective instinct toward anyone else. Sometimes I wonder if things might have been different if..."

She trailed off again, and Soren felt a wave of sadness wash over him. The weight of what this Jane had lost—what this entire dimension had lost—seemed to hang heavily in the air between them.

"It's not your fault," Soren said softly. "You obviously did the best you could do with the circumstances you were given."

"Perhaps. But it's hard not to wonder about the *what ifs*. Especially now, seeing you and hearing about your family. It's like a glimpse into a life I could have had."

"I understand," Soren said. "But focusing on what might have been won't help us now. We need to concentrate on the future—on stopping the Convergence and giving all three of our dimensions a chance at a better tomorrow."

"You're right, of course," Yarborough agreed. "It's just...seeing you, talking with you like this. It brings back a lot of memories, some of them very good."

"It's the same for me," Soren said. "But we can't let that cloud our judgment. We have a mission to plan, and a lot of lives are depending on us getting it right."

Yarborough nodded, visibly pulling herself together. "Of course. You're absolutely right. Let's get back to the matter at hand."

They turned their attention back to the holographic display, diving deeper into the specifics of their plan. As they discussed troop movements and contingencies, Soren found himself marveling at how easily they worked together. Despite the strange circumstances, there was a familiarity to their interactions that made strategizing feel almost effortless.

"What about the internal security systems?" Soren asked, zooming in on the station's central hub. "Once we're inside, we'll need to stifle alarms and disable them quickly to prevent lockdowns. We have software to crack most security protocols, but if the station is using anything unexpected..."

"I'm not sure if your tools are up to the task," Yarborough admitted. "The control systems are heavily encrypted and isolated from the main network. What we need is someone with exceptional hacking skills to breach them in time."

"Do you have anyone in mind?" Soren asked.

"Yes. He's handled similar efforts for us in the past, though not usually in the middle of a raid. We'll need to provide him with cover, though. The control room is likely to be heavily guarded."

"Agreed," Soren nodded. "I'm starting to think we need more Marines on the initial infiltration than just the Scorpions."

"Do you have any extra power armor?"

"No. But what if, instead of sending the Scorpions EVA, we take a shuttle across to the station? Bigger profile, greater risk, but as long as we maintain the cloaking envelope correctly, we can hide anything without it being seen."

"It would be helpful to have a larger force inside during

the ingress. We could cover more of the strategic positions more quickly."

"We can split the Scorpions up, one per unit," Soren said. "They can provide cover and heavy firepower for each team."

"I like it."

"There is one problem I should mention. The Wraith is currently equipped with a transmitter that reveals its location to anyone who knows how to locate the signal. It needs to be actively searched for to be detected, but we believe the SF might know how to find it."

"You should have mentioned that at the beginning of our meal," Admiral Yarborough said.

"Well, we have a potential solution. We just haven't had time to search the hull for the transmitter. It may be a moot point, but I wanted you to know about it. Even if we can't disable the transmitter, again, as long as the enemy doesn't suspect we're in the area, there's little reason for them to look for the transmitter."

She shook her head. "If they spotted you with it once, they'll be sure to search for you again."

"Strickland won't take any chances," Soren said, since he wouldn't either. "We'll have to do more than just try to find the transmitter; I'll make it a priority."

"We can spare a few days."

"I'm not sure we can, but we don't have much choice."

As they continued to refine their plan further, a soft chime sounded. Yarborough glanced at her datapad. "We're approaching the rendezvous point," she said. "We'll be exiting fold space soon. I think we have a workable strategy here. It might be best to sleep on it in the meantime to see if we come up with any new angles. For now, I'm sure you're eager to get back to your ship."

"And share everything we've discussed with my crew," Soren agreed, placing his napkin on his chair as he stood from the table. As he did, Yarborough reached out, gently touching his arm.

"Thank you, Soren," she said softly. "For coming to dinner, for the planning session, and for giving me one last normal meal with the Soren Strickland I remember."

Soren felt a lump form in his throat. "Admiral, I—"

She shook her head, cutting him off. "No, don't. Please. Just...thank you."

As Soren left her quarters, his mind was a tornado of emotions and tactical considerations. The upcoming mission could be a huge win for the FUP. But as he made his way back to rejoin Lukas, one thought kept pushing its way to the forefront of his mind:

What if the vortex cannons had some connection to the Convergence? And if they did, what then?

He quickened his pace, eager to share his thoughts with Lukas.

They had a lot to do and precious little time to do it.

CHAPTER 21

Soren followed the Marines back through the corridors, still wondering about the potential implications of the vortex cannons. As they approached the officer's lounge where he had left Lukas, he couldn't wait to share his idea with the scientist.

The door slid open, revealing Lukas still hunched over his datapad, seemingly oblivious to the passage of time. He looked up as Soren entered, blinking rapidly as if coming out of a trance.

"Ah, Captain," Lukas said. "Back already? How did it go?"

"We made some progress," Soren replied. "It's time to go."

"Oh. Already?" Lukas hopped to his feet, and they fell into step behind the Marines.

"I have a question for you," Soren said as they walked. "What do you know about the vortex cannons and their effect on spacetime?"

Lukas glanced at him. "I think I know what you're thinking, Captain. Yes, the cannon does affect spacetime, as you saw when we were in the Eye. But its disruptive energy is actually pretty minimal compared to something like a space fold. The main difference is that the cannon focuses the disruption in a specific manner. Technically very complex to do, but mathematically simple to explain."

Soren felt a pang of disappointment. "Darn. I thought I might have been onto something. The SF has similar weapons, and I wondered if they could be connected to the Convergence somehow."

Lukas shook his head. "I'm afraid not, Captain. Unless they have...say, a thousand of them firing at once, they aren't capable of causing the kind of instability we're seeing. It was a good thought, though. Dana and I eliminated the possibility soon after we learned about the weapon. With Tashi's help, of course."

"I see," Soren said, trying not to let his frustration show. "Worth asking about, anyway."

"How did the planning session with the Admiral go?" Lukas asked again. "Did you learn anything useful?"

"It went well," Soren replied. "We've agreed to a joint operation against an SF space station. I'll brief the team on the details once we're back on the Wraith. But I think it's a solid plan, and it could help us solidify our alliance in this dimension."

"I just hope we can get more information from the FUP's spies," Lukas said. "We may gain allies, but they won't help if we can't find the source of the Eye."

"I know. And I agree. By gaining access to a network of operatives, we've expanded our search radius and velocity significantly."

Lukas laughed. "Now you're sounding like a mathematician, Captain. I must be rubbing off on you."

They entered the hangar, where the same shuttle that had brought them waited. As they boarded, Soren couldn't help but feel relieved. He had enjoyed spending time with this dimension's Jane, planning the mission, but he was glad to be heading back to his ship and crew.

The trip back to the Wraith took only a few minutes. As the shuttle's hatch opened, Soren saw a familiar face waiting for them. Dana stood in the hangar, a smile breaking across her face as she saw her father and Lukas emerge unharmed.

"Dad!" she called out, stepping forward to embrace him. "We were starting to worry. You've been gone for twenty hours."

Soren returned the hug. "It was eight hours each direction, and there was a lot to discuss in between." As they broke apart, Soren activated his comms. "Tashi, Ethan, do you copy?"

"We're here, Captain," Ethan's voice came back. "What do you need?"

"I need you to prioritize locating that transmitter. It's become even more critical now."

"Understood, sir," Ethan replied. "We've already made a second EVA and eliminated more of the hull from consideration."

"Good work. Keep at it. I want that thing found and disabled as soon as possible."

"Aye, Captain."

Soren turned to Dana and Lukas. "I need to brief the team on what's happened. I want both of you there as well."

"We're right behind you, Captain," Dana said, smoothly switching from daughter back to subordinate officer.

Fifteen minutes later, Soren stood at the head of the conference table, looking out at his assembled team. Keira, Jack, Liam, Alex, Minh, Dana, Lukas, and Wilf all sat waiting for his briefing.

"I'm sure you're all eager for an update," Soren said.

"We've agreed to assist the FUP in a joint operation against a Strickland Federation space station."

He activated the holographic display in the center of the table, bringing up the schematics of the target station from his datapad. "This is our objective. It's a major forward operating base for the SF, heavily defended and well-supplied. Taking it would be a significant blow to the SF and a much-needed boost for the FUP."

Soren went on to outline the general plan they had developed with Admiral Yarborough, detailing the use of the Wraith's cloaking technology to insert a team for sabotage, the potential use of the vortex cannon to disrupt the defenses, and the coordinated assault that would follow.

As he finished his summary, Soren looked around the table. "Questions?"

Jack leaned forward, his expression skeptical. "This all sounds well and good, Soren, but how does it get us any closer to solving the Convergence? That's supposed to be our primary mission here."

Soren understood his concern. "Fair question, Jack. For one, this operation was a condition of meeting with Yarborough in the first place. And before you think that was a dead end, she's agreed to reach out to her spy network to see if they might have any leads on any new Strickland Federation developments that might be behind the Convergence. She's putting her people at risk to gather intel for us. That's far more than we could have accomplished on our own in this dimension, and at a much faster pace."

"I'm glad to hear it," Jack replied.

Alex spoke up next. "Captain, I've been thinking. My team would be a lot more effective if we could get our neural augments activated. From what Tashi told me, we don't have the capability to enable them on the Wraith, but if Admiral Yarborough has access to a skilled hacker and the right equipment, they might be able to help us with that."

Soren considered this for a moment. "That's an interesting thought, Alex. I'll look into it. I'm not familiar with the neural augments, but I assume it will give us an edge in the operation?"

"Absolutely, sir."

"Speaking of edges," Minh said, "what kind of air support can we expect for this operation? My pilots are itching for some action, but I'd like to know what we're up against."

"The station has a significant defensive presence in the form of patrol ships," Soren replied. "We don't have all the details worked out yet, but my intention is for the Hooligans to assist in disabling the ships. Once we make ourselves known to the enemy, we'll need those craft too busy trying to swat you away to focus on the larger ships moving in on the station. I'll make sure you get all the details once we have them, so you can brief your pilots thoroughly."

"Understood. Thank you, sir."

Keira spoke up next. "Captain, what's our contingency plan if the SF detects us before we're in position? Even with the cloak, if they're actively scanning for that transmitter..."

"That's why finding and disabling that transmitter is our top priority right now," Soren answered. "But you're right, we need to be prepared for that possibility. I want you and Jack to work on developing a fallback plan. We need options if things go badly."

"Aye, sir," Keira replied.

Soren looked around the table once more. "Any other questions?" When no one spoke up, he nodded. "Alright then. We have a lot of work to do and not much time in which to do it. Let's get to it. Dismissed."

Soren watched his team file out of the conference room

with pride. They were preparing to embark on a dangerous mission in an unfamiliar dimension against a powerful enemy. But looking at the determined faces of his crew, he knew they were up to the challenge.

He caught Alex just before he left the room. "Alex, hang back a moment. I want to ask you about your neural augments."

Alex nodded, stepping aside as the others left. "What do you want to know?"

Soren leaned against the conference table. "Everything. What exactly are we dealing with here? And why haven't they been activated already?"

"The augments are relatively new technology. Still classified. Only six units in the entire FUP Marines had them. They're designed to boost our reaction times, improve sensory processing, and enhance our ability to interface with our armor and weapon systems. They can also deliver stimulation to the brain that can increase adrenaline production for increased strength, but only in short bursts. And, they're like mental comms between the Scorpions. We can always talk to one another, up to a distance of about fifty klicks, depending on the environment and terrain. The thing is, they're considered too dangerous to keep active all the time. You know the one thing the military least wants to lose is control. A unit of Force Recon with augments active could easily assassinate the president without ever uttering a word about it. I tried to turn them on when we were stuck on Jungle, but I couldn't guess my CO's password to gain access."

"It sounds like they'd give us a significant advantage in this operation," Soren said.

"Absolutely," Alex nodded emphatically. "With the augments active, we'd be faster, more precise, and better coordinated. In a high-stakes infiltration like this, that could make all the difference."

"And you're certain these augments are safe? No risk of long-term side effects?"

"They've been thoroughly tested," Alex assured him. "The brass wouldn't have cleared them for field use otherwise. The only reason they're not standard issue is the complexity of the activation process and the specialized training required to use them effectively."

"Okay," Soren said after a moment's consideration. "I'll reach out to Admiral Yarborough about getting her engineer to take a look. But Alex," he added, his voice taking on a more serious tone, "I need you to be absolutely certain about this. We're in uncharted territory here, and I can't afford to take unnecessary risks with you and your team."

Alex met his father's gaze. "I understand. But I wouldn't suggest it if I wasn't completely confident in the safety and benefits."

Soren nodded, a small smile tugging at the corner of his mouth. "You remind me of me when I was your age, always pushing for that extra edge. In the meantime, let's assume we'll get those augments online."

"Copy that," Alex replied. "Thanks for hearing me out on this, Dad."

"Always, son," Soren said, clapping Alex on the shoulder. "Now get going. We've got work to do."

CHAPTER 22

Alex stood on the hull of the Wraith, the vastness of space stretching out around him. His power armor anchored him to the ship's surface, magnetic boots keeping him firmly in place despite the lack of gravity. In his gloved hands, he held Tashi's makeshift transmitter detector, its screen casting a soft blue glow across his faceplate.

"Anything yet, Gunny?" Sarah's voice came through the comms.

"Negative, Two," Alex replied, slowly sweeping the device in an arc before him. "But we've only covered about half of the hull so far. Keep looking."

They had been at this for a few hours now, methodically searching every inch of the Wraith's exterior for the elusive transmitter. The device that could potentially give away their position to the enemy, jeopardizing not only their mission but their very lives.

"I still can't believe the FUP managed to plant this thing so well," Jackson grumbled, his frustration evident even through the distortion of the comms.

"They're crafty bastards," Malik replied. "Gotta give 'em that much."

Alex tuned out the chatter. He took a few careful steps forward, eyes locked on the detector's readout. For a moment, he thought he saw a faint blip on the screen, but it vanished as quickly as it had appeared.

"Hold up," he said, halting his squad's movement. "I might have something here."

He continued forward a few more steps, moving the detector in increasingly tight circles. There it was again—a faint, intermittent signal. Alex's heart began to race.

"I've got a ping," he announced, excitement creeping into his voice. "It's weak, but it's definitely there."

"Location, Gunny?" Zoe asked.

"Amidships, between the port and starboard railgun batteries."

"On my way." Zoe confirmed, the others acknowledging their arrival shortly as well.

As Alex carefully made his way toward the source of the signal, the ping on the detector grew stronger and more frequent. Alex felt a surge of triumph. They were close, he could feel it.

"Ethan," he called over the comms. "I need you up here. I think we've found it."

"On my way, Gunny," the chief engineer replied, excitement rippling through his voice.

While he waited for Ethan to arrive, Alex continued to sweep the area with the detector. The signal was definitely strongest here, but he couldn't see anything out of the ordinary on the hull's surface.

Ethan's bulky form appeared over the curve of the hull, moving with the careful precision of someone well-versed in EVA operations. He made his way to Alex's position, the toolkit clipped to his suit swaying gently at his hip with every step.

"What have we got?" he asked as he reached Alex's side.

Alex handed him the detector. "The signal's strongest right here, but I can't see anything obvious."

Ethan took the device, his experienced eyes scanning both it and the surrounding hull. After a few moments, he shook his head. "You're right, the transmitter has to be in this vicinity. But it's not immediately visible."

"Scorpions," Alex called out to his squad as they approached. "Fan out and search this area." He swung his right arm in an arc, encompassing the area he wanted them to search. "Look for anything that might be a good hiding spot for the transmitter—access panels, irregularities in the hull plating, anything that seems out of place."

"What does the transmitter look like, Gunny?" Sarah asked.

"Damned if I know," he replied.

"So how will we know when we find it?"

Alex glanced at Ethan, who answered by holding up Tashi's tracker. "Once it's out in the open, this thing should start going crazy."

The Scorpions began their search, methodically examining every pertinent inch of the hull. Nearly ten minutes passed, the silence while they searched interrupted only by the sound of the oxygen flowing into Alex's helmet.

"Gunny!" Jackson's voice suddenly cut through the comm channel. "I think I've got something!"

Alex and Ethan quickly made their way to Jackson's position. The Marine was crouched next to an external access panel for one of the missile batteries, about twenty meters astern from where they'd initially gathered.

"What have you got there, Three?" Alex crouched down beside Jackson.

"This doesn't look right." Jackson pointed to a small, almost imperceptible seam along the edge of the panel. "The panel's slightly misaligned."

Ethan leaned in for a closer look, running a gloved hand

along the edge of the panel. "Good eye, Marine. This defi-nitely isn't a standard install." He turned to Alex. "It's a clever hiding spot though. Easy to overlook. We're lucky this small gap in the nano-coating didn't cause its own set of issues. The good news is, it proves we can scratch the paint job and still remain hidden."

"Maybe," Alex replied. "We just don't know how badly we can scratch it."

"I'm pretty sure I don't want to find out."

"Can you open it?" Alex asked.

"Good question." Ethan reached for his toolkit. "Give me a minute here."

It didn't even take that long. Ethan removed four screws, careful not to damage their nano-coating and slowly pried at the panel. With a soft click, the panel came loose. Ethan slowly pulled it away, revealing a small, innocuous-looking device nestled among the wiring of the missile launcher.

"That's it," Ethan confirmed. "They hid it surprisingly well. Without Tashi's tracker, we never would have found this thing."

"Not bad for a revo, eh?" Alex said.

"Not bad at all," Ethan agreed, grinning behind his helmet. "Let's get this thing out of here and—" He froze in place. The moment his gloved hand made contact with the transmitter, a small LED on the surface began flashing red, its frequency increasing rapidly.

"Shit!" Ethan exclaimed, jerking his hand back. "It's rigged!"

"Can you disarm it?" Alex asked, his voice calm.

Ethan shook his head. "I don't know. This isn't my area of expertise. If we remove it now, it might trigger some-thing worse."

The red light continued to flash, its pace quickening

with each passing second. Alex still didn't panic. He put his hand on Ethan's shoulder. "Step back, sir."

"What do you mean?" Ethan asked.

Zoe stepped forward. "Please step aside, sir," she said, her voice calm and authoritative. "Let me take a look."

Ethan hesitated for a moment, then moved out of her way. Zoe crouched, her eyes fixed on the device. Without a word, she opened a compartment on her armor and pulled out a set of tools.

"Zoe, what are you—" Ethan began, but she cut him off.

"Trust me. I've got this."

Before the engineer could protest further, Zoe's hand darted out. She severed two of the three wires connecting the transmitter to the ship's systems with two quick, precise movements. The flashing red light abruptly stopped.

For a moment, no one moved. Then, slowly, Ethan leaned in to examine the device. "It's deactivated," he said, disbelief in his voice. He turned to Zoe. "How did you know which wires to cut?"

Zoe shrugged. "I've got over three hundred hours of training in disabling various types of explosives and booby-traps. This was actually pretty simple compared to some of the stuff they threw at us in the sims."

Ethan glanced at Alex. "No wonder you stayed so calm."

"I have total faith in my squad," he replied. "Well done, Five."

"Easy peasy," she replied.

"What if you had cut them out of order?" Ethan asked.

"Boom," she answered. "But it's safe to cut the third wire now." She snipped it and passed the transmitter to Ethan. "Here you go, sir."

"Thank you, Five," he replied.

Alex activated his comms to report in. "Captain, this is Scorpion One. We've located and disabled the transmitter."

"Excellent work, Gunny," Soren's voice came back, a note of relief evident even through the comm distortion. "And your timing couldn't be better. Once you're back inside, I need you and your squad to change out of your armor and report to the hangar. We're taking a trip over to Admiral Yarborough's ship."

"Copy that, sir. May I ask what for?"

"We're meeting with their software and systems expert," Soren replied. "It's time to see about getting those neural augments of yours activated."

A thrill of excitement ran through Alex at his father's words. "Understood, sir. We'll be there ASAP."

The Scorpions quickly shed their armor once they got back inside the Wraith, joking with one another about the look on Ethan's face when he discovered the rigged transmitter.

"I have to say," Jackson said. "It's kind of crazy that the FUP rigged their own transmitter to explode like that."

"What's crazier is the question of whether the detonation would have been powerful enough to hit the ordnance inside the missile launcher and set off a chain reaction," Sarah said.

"Oh, damn," Malik hissed. "Would they really do that?"

"What's even crazier than that," Alex said, "is if they had the ability to remote detonate the transmitter."

"See, now you're just taking things a step too far, man," Malik said.

"No, he's right," Zoe said. "Think about it. You build a ship that can make itself invisible. What if it falls into the wrong hands? Like what if this dimension's Captain Strickland had the Wraith? It's an incredibly dangerous weapon, and it needs redundancies to keep it under control. That's what the transmitter is. There'd be no reason for them to ever use it on their own spacers."

"I guess you have a point there," Malik said.

The Scorpions finished shedding their shells and headed for the hangar. They were nearly there when Tashi and Wilf met them at an intersection, looking apprehensive.

"Hey, Gunny," Wilf said, wiggling his fingers in greeting. "Are you heading over to the Spirit of War, too?"

"To where?" Alex asked.

"Spirit of War. Your dimension-mom's ship."

"Don't call Admiral Yarborough that, Wilf," Alex chided.

His fingers curled in embarrassment. "Sorry."

"Yes, we're headed to the hangar to hop over there and meet with their engineer. You?"

"Same," Tashi replied.

"Cool name for a ship though," Malik said.

Soren was waiting for them by the Stinger. As they approached, he nodded in acknowledgment. "Good work out there. You've given us a much better chance at maintaining the element of surprise and considerably raised the odds of our mission's success."

"Thank you, sir," Alex replied. "It was a team effort. Zoe's the one who disabled the device."

Soren turned to her. "Well done, Private Andersson. I'll make sure that goes in your file."

Zoe straightened, a hint of pride in her voice. "Thank you, Captain. Just doing my job."

Sang's voice came over the comms as they boarded the Stinger and settled into their seats. "Next stop, the Spirit of War. Keep your arms and legs inside the vehicle at all times, and remember—if you can see the stars, you've gone too far."

"What does that mean?" Wilf asked.

"It means you're in deep shit," Jackson replied while the other Scorpions chuckled.

As the Stinger lifted off and maneuvered out of the Wraith's hangar, Alex found himself studying the looming form of the Spirit of War through the viewscreen. The FUP flagship was a formidable sight, its battle-scarred hull a reminder of the long and brutal conflict they had been fighting.they're

"So," Jackson said, breaking the silence that had fallen over the group, "anyone want to place bets on what this hacker's going to be like? I'm thinking either a wiry kid with thick glasses or some grizzled old vet who looks like he hasn't slept in a decade."

"My money's on the kid," Malik replied with a grin. "Probably thinks he's hot shit, too."

"Or she," Zoe pointed out.

"Whatever they're like, remember we're guests on their ship," Alex said. "Best behavior, all of you."

"Yes, Mom," Sarah quipped, earning a few stifled laughs from the others as she elbowed Alex in the ribs.

The Stinger touched down smoothly in the FUP flagship's hangar. As the hatch opened, Alex saw Admiral Yarborough waiting outside. His heart immediately started pounding, drawing a steadying hand on his arm from his father.

"Strange, isn't it?" Soren asked.

"Yeah, you could say that," Alex replied.

"She's a fine woman, like our Jane. But she chose a different path in life, and she's been through a lot. Just be yourself, and remember that it will be even stranger for her."

"Right." Alex breathed deeply, preparing himself. "I'm ready."

"Then let's go."

CHAPTER 23

Alex stepped out of the Stinger, his eyes immediately traveling toward Admiral Yarborough. Despite his father's warning, he felt his breath catch in his throat. The resemblance to his mother was uncanny, yet there was a hardness to the Admiral's features that spoke of years of struggle and loss.

As she approached and he noticed her composure falter for a moment, his heart went out to her. Her eyes glistened with unshed tears, and he could see the slight tremor in her hand as she extended it towards him.

"Gunnery Sergeant Strickland," she said, her voice steady despite the emotion playing across her face. "It's...a pleasure to meet you."

Alex took her hand, giving it a firm shake. "The pleasure is mine, Admiral. I've heard a lot about you." He managed to keep his voice level, though it took some effort.

"All good things, I hope," she replied, lower lip still quivering.

"Of course, ma'am," Alex said. He turned slightly, gesturing to his squad. "Allow me to introduce the rest of the Scorpions. This is Corporal Sarah Chen, Lance Corporal

Jackson Holt, Private First Class Malik Johnson, and Private Zoe Andersson."

Each of the Scorpions nodded in turn as they were introduced. Admiral Yarborough greeted them all, but Alex couldn't help noticing how her gaze kept drifting back to him.

Soren stepped forward, breaking the moment of awkwardness. "Admiral Yarborough," he said warmly. "Thank you for arranging this. I'd also like you to meet Tashi Sato and Wilf Delaney, two of our civilian specialists."

Tashi and Wilf both offered polite greetings, with Wilf's fingers doing a little dance as he spoke.

"A pleasure," Yarborough replied. She gestured to a young man standing slightly behind her. "This is Aster, our software and systems expert. He'll be working with you on activating your neural augments."

Aster stepped forward, and Alex found himself reassessing his initial expectations. The hacker was far from the stereotypical image of a tech expert. He was tall and well-built, with an athletic physique that suggested he was no stranger to physical training. His sharp, intelligent eyes scanned the group, and Alex had the distinct impression that Aster could hold his own in a fight just as easily as he could behind a computer terminal.

"Nice to meet you all," Aster said, his voice carrying a hint of an accent Alex couldn't quite place. "I'm looking forward to digging into those augments of yours. It's been a while since I've had a challenge like this."

Admiral Yarborough turned to Soren. "Captain, if you'd like to join me in my ready room, we can discuss the finer points of the upcoming mission while Aster works with your squad."

Soren nodded. "Of course, Admiral." He glanced at Alex, giving him a reassuring nod before following Yarborough out of the hangar.

As they left, Aster clapped his hands together. "Well then, shall we get started? My lab's this way."

The group followed Aster through the corridors of the Spirit of War. Alex couldn't help but notice the stark contrast between this ship and the Wraith. Where the Wraith was sleek and advanced, the Spirit of War bore the scars of prolonged conflict. Patches of mismatched metal covered battle damage, and exposed conduits ran along walls where panels had been removed for quick repairs.

Tashi fell into step beside Aster, his curiosity evident in his rapid-fire questions. "So, these emitters you mentioned—how exactly do they work? Is it a direct interface, or more of a wireless system?"

Aster grinned, clearly pleased by Tashi's interest. "It's a bit of both, actually. The emitters use quantum encrypted signals to securely transmit to the neural augments. The encryption itself is unbreakable—believe me, I've tried—but the code generation algorithms can be modified."

"Fascinating," Tashi replied, his eyes wide with excitement. "And the bandwidth? How much data can you push through the connection?"

"More than you'd think," Aster said. "But let's save the technical deep dive for when we're in the lab, yeah?"

They reached Aster's workspace, a cluttered room filled with various computer terminals, displays, and what looked like partially disassembled pieces of equipment. The hacker reached a central workstation, gesturing for Alex to join him.

"Okay, Gunny," Aster said, picking up a small, hand-held device. "Let's start by scanning those implants of yours."

Alex stepped forward, tilting his head to give Aster better access. The hacker ran the device along both sides of Alex's head.

"Yup, you have augments," Aster said lightly. "And

they appear to be functional, but offline. Let's try a basic activation signal first. It probably won't work, but you never know."

He tapped a few commands into his terminal, then activated the emitter. Alex felt...nothing.

"No dice," Aster said, unsurprised. "It was worth a shot. Now it's time to get creative."

For the next hour, Tashi and Wilf leaned over each of Aster's shoulders while he tried various modifications to the activation signal, each attempt failing. His initial bravado began to waver, replaced by a growing frustration.

"Damn," Aster muttered, tapping his fingers on his desk. "I hate to admit it, but I'm starting to run out of ideas here."

"There has to be something we can try," Alex said.

Aster leaned back in his chair, considering. "There is one option, but it's a bit more invasive. To really crack this system, I need to pull the source code from one of the implants themselves."

Alex didn't like the sound of that. "What exactly does that entail?"

"Surgery," Aster replied. "But it's minor. I promise. We'd need to put a small hole in your skull so we can connect a wire to one of the implants and download its core programming. Once I can see how the implant expects the signal, it will be much easier to change the emitter to match."

"Gunny, we didn't come here to get our skulls cracked open," Malik said.

"Not all of your skulls," Aster said. "We only need to do this once. Don't worry," he added quickly, seeing the concern on Alex's face, "our medical team is more than capable of handling it."

Alex hesitated. The idea of letting an unknown doctor poke around in his brain, even for a good cause, didn't sit well with him. "I'm sure your people are great, but if this is the only way to get these things working, I'd rather have our doctor handle the procedure."

"Whatever works for you," Aster replied.

Alex activated his comms. "Captain, this is Scorpion One. We've hit a snag with the augment activation. Aster says he needs direct access to one of the implants. It would require minor surgery."

There was a pause before Soren's voice came back, tight with concern. "That sounds risky, Alex. Are you sure it's necessary?"

"I believe it is, sir," Alex replied. "Without it, we're not going to make any progress here. And you know the benefits of getting us online."

Another pause. "Very well," Soren said finally. "Admiral Yarborough tells me her medical team is quite skilled."

"Aster said the same, sir. But I'd prefer if Asha performs the procedure. As a matter of familiarity, not trust."

"Of course," Soren replied. "I'll send Sang to pick her up."

"Thank you, sir," Alex said, relieved.

While they waited for Asha to arrive, the group made their way to the Spirit of War's sickbay. Alex paced, while the other Scorpions tried to lighten the mood with increasingly bad brain surgery jokes.

"I've got one," Sarah said. "Why did the brain surgery go wrong?"

"I don't know, why?" Jackson asked.

"Because the surgeon had a lot on his mind!"

"That's terrible," Zoe said.

"The worst. Seriously," Malik agreed.

"What did I miss?" Asha asked, entering sickbay escorted by the ship's lead doctor, Lieutenant Patil, concern plastered on her face.

"Nothing," Alex said. "You just saved me from something much more painful than brain surgery."

"I don't like this, Alex," she said, frowning. "It's not exactly a standard procedure. According to Doctor Patil, you'll need to be awake and alert throughout."

"I have years of experience, Gunny," Patil said. "If you would prefer—"

"No, I wouldn't," Alex replied. "But thank you, Doctor. I understand the risks. We need these augments online. It could make all the difference going forward."

"Let me do it instead, Gunny," Zoe volunteered. "I'm less crucial to the operation. If something goes wrong—"

"No," Alex cut her off firmly. "It has to be me. I'm the squad leader. It's my responsibility."

Asha sighed, recognizing the determination in Alex's eyes. "Let's get started then."

The next hour was one of the most surreal experiences of Alex's life. He lay on the operating table, a local anesthetic dulling the sensation behind his right ear as Asha carefully cut through skin and bone to access the implant. He could feel the pressure of her instruments and hear the soft murmur of her voice as she conferred with Aster, but there was no pain.

"Okay," Asha said finally. "We've exposed the implant. Aster?"

He held a thin wire out to Asha. "We need to connect this to the small protrusion on the implant. It's magnetic, so it shouldn't be too hard."

Asha took the end of the wire and used a pair of tiny tweezers to hold it and put it in place. "Done," she announced.

"Let's see what we've got here," Aster muttered, tapping on his datapad.

Time seemed to stretch as Alex lay there, hyper-aware of every sound and movement around him. He focused on his breathing, using the techniques he'd learned in training to keep himself calm.

"I have the source code!" Aster exclaimed suddenly, startling Alex. "You can disconnect the cable and patch him up, Doc. We're done here. Meet me back in the lab when you're ready. This shouldn't take long." He hurried out of sickbay.

"Gunny, should we—" Sarah started to ask.

"Go," Alex said as best he could without moving. The others chased after Aster, leaving him alone with Asha and Doctor Patil.

Asha pulled the wire from inside his skull and quickly closed the incision. "All set," she said. "How are you feeling?"

"Like I've got a splitting headache," Alex replied with a weak grin. "But otherwise, it was nowhere near as bad as I thought it might be."

Asha chuckled. "Here, this should help." She pressed a hypospray to his neck, and Alex felt the pain begin to recede.

"Thanks, Doc," he said, sitting up slowly.

"Take it easy for a few minutes," she advised. "No sudden movements."

Alex nodded, then immediately regretted it as a wave of dizziness washed over him. Asha steadied him, her hand lingering on his arm.

"You know," she said softly, "you didn't have to do this. It was a big risk."

"It was necessary," Alex replied. "For the mission, for my squad."

Asha shook her head, a mix of admiration and exasperation in her eyes. "You Stricklands and your sense of duty. It'll be the death of you one day."

"Maybe," Alex said with a small smile. "But not today."

They made their way back to Aster's lab, where they

found the hacker once more hunched over his terminal. The other Scorpions stood nearby, a palpable sense of anticipation in the air.

"How's it going?" Alex asked as they entered.

Aster didn't look up, his focus entirely on his work. "Almost there. Your implants use a fascinating encryption algorithm. It's like nothing I've ever seen before."

"Is that good or bad?" Sarah asked, a note of concern in her voice.

"Good for security, bad for me trying to crack it," Aster replied. "But I think I've...got it!" He spun in his chair, a triumphant grin on his face. "Ready to light up those augments, Gunny?"

Alex nodded. "I was ready yesterday."

Aster activated the emitter, and for a moment, nothing happened. Then, suddenly, Alex's world exploded with information.

A heads-up display materialized in his field of vision, offering a dizzying array of data. He could see his own vital signs, the status of his squad mates, a targeting reticle, and more. With a thought, he could also activate various "boost" modes, enhancing his strength, speed, sensory perception, or everything at once.

Scorpions, augment check, he thought silently.

They each checked in without making an audible sound. Their augments were active at last!

"Well?" Aster questioned.

"It worked," he said aloud, his voice filled with excitement. "It actually worked."

Aster grinned. "Of course it did. I told you I was good."

Alex looked at his squad, a smile spreading across his face.

Alright, Scorpions. Now we're ready for war.

CHAPTER 24

Six days later, the Wraith emerged from fold space in the Gliese 876 system. Soren stood on the bridge, his eyes fixed on the main viewscreen as the flash of light surrounding them faded, allowing him a view of the FUP Navy fleet. Soren counted nearly thirty ships of various sizes and configurations, according to the Admiral, every single battle-ready vessel they possessed, every one bearing the scars of prolonged conflict. At the center of the formation sat the Spirit of War, its imposing bulk a reminder of the power the FUP still wielded.

Just thirty ships against the entire Strickland Federation. He suddenly wondered if Jane had been right to question his loyalty to them. Seeing the state of the FUPN's remaining war machine, maybe they would have been better off trying to negotiate with Grand Admiral Strickland.

He pushed that thought aside. Someone like this dimension's version of himself couldn't be trusted. This was the only way forward, and his doubts were just his nerves trying to get the best of him.

"Status report," Soren called out, his voice carrying across the bridge.

"All systems nominal, Captain," Mark announced from his station. "Current position is approximately two AU from Gliese 876b."

Soren turned to Jack. "Let's get the team assembled in the conference room." Jack nodded, calling Vic to the bridge to take the conn.

Fifteen minutes later, Soren stood at the head of the conference table, looking out at his assembled crew. Jack, Keira, Liam, Alex, Minh, Dana, Lukas, Ethan, Tashi and Wilf sat around the table. Nervous energy left most of them fidgeting. Only Alex seemed unaffected, and Soren wondered if he might be having a conversation with the other Scorpions right now, venting his concern to them instead of relieving his tension with a tapping foot or a restless hand. Soren immediately realized why Aster had given him the emitter—an off switch allowing him to turn off their neural implants whenever he wanted—but he preferred to let the Scorpions get as comfortable with them as possible before they needed to use them in combat.

"Captain," Wilf said, raising his hand. "Do you mind if I ask why we're here?"

"Admiral Yarborough is organizing a meeting of all the ship's captains," Soren replied. "I could have taken it alone, but I want them to see all of you as well. That the Wraith is in the hands of more than just a doppelgänger of Grand Admiral Strickland."

Before he could continue, Samira's voice came over the intercom. "Captain, we're receiving an incoming video transmission from the Spirit of War."

"Put it through to the conference room, Samira."

The large display on the wall flickered to life, revealing Admiral Yarborough seated at her desk in her ready room. A few seconds later, the image fractured, splitting into multiple windows. Each new frame showed the face of a different ship's captain, their expressions stoic and focused.

"Captain," Tashi whispered. "Shouldn't we turn our camera on." He motioned to the red light beneath the display.

"Not yet," Soren replied just as softly.

"Admiral, what's going on?" one of the captains asked. "Where did we get this new ship?"

Another captain chimed in, her voice suspicious. "And why is their feed turned off?"

Yarborough raised a hand, effectively silencing the chatter. "I need you all to listen carefully to what I'm about to say." She paused, taking a deep breath before continuing. "We've come across a new, unexpected ally in our fight against the Strickland Federation. They're connected to this conference, but I've asked them not to reveal themselves just yet. What I'm about to tell you may sound impossible, but I assure you, it's the truth."

Yarborough leaned forward slightly. "I've recently learned that despite all of our advances, despite our ability to traverse the stars and colonize planets of all kinds, there are still great forces of nature that we've never encountered before. Greater powers than we can fully understand. I've learned that we aren't alone in our existence. We aren't even quite as unique as we may have thought."

The captains wore bewildered expressions, but remained silent as Yarborough continued.

"There's a threat to our galaxy that's bigger than the SF, but also possibly caused by them. A rift between universes. The ship on your sensors came through that rift, searching for a way to end that threat." She paused again, letting her words sink in. "Captains, let me introduce you to another dimension's Captain Soren Strickland."

At her words, Soren nodded to Keira, who activated their feed. The reaction was immediate and chaotic.

"What the hell?"

"Is this some kind of joke?"

"Admiral, have you lost your mind?"

The voices overlapped, each captain trying to make themselves heard over the others. Some looked angry, others terrified. A few seemed on the verge of ending their transmission entirely.

Yarborough's voice cut through the noise like a knife. "Enough!" The single word, delivered with the full weight of her authority, brought immediate silence. "I understand this is shocking. But I assure you, this Captain Strickland is not our enemy. He and his crew are here to help us in our mission, and in return, we're going to help them with theirs." Her gaze fixed on the Wraith's feed. "Captain Strickland, you have the floor."

Soren took a deep breath, keenly aware of the skeptical and hostile gazes fixed on him. "Captains, I understand your concerns. I know how this must look to you. But while I am Soren Strickland, I'm not Grand Admiral Soren Strickland. As the Admiral said, I'm not even from your dimension." He paused, waiting for another outburst that never materialized. The captains looked too shocked to speak. "In my dimension, I never betrayed my oath or my duty. I remained loyal to the FUP, just as all of you have. And now, my dimension and yours face a threat greater than anything we've encountered before."

Soren explained the basics of the Convergence, the rift between the three affected dimensions, and the desperate search for its cause. As he spoke, he could see the captains' expressions slowly shifting from outright hostility to cautious curiosity.

"I've earned Admiral Yarborough's trust," Soren concluded. "And now I'm asking for yours. We have a plan to deal a significant blow to the SF, one that could turn the tide of your war. In return, we need your help to uncover the source of the Convergence before it's too late for all of us."

There was a moment of silence as the captains processed his words. Then, one by one, they began to speak.

"I don't like it," a grizzled captain with a scarred face said bluntly. "But if the Admiral vouches for you, I'm willing to accept your presence here."

Another captain, a younger woman with sharp eyes, leaned forward. "This plan of yours...how confident are you of its success?"

"Very," Soren replied without hesitation. "It's risky, I won't deny that. But with your help, the FUPN has a real chance of scoring a major victory."

The discussion continued, with Soren and Yarborough fielding questions and addressing concerns. Most of the captains seemed to come around, but Soren could tell that a few remained skeptical. He caught Yarborough's eye, and she gave him a slight nod, as if to say, *I'll handle the holdouts.*

As the meeting wound down, Yarborough spoke up once more. "I'll be sending each of you detailed plans within the hour. You have two days to review them and prepare your crews. If you have any questions or concerns, bring them to me directly."

The captains acknowledged her orders, and one by one, their feeds winked out until only Yarborough remained.

"Well handled, Captain Strickland," she said with a hint of a smile. "For the most part, I think we've won them over."

"I hope so," Soren replied. "We'll need everyone's full commitment if this is going to work."

Yarborough nodded. "I'll speak to the few who still seem hesitant. Don't worry, they'll fall in line." Her expression grew serious. "Two days, Captain. Make sure your people are ready."

"We will be," Soren assured her. "Good luck, Admiral."

As the transmission ended, Soren turned to face his team. The weight of what they were about to attempt hung heavy in the room.

"Well," Jack said, breaking the silence, "I guess this is really happening."

Soren nodded, his eyes sweeping across the faces of his crew. "It is. And we're going to make it count." He activated the holographic display in the center of the table, bringing up a detailed schematic of the SF station. "Let's go over the plan again. I want to make sure we've accounted for every possible snafu that could occur."

In two days, they would go over the plan one last time before either striking a crippling blow against the SF and moving one step closer to stopping the Convergence or failing spectacularly, potentially dooming multiple universes to whatever end the Convergence wrought.

The thought should have terrified him. Instead, he felt a familiar surge of determination. He had faced impossible odds before and had come out on top. This time would be no different.

As the meeting stretched into its third hour, Soren could see fatigue starting to set in among his crew. But there was also a palpable sense of readiness, a shared understanding of the monumental task ahead.

"I think that covers everything," he finally said, straightening up from where he had been leaning over the holographic display. "Unless anyone has any last-minute concerns?"

The room fell silent for a moment. Then Wilf spoke up.

"Captain," he said, his fingers twisting nervously, "what if we're wrong about all this? What if helping the FUP doesn't get us any closer to stopping the Convergence?"

The question hung in the air, giving voice to a fear Soren guessed was lurking in everyone's mind.

"It's a fair point to make, Wilf," Soren admitted. "We're

taking a big risk here, and there's no guarantee it'll pay off in the way we hope it will." He paused, looking around at each member of his crew. "But sometimes, the right path isn't always clear. We have to make educated decisions we can come to with the information we have." His voice had taken on a tone of quiet conviction. "I believe this is the right move. Not just because it might help us stop the Convergence, but because it's the right thing to do. These people are fighting against tyranny and oppression. If we can help them, even a little, then we have to try."

The room fell silent for a moment as Soren's words sank in. Then, one by one, heads began to nod in agreement.

"Well said, Captain," Jack said softly.

Soren looked around the room one last time, meeting each person's gaze. "Get some rest," he said. "We've got a long couple of days ahead of us. Dismissed."

CHAPTER 25

Soren stood on the bridge of the Wraith, his eyes fixed on the main viewscreen. The vast expanse of space stretched out before them, the large, bluish bulk of Gliese 876b occupying the entire port side of the monitor. His fingers tapped a restless rhythm on the arm of his command chair as he waited for the signal to begin their assault, more impatient than nervous.

He didn't have to wait long.

"Incoming hail, Captain," Samira said.

"Put it through."

"Captain Strickland," Admiral Yarborough greeted, her voice stiff. "Our ships are in position. Are you ready to proceed?"

"We're ready, Admiral," Soren replied, his voice steady despite the tension coiling in his gut. "Awaiting your order."

"Very well. You may commence the attack. Good hunting, Captain."

As the transmission ended, Soren turned to his crew. "Keira, engage the cloak. Sang, take us in."

"Aye, Captain," Keira responded. "Cloak engaged."

Sang's voice was cool and professional as she acknowledged the order. "Course laid in, Captain. Commencing approach."

The Wraith surged forward, its powerful thrusters propelling them toward their target.

"Mark, keep a close eye on those sensors. I want to know the moment we pick up any contacts."

"Understood, sir," Mark replied, his attention focused on the sensor readouts before him.

As they rounded Gliese 876b, using the gas giant's bulk to mask their approach and started on their intercept vector toward the station, Mark's voice cut through the tense silence on the bridge. "Captain, I'm picking up multiple contacts. Patrol ships, sir. Scutum-class, by the look of it."

Soren leaned forward in his chair. "How many?"

"I count twelve, sir."

"As expected," Jack said. "Jane's spies were right on the money."

"FOB Alpha just appeared on sensors. It's massive, Captain."

"Put it over the barrel," Soren said.

The sensor grid projected ahead of his station, allowing him his first look at the target. Right now, it was a basic wireframe, but comparing its size to the Scutums, it had to be at least twice as large as Omega Station.

Soren activated his comm link. "Liam, status report on the boarding party."

Lieutenant Moffit's voice came back crisp and clear. "All units ready and standing by in the Stinger, sir. The Scorpions are suited up and itching to go."

"Good. Stand by for launch."

Soren switched channels. "Phoebe, are the Pilums prepped and ready?"

"Affirmative, Captain," came the quick reply. "All

fighters are fueled, armed, and ready for immediate launch."

"Excellent." He changed channels once more. "Captain Pham, this is Strickland. Be prepared to scramble on my command."

"Copy that, sir," Minh responded. "The Hooligans are ready for the party."

As the Wraith drew closer to its target, the massive space station came into view on the main screen. Soren felt his breath catch at the sight of it. The station was even more of a behemoth up close. Its central hub sprouted multiple arms, each dotted with docking ports, weapons emplacements, and sensor arrays. Warships were currently docked on at least ten of the hub's arms.

But those ships weren't alone.

Surrounding the station were the Scutum patrol ships, their boxy, heavily armored forms drifting back and forth in automated patterns. Beyond them, Soren could make out what appeared to be a strike force of a dozen additional ships, four Komodos and eight Valkyries that looked like they were preparing to head out on a mission. No doubt, they were set to search for the FUP rebels and/or the Wraith, the unidentified ship that had escaped the Eye.

"The intel didn't mention the presence of a strike force," Jack said.

"No, but we accounted for that possibility in the planning for a reason."

"True. We prepared for so many possibilities, this seems almost too easy," Jack mused, a hint of excitement creeping into his voice. "Like taking candy from a baby."

Soren shot him a warning glance. "Don't get cocky, old friend. The best-laid plans have a habit of going sideways at the worst possible moment. Nothing is guaranteed in war."

Jack nodded. "Right. I should know better by now."

As they penetrated the outer defensive perimeter, slipping past the Scutum patrols with ease, the tension on the bridge ratcheted up another notch. Soren could feel the nervous energy radiating from his crew, each person acutely aware of their precarious position.

Sang's voice broke the silence, an edge of concern evident in her tone. "Captain, we have a problem. One of the capital ships is blocking our planned approach vector to the entry point."

Soren's jaw tightened in frustration, but he didn't let it show. He glanced at Jack, who had the grace to look sheepish. "You were saying something about this being too easy?"

"Noted," Jack replied.

Soren quickly assessed their options. They couldn't risk contacting Yarborough for new orders. The SF might detect any transmission, blowing their cover before the operation even began. He studied the station schematic on his display, searching for an alternative option.

"There," he said, pointing to a maintenance airlock closer to the station's center. It would mean breaching closer to the station's more populated areas than he would have liked. There would probably be more security to deal with, but he had faith in Alex and the other Marines. "We'll use that as our entry point instead. Sang, can you get us there?"

Sang's eyes narrowed as she calculated the new approach. After a moment, she nodded. "It'll be tight, but I can do it, sir."

"Make it happen." Soren opened a channel to the hangar bay. "Liam, we've had to change our insertion point. I'm sending you the new coordinates now. You'll need to adjust your internal route, but the primary objectives remain the same."

"Understood, Captain," Liam replied. "We'll update our

tactical maps and brief the teams. It might slow us down a bit at the start, but we'll make up the time."

As Sang maneuvered the Wraith into position, Soren found himself gripping the arms of his seat more tightly. They were deep in enemy territory now, surrounded by SF ships and defensive systems. Discovery at this point would be catastrophic.

"Almost there," Sang muttered, her focus absolute as she guided the ship through the maze of patrol routes and sensor sweeps. After what felt like an eternity, her voice rang out again. "We're in position, Captain."

Soren allowed himself a small sigh of relief before straightening in his chair. This was it—the point of no return. "Bastian, you're cleared for launch. Get our people over there and get back here fast."

"Aye, sir," came the reply. "Launching now."

On the viewscreen, Soren watched as a small icon representing the Stinger passed out of the Wraith's hangar and began its short journey to the station. He shifted his attention to the sensor grid, confirming the Stinger was invisible to their sensors, which meant it would be invisible to the enemy, too.

As the Stinger disappeared from view, melding with the station's bulk, Soren turned his attention to the next phase of the operation. The real fireworks were about to begin, and he intended to give the SF a show they wouldn't soon forget.

"All hands," he announced over the ship-wide comm, "this is it. Let's show them what the Wraith can do. Godspeed everyone." The bridge crew tensed, hands hovering over consoles, ready to spring into action at a moment's notice.

Soren's eyes remained fixed on the tactical display, watching for any sign that their presence had been detected. "Minh, status report on the Hooligans."

"Locked, loaded, and ready to raise hell, sir," came the immediate reply.

"Good. Stand by for my signal. When we decloak, I want you to hit those patrol ships hard and fast. Keep them off balance and draw their attention away from the station."

"With pleasure, Captain," Minh said, a hint of eagerness in his voice.

Soren switched channels. "Keira, charge up the vortex cannon. I want it ready to fire the moment we reveal ourselves."

"Already on it, sir," Keira replied. "Cannon will be at full charge in thirty seconds."

As the seconds ticked by, Soren felt the familiar surge of adrenaline that always preceded combat. Despite the gravity of their situation—or perhaps because of it—he relished the challenge ahead.

"Stinger is in position, Captain," Bastian reported. "Deploying the Scorpions now."

Soren exhaled, trying to push his fear for Alex's safety out with a breath. His son and his team were the best in the galaxy, and the augments made them even better.

"Captain, we're crossing to the hatch," Alex said. "Contact with the station in five. Four. Three. Two. One. Contact."

Soren's mind created the soft thunks of the Scorpions' magboots against the station's hull.

"Preparing for infil," Alex said. Soren knew that Zoe would be opening up panels on the external part of the station and disabling security alarms before they opened the airlock, similar to how they had gone after Harper on his ship.

"Captain, we have movement from the Scutums," Mark reported. "They're breaking the perimeter."

Soren's eyes snapped to the grid. Indeed, two of the ships were moving toward the station. Was it a routine shift change, or had they noticed the anomaly the Wraith's cloak may have created on their sensors? Either way, they were nearly out of time. "Keira, get ready to raise the shields."

"Aye, Captain," she replied.

Soren remained tense. They couldn't make their move until the Marines were inside and the Stinger back inside the hangar. His fingers dug deeper into the armrests a little harder, heart pounding as the seconds passed. The Scutums continued their approach, slowing as they angled toward where the Wraith had tucked in beside the station.

"Come on, Alex," Soren whispered.

"Airlock disabled and opened," Alex reported.

"Stinger initiating docking seal," Bastian said.

"Captain," Mark said, getting too nervous to remain silent.

"Almost there," Soren replied.

The Scutums cut their thrusters, drifting in on the station, their vector carrying them toward a collision with the Wraith.

"Captain," Mark repeated even more nervously.

"Almost there," Soren repeated.

"Docking seal complete," Bastian reported. "Stinger hatch open, Scorpions leading the charge." Then, a handful of seconds later. "Station hatch is sealed. Stinger on its way home."

Soren eyed the sensor grid. The Scutums were about ten seconds from smashing right into the Wraith. When they did, not only would they know the ship was there, but they would also damage the hull, destroying the cloak.

They were out of time.

"Phoebe, launch the Pilums now!"

CHAPTER 26

Alex's heart raced as he led the Scorpions into the Strickland Federation space station. They were in hostile territory now. Every second counted.

"Zoe, get that inner lock network connection disabled," he ordered, sticking to regular comms for now.

"On it, Gunny," Zoe replied as she deftly unscrewed the airlock control panel.

Behind them, the rest of the Marine contingent poured into the airlock, the space quickly filling with bodies in power armor and standard issue Marine body armor.

"Last one in," Jackson called out. "Sealing the hatch."

The outer door slid shut with a hiss, cutting them off from the Stinger. Alex could see the ship as it detached from the station and darted back to the Wraith.

"How's it coming, Five?" Alex asked, his eyes scanning the inner door for any sign of movement on the other side.

"Almost there," Zoe muttered.

"Hurry it up," Sarah chimed in. "We're literally sitting ducks in here."

The seconds ticked by too slowly. Alex knew that every

moment they spent in this airlock increased their chances of detection. Finally, Zoe let out a triumphant, "Got it!"

"Malik, get us in," Alex ordered aloud.

The burly Marine stepped forward, his augmented strength making short work of the manual release. The door slid open, revealing an ordinary, quiet corridor.

If only it would stay that way.

Alex took point, his weapon at the ready as he stepped out into the station proper. The Scorpions followed close behind, with the rest of the Marines filing out after them. They had barely made it a few steps when a spacer crossed an intersection up ahead. He froze, head turning toward them, his mouth falling open. "What the—"

Jackson's reaction was instantaneous. His sidearm came up, and a single round caught the unfortunate crew member squarely in the chest. The man went down without another sound, his body twitching as blood rapidly soaked his uniform.

"Nice shot, Three," Alex said. "Alright Marines, you know the plan. Let's move."

The Marines began to split off into their pre-assigned groups, each led by one of the Scorpions. Alex saw Zoe gesture to Aster, the FUP hacker falling in line with her team as they headed off towards the fire control systems.

Jackson, Malik, Alex's call went out mentally, *get to those barracks and lock 'em down before we have the entire Marine complement breathing down our necks.*

Roger that, Gunny, Jackson replied. *We'll keep them busy.*

And try not to have too much fun, Malik added. *Boring is good, right?*

Boring is very good, Alex replied, motioning to his squad. As usual, they had been assigned to storm the CIC and do whatever they could to wreak havoc from the top down.

They started down the corridor, Alex following a map displayed on his augmented HUD instead of his helmet display. They made it to the first intersection and changed direction, keeping a quick pace toward the elevators that would carry them to the same deck as their objective. It would have been easier to reach from their initially planned entry point, and they probably wouldn't have already had to kill anyone, but he was nothing if not adaptable.

Alex and his squad had barely made it halfway to their objective when they rounded a corner and came face-to-face with a group of startled crew members. Unlike the first encounter, these weren't unarmed technicians. Each carried a sidearm.

"FUP scum!" one of them shouted as they reached for their weapons and opened fire.

Alex advanced ahead of his unit, his armor deflecting the rounds while his team remained under cover behind him. He swept a burst of rounds across the enemy. Each bullet, precisely guided by his neural implants, hit its mark, quickly dropping the SF crew save for the one who managed to duck down the adjoining corridor. A quick burst from his jump jets allowed him to leap the length of the corridor. Swinging just his rifle around the corner, he fired when the reticle in the transparency in front of his eyes turned green. The single round brought the man down, sight unseen.

As Alex silently asked for sitreps from his squad, his implants quickly replaced his vision with the view of each squadmate as they spoke.

Halfway to Marine berthing, Gunny, Malik reported. *Had to cut a few stragglers in the wrong place at the wrong time, but not much resistance so far.*

Alex confirmed the report, looking down the nearly empty corridor Malik moved down. He switched over to Zoe's visuals. She wasn't quite as far along to her target, but he could see why. *Ran into some tangos on their way to who cares,* Zoe explained. *Five less bad guys to worry about.* The SF Marines lay on the deck at the end of her corridor.

Nice work, Five, Alex checked in on Sarah next. She was inside a dark storage compartment. *Two, are you taking a break already?*

Nearly got caught by a security patrol. They're wearing Karuta armor, Gunny.

Alex winced. *If they have augments too, that puts us on even footing.*

Yeah, except I bet there are a lot more of them than there are of us.

Don't panic. Stick to the plan. Good job not being seen.

It won't last.

No, but the further we get before... He stopped his thought as alarms began blaring throughout the station. Red emergency lights bathed the corridors in an eerie glow.

"And there it is," Sarah said out loud. "I didn't do it."

"It was bound to happen sooner or later," Alex muttered; it was second nature under pressure. "Which of you was made? If it was you again Mal, you're up for reprimand."

"Not me, Gunny," he replied.

"Gunny, we've got a problem," Zoe said. "We ran right into a unit of Karutas on our way to the FCS. I lost two Marines, and we're backpedaling to get clear of them, but they're going to catch up in a hurry."

"Copy that. Malik, I need your team at Zoe's position ASAP."

"On it, Gunny," Malik replied. "Oh hell, we've got company of our own. Looks like somebody kicked the hornet's nest."

"Yeah, we did," Jackson said. "Sorry, Gunny."

Alex checked Malik's visuals. SF defenders were rounding the corner of the bulkhead into the corridor where Malik and his team had advanced down. They were already trading fire, the tangos taking cover around the junction they had emerged from. He switched to Jackson's view. The other Marine had taken a different route toward berthing and remained unencumbered.

"Change of plans, Jackson, get to Zoe, now!"

"On our way," Jackson replied.

Alex motioned his team forward, using his jump jets to shoot ahead of them. Reaching the next intersection, he slid into the center of it and came to a stop, rifle already up and ready.

A dull metal fist swung toward his helmet, nearly connecting. Alex ducked below it, triggering a boost with his augments. Time seemed to slow, and when the power-armored defender in front of him tried to gut-shoot him at close range, he used his jets to slip aside, the rounds whizzing past him, straight into the hardened bulkhead behind him. He grabbed the enemy's arm and squeezed, crushing the SF Marine's armor and throwing the man aside. Alex squeezed off three rounds as he struggled to recover, penetrating his faceplate. Blood and brain matter exploded inside his helmet, his body instantly falling limp.

"They have a lot more security in Karuta than we antici-pated," he said to the Scorpions.

"So much for Yarborough's intel," Malik replied.

As a trio of armored Marines swung around the corner ahead, Alex turned and sprinted back where he had come. Moving up on their six, he warned his unit back, putting himself between them and the incoming tangos.

A soft thump preceded a grenade that ricocheted off the opposite bulkhead and landed at his feet, sticking to the deck just in front of him. He scooped it up smoothly with augmented reflexes and hurled it back the way it had come.

It went off in a bright flash of light as it neared the corner, followed by arcing daggers of energy. The light blinded Alex, leaving him stumbling back as the energy speared his armor, threatening to overload its systems. Warning tones echoed through his helmet.

By the time his vision cleared, the three enemy Marines were on him. But their sluggish, uncoordinated movements told Alex one thing. The explosion had affected them as much as it had him. His approaching Marines opened fire, bullets pinging off the enemy's Karuta armor and sending two of them stumbling back.

Every little bit helped.

Alex grappled with the one remaining SF Marine, his augmented strength allowing him to lift the man off the deck and slam him into the bulkhead. As he slid to the deck, stunned, Alex spun around and grabbed the muzzle of the rifle aimed at him. He squeezed the barrel closed just as the Marine pulled the trigger. The gun exploded, blowing off the front of the man's helmet taking his face with it. Alex left him lying there, screaming and thrashing around, his hands clasped to his mangled features. Blood streamed through his fingers.

Alex swung around just in time to slam the butt of his rifle into the helmet of the Marine who'd regained enough of his faculties to get back up. The man stumbled back, giving Alex enough time to bring the rifle butt up to his shoulder and blast him point-blank in the chest. A fist-sized hole blossomed in the armor squarely over his heart, killing him instantly. By the time Alex spun back to the last remaining tango, his Marines brought him down. Just like they had practiced, thanks to their updated playbook.

"Gunny, it's Zoe," her breathless and strained voice came through the comms. "Malik got us out of that jam, but we're still nowhere near the fire control center. This resistance is insane."

"It's like they knew we were coming," Jackson added.

"Maybe they did," Sarah suggested. "What if Yarborough sold us out?"

"No way," Alex growled so forcefully none of the Scorpions would question it.

"They could have a mole, though," Zoe said.

"It doesn't matter now," Alex pressed. "We're here, and we have to deal. Can you get to the FCS?"

"Negative, Gunny," Zoe replied. "At least, not in time to make it worthwhile."

"Copy that." Failing to disable the big guns would put a major strain on their forces outside the station, but at least they'd baked that possibility into their contingencies. "What's near your position, Five? Anything we can take out to press our advantage?"

There was a pause as Zoe presumably consulted her tactical map. "Not much, Gunny. Lots of access tunnels and utility rooms, but nothing mission-critical."

Alex was about to reply when an idea struck him. "Wait. What about network relays? Any of those nearby?"

"Hold on," Zoe said. After a moment, she came back, excitement evident in her voice. "Yes! There's a major network hub about fifty meters from our position."

"Perfect," Alex said, a plan already forming. "Get Aster to the hub. If we can't reach the fire control center directly, maybe he can work some magic from there."

"What exactly am I supposed to do?" Aster's voice cut in, sounding both nervous and intrigued.

"Whatever you can," Alex replied. "Jam their communications, overload their systems, block some of the hatches. Hell, turn off their coffee makers just to piss them off. If we can't kill the FCS, our next best hack is to keep those docked ships from launching and getting into the fight."

"I'll do my best," Aster said, determination replacing the uncertainty in his voice.

"That's all I ask," Alex said. "Five, get him there in one piece. Three, make sure they reach the target."

As he signed off, Alex turned his attention back to his

own situation. They were still a good distance from the CIC, and the resistance was intensifying with every step.

"Gunny," Sarah's voice came through the comms. "We've reached the hangar, but it's a mess down here. They're trying to launch ships, and we're doing our best to stop them. But I don't know how long we can hold out."

Through their connection, Alex caught flashes of the scene—a massive hangar bay filled with the sleek shapes of SF fighters. Sarah's team was spread out along an upper catwalk, raining fire down on SF pilots and ground crews as they scrambled to get their ships airborne. A burning starfighter already blocked a portion of the hangar, which would slow launches until they could clear the debris away.

Alex's jaw clenched. Everything was balanced on a knife's edge. It wouldn't take much more for the entire operation to come crashing down around them.

His focus homed in on Sarah's neural signature. *Hold that position as long as you can, Two. Help is coming.* He switched his focus to Jackson. *Four, what's your status?*

I've got the exit to berthing pinned down, Gunny, Malik returned, the sound of weapons fire punctuating his thoughts. *But it'll only last until some of those tin can soldiers make their way up to me.*

You're a tin can soldier, too, Alex reminded him.

But the rest of my squad isn't.

Copy that. Do what you can to keep them contained for as long as possible, Alex ordered. *We can't afford to have them reinforcing what's already out here.*

Alex took a moment to survey his own team. They were holding up better than he might have hoped. All of those drills they had done over the last few months had really paid off.

"Alright, Marines," Alex said. "We're not there yet, but

we're making progress. Keep pushing forward. We take the CIC, the enemy falls apart."

"Oorah!" the Marines shouted.

As they pressed forward, Alex couldn't help but wonder how the battle was progressing outside the station. Had the Wraith revealed itself yet?

He could only hope his father's side of the mission was unfolding as they had planned.

CHAPTER 27

The original plan called for the Wraith to slip silently away to a better offensive position while remaining cloaked until the station's fire control system was offline. Only then would the ship materialize into view to launch fighters, fire the vortex cannon and disrupt as many ships around the station as possible.

That plan had already gone to hell.

It didn't mean they were out of the fight. Not by a long shot. Their passage through the Eye had forced them to bolster shields beyond what the Navy bean counters found rational.

As the Pilums poured out of the hangar bay and opened up on the surprised Scutums—drawing the attention of station control, the surrounding capital ships, and the rest of the defensive positions—Soren knew they would need every last ounce of deflection power those shields could handle. He turned to the tactical station. "Keira, disable the cloak and activate shields. Sang, evasive maneuvers. Get us clear of the station as fast as you can."

"Aye, Captain," they replied.

"Here we go," Jack muttered.

"Captain," Phoebe came over the comms from the hangar. "Stinger is aboard."

A mote of relief washed through Soren. At least Bastian had made it back before things got dicey.

On the sensors, the Hooligans swept in a wave toward the nearby Scutums, already unleashing hell on the defenders who had forced their hand. On the secondary viewscreen, Soren watched their missiles pound the defenders' shields, failing to break through on the first pass. The Pilums split up, their movements coordinated by Minh as they prepared to circle back around for another attack.

"Captain," Mark called out, his voice urgent, "it looks like we have their attention. The entire strike force is moving to engage."

Soren nodded, having expected as much. "Samira, get me Admiral Yarborough."

"Aye, Captain," she replied.

"Captain Strickland," Yarborough said a moment later, tension obvious in her tone. "You're early."

"Best laid plans," Soren replied. "The situation has deteriorated faster than anticipated. We need immediate reinforcements."

"We're on our way, Captain. Just hold on, the cavalry's coming." Yarborough disconnected.

"Samira, establish a connection with the Scorpions."

"Connection established, Captain," she replied a moment later.

"Alex, status report."

"Captain, we've run into much more resistance than anticipated," Alex replied, the muffled report of his rifle in the background. "All five teams are taking fire, and the enemy has more Karuta armored sentries than we thought."

Soren's jaw clenched. Everything seemed to be going

wrong. He didn't panic or waver. This wasn't the first time the odds had looked bleak, and it wouldn't be the last.

"What about the FCS?" he asked.

"Negative, sir," Alex replied. "Five got cut off before she and her team could reach it. They've diverted to secondary systems, trying to keep those additional warships docked."

"Understood. And the CIC?"

"We'll get there...slow but steady, Captain."

"Understood. Stay safe in there."

"You stay safe out there."

Soren muted the channel and sat back, considering their next move. The vibrations of missiles detonating against their shields vibrated across the hull, into the superstructure, and ultimately through the padding of his seat.

"Captain," Mark's voice cut in, "the station's defensive batteries are coming online!"

"We need to slow them down. Buy us more time," Soren said. "Sang, Keira, contingency B. We need to hit the station with the vortex cannon. Sang, I want a full vertical rotation with an added lateral roll. Let's keep our profile shifting as much as possible. Keira, as soon as the vortex cannon is pointed at the station, fire it." He used his command surface to switch to Minh's channel. "Minh, we're switching to contingency B. Clear your fighters from the target area."

"Copy that, Captain," Minh replied. "Just mopping up."

Soren glanced at the secondary viewscreen in time to see the second Scutum near the station succumb to a heavy volley of missiles from the Pilums. The fighters immediately peeled away, thrusters firing full blast to clear the area quickly.

"Captain, the strike force is vectoring to box us in," Mark said. "If we don't get clear, we're going to be in a world of hurt."

"If we don't take care of those station guns, we're going

to be in a bigger world of hurt," Soren replied. "So will the Admiral and her fleet. Sang, execute rotation."

"Aye, Captain," she replied, cutting the main thrusters and firing the vectoring jets. Inertial forces tugged at them as she threw the Wraith into a roll while pushing the bow up and eventually over.

"Fighters are launching from the station," Mark announced.

"They won't get far," Soren replied, the universe flipping and rolling in the primary viewscreen. "Keira, standby to fire."

"Ready, Captain."

As the Wraith's bow swung toward the station, Soren saw the strike force moving in behind it, working to surround them. Of the Scutums closing the distance from their defensive perimeter, only a handful of seconds away from fully joining the fray. Of the station's gun batteries, swiveling to open up on them. Of the Hooligans, already down one but clear of the cannon's range, ready to jump back into the fight.

Keira didn't wait for his order to fire. A wave of disrupted spacetime erupted from the Wraith's bow, spreading out in a cone as it raced toward the station. The effect was immediate but not as devastating as Soren had hoped. Sections of the station's outer hull rippled, and several defensive batteries went dark. But they were too close, and the dispersal was too narrow to have the full effect they needed.

The good news was that the shot disrupted the launching starfighters and continued out past the station, spreading as it went and reaching some of the strike force in the distance. It wouldn't permanently harm them, but it did rattle them a little, and every second they were distracted mattered.

The Wraith continued its rotation, the station vanishing from the viewscreen within seconds.

"Sang, full thrust. Get us clear of this mess." He glanced at the sensor grid, marking a pair of Valkyries closing on them from the flanks. "Keira, hit those Valkyries with everything we've got."

"Aye, sir. FCS online and tracking. Vortex cannon recharging."

The Wraith's arsenal came to life, railgun rounds streaking across space while missiles launched in rapid succession. The nearest Valkyrie's shields flared brilliantly as they absorbed the initial barrage. Soren could see them weakening under the sustained assault.

"Enemy ships returning fire," Mark called out. "Multiple missile locks detected!"

The bridge shuddered as explosions blossomed against their shields.

"Shields down to seventy five percent," Keira reported, her voice tight.

Soren eyed the sensor grid, noting the positions of the enemy forces. They had bought themselves ten to fifteen seconds, but that was all. The strike force was still bearing down on them. While they could handle a Valkyrie or two alone, things would escalate quickly once the bulk of the group reached a firing solution.

And most of the station guns were online. It was only a matter of time before…

The guns suddenly shifted, nearly three dozen emplacements rotating to find targets. Only thin slips of light signaled the ejection of flechettes from the railguns in an assault Soren was sure they couldn't absorb. At least not for long.

He wasn't pleased to find they didn't need to absorb the rounds. Rather than target them, the guns had aimed at the

Pilums. Within seconds, three vanished from the grid, succumbing to overwhelming force. The others broke formation, spreading quickly and scrambling to get clear. Another vanished from the grid. And another. The Hooligans needed help that was still too far away.

"Sang, bring us about," Soren said.

"Captain?" she questioned. Every crew member on the bridge knew what turning back toward the station meant. They would have to burn their velocity to reverse course, leaving them a sitting duck.

But that's exactly what Soren wanted.

"We need to be the biggest, juiciest target in space right now," he explained. "Draw all the fire from the Pilums, and from the reinforcements when they arrive."

"We can't absorb that much firepower," Keira said.

"We have to," Soren replied. "Divert power from the cannon, pull it from life support if you need to. And hope those upgrades hold up."

"This is strategic insanity," Jack muttered beside him.

Soren glanced at his old friend, a devilish grin on his face. "I hear they teach my tactics at the Academy."

"Only the ones that pay off," Jack replied.

"Sang, execute."

"Aye, Captain," she replied without hesitation.

Sang guided the ship in a second rapid turn, facing it toward the station and firing the mains at full power, slowing their reversed velocity. Soren envisioned the station's tactical officer seeing them slow, prompting him to turn all his available guns their way. The station guns joined the incoming Scutums and Valkyries in a withering railgun and missile fire barrage. The remainder of the strike force, including the Komodo, waited further afield.

Soren's eyes remained fixed on the edge of the sensor grid as the ship shuddered, rocked by the assault. His hands tightened on his armrest while he waited inter-minable moments for the FUPN fleet to arrive.

Their time was running out.

CHAPTER 28

Alex led his team through the winding corridors of FOB Alpha. The resistance was fierce, slowing their progress at practically every turn.

"Gunny, we've got more incoming!" one of his Marines cried out, her voice tight. "Six o'clock."

Alex spun, his weapon snapping up as he tracked the movement at the far end of the corridor. A group of the station's crew, clad in nothing more than jumpsuits, rushed toward him firing their sidearms. Alex stood there, bullets pinging off his armor. He barely felt the impacts, the projectiles leaving behind no more than minuscule dents. Raising his rifle, he shot one of the men in the leg, hoping it would be enough to send them running. The man went down, but the others hunkered down where they were and continued shooting. Behind him, his team each took a knee and returned fire, killing another two.

"Gunny, man down," one of them shouted.

Alex glanced over to see young Corporal Barnard sprawled on the deck, a wound in his chest gushing blood. "Get him patched," he barked. Turning back around, he tossed his rifle over to his left hand, and pulling his sidearm, he began walking casually toward the defenders, firing until they finally fled back around the corner, leaving their dead and dying behind. They didn't return, obviously unwilling to go toe-to-toe with a power armored Marine.

Alex stood there, wondering why they were fighting at all. These weren't trained Marines, just technicians and other support personnel. Rather than hide or surrender, they were out here with nothing more than handguns, and he couldn't understand why.

Only one reason came to mind. Fear. They had to believe that what their superiors would do to them if they didn't stand and fight—what Grand Admiral Strickland might do to them—would be much worse.

His train of thought collapsed as the entire station suddenly shuddered violently beneath his feet. A series of loud clangs and the screech of rending metal reverberated through the structure.

"What the hell was that?" one of the Marines gasped, stumbling against the bulkhead as the deck continued to vibrate in response to whatever had just hit them.

Alex's mind raced, quickly putting the pieces together. "The vortex cannon," he realized aloud. "Contingency B."

Before he could elaborate further, the effects of the weapon hit them. For a moment, it was as if reality itself warped around them, twisting and bending in ways that defied comprehension. Alex's stomach lurched, his inner ear on both sides rebelling against the sickening sensations.

Alex fought down his nausea, forcing himself to stay focused. Two of his Marines weren't so lucky. They doubled over, retching on the deck. "Shake it off, Marines," he ordered. "We've got a job to do."

As they regrouped and pressed onward, Alex's comm crackled to life. Sarah's panicked voice came through. "Gunny! We need immediate backup!"

Her words cut off abruptly, replaced by the sound of

intense weapons fire. Alex's blood ran cold as he tapped into Sarah's visual feed.

The scene that greeted him was chaos incarnate. The situation in the hangar bay had rapidly dissolved as a unit of Karuta-armored Marines stormed in. Alex watched them activate their jump jets, arcing upward towards Sarah's position on the upper catwalk. Her team opened fire, their weapons flashing desperately in the cavernous space.

"Fall back!" Sarah's voice rang out, both over the comm and through her visual feed. "We can't hold this position!"

Her Marines began to retreat, laying down covering fire as they withdrew. Combining to target one power-armored Marine at a time, just like they had practiced, their concentrated rifle fire took out the first one's jump jets in mid-flight. The armored figure plummeted back to the deck, the clangoring impact resonating throughout the bay. It was a small victory, quickly overshadowed by the overwhelming force bearing down on them.

Sarah herself managed to take down another, her precise fire pounding through the attacker's faceplate.

"Four, what's your status?" Alex asked, hoping he could get reinforcements to her in time.

"Not much activity from the barracks now, Gunny," Malik replied, "I think all the Marines are already out there on patrol."

"Like they knew we were coming," Alex reiterated. "Get down to the hangar. Move, move, move! Two's in trouble."

"On our way!"

Still watching the scene unfold, Alex watched the SF Marines land on the catwalk with Sarah and her unit. At close quarters, the difference in firepower became painfully apparent. Like his team and those of Jackson, Malik and Zoe, Sarah's team was equipped only with standard body armor. They stood little chance of survival against the superior force.

Understanding the disparity, Sarah charged the armored opponents, desperate to protect her team. Better trained and equipped than the SF Marines, she boosted her strength and speed, slipping under the guard of one, easily lifting and throwing him back off the platform. Turning to the second, she ducked his jab and countered with a hard hook that knocked her off balance. She lunged forward, shouldering the woman over the catwalk railing. Alex could hear the hiss of her jump jets as she tried to recover from the fall.

Pivoting toward the third Marine, both Sarah and Alex froze as the muzzle of his rifle pressed against her faceplate.

Alex forced himself to keep his eyes open and watch the explosive flash shatter Sarah's faceplate just before the feed went dark.

"No!" he roared, the cry tearing from his throat before he could stop it. He slammed his fist into the bulkhead, the impact leaving a dent and reverberating up his arm through his armor.

He took a shuddering breath, forcing down the surge of grief and rage that threatened to overwhelm him. He couldn't afford to lose focus now. Sarah's death would mean nothing if they failed in their mission.

"Two's down," he growled through he comms. "We've lost the hangar." He paused to give them a brief moment to process. It was all they could spare. "Four, redirect to the CIC. Approach from the starboard side. I'll come in from port. We'll take it together. For Sarah."

"Copy that, Gunny," Malik replied, his usual jovial tone noticeably absent.

"Five, sitrep."

"We've reached the network relay, Gunny," Zoe answered, voice quivering with barely contained rage and hurt. "Three's squad is holding back the enemy forces, but it's tough going."

"Aster?"

"He's working on getting access through the terminal now."

"Keep at it. We need him to work his magic if we're going to pull this off."

As Alex once more led his team forward, Sarah's loss settled over him like a cold shroud. The Scorpions had always been a tight-knit unit, and losing one of them hit him hard. He knew it did the others as well.

She died fighting, Alex said, his words carrying to the other Scorpions team through the neural link. *The best way we can honor her memory is by completing this mission. So let's get it done.*

A chorus of determined affirmatives came back, the shared grief transforming into renewed resolve.

They had covered more ground without incident than Alex expected when he heard heavier footsteps up ahead. He raised a fist, bringing his team to a halt, waving them into the alcove of a sliding door just before three Karuta-armored figures barreled around the corner ahead. The one in the lead had a significant dent in the shoulder of his armor, allowing Alex to recognize him as one of the SF Marines from the hangar bay.

The one who had killed Sarah.

Controlled anger burned like a hot shard in his gut, his vision narrowing down to the man who'd killed Sarah—and only him—as he activated his jump jets. Full power propelled him toward the man, his startling speed catching the SF Marine off guard.

It gave Alex the crucial edge he needed.

He slammed into the Marine, the impact sending them both crashing into the bulkhead at the end of the corridor. Alex's augmented strength allowed him to pin his opponent for a precious few seconds, just long enough for him to jam his rifle muzzle against the weak point where his helmet snapped into the body of his armor and squeeze off a burst.

The Marine went limp, and Alex held him there, pinned to the bulkhead, taking satisfaction in the fear filling the man's eyes as blood filled his helmet. It was gratifying watching him die but a stupid distraction to allow himself. He'd left himself wide open to retaliation, movement in the corner of his eye revealing the other two SF Marines bringing their weapons to bear on the back of his head.

Alex's Marines opened fire, forcing the SF troops to divide their attention. It was the reprieve Alex needed. He pushed off from the dead Marine, letting the man's body fall to the deck. His neural augments allowed him to boost his reflexes, his perception slowing the fight down as he grabbed one of the Marines by the arm and spun him around with the speed and strength few of his peers had ever been able to match. Throwing him down on his back, he stomped his faceplate in, crushing his skull behind a concave spider web of cracks. Blood seeping up through them, Alex spun away, leaping and pushing off the other corridor's bulkhead with one foot. He turned in mid-air and slammed into the other Marine, knocking her to the deck. Jamming his foot down on her chest, he stared down through her faceplate into her narrowed, hate-filled eyes.

Casually, he swung his rifle barrel over, resting the business end of it against her helmet's transparency. And then, he pulled the trigger.

"Gunny."

Zoe's voice coming through the comms pulled Alex out of his cold rage. He blinked back to the reality around him. "Report."

"Aster's made some progress. He's managed to lock out the docking clamp release for the warships still attached to the station."

"Fantastic," he replied, allowing himself a small

measure of relief. That would buy them some much-needed time. "How long will it hold?"

"Hard to say," she admitted. "Aster's good, but these systems are complex."

"Tell him to keep at it," Alex said. "Every second those ships stay docked is a second in our favor."

"Will do," Zoe replied.

As they pressed on toward the CIC, Alex could sense Malik's team drawing closer. They approached from opposite sides, a pincer movement that would catch the CIC's defenders off guard.

Four, Alex passed through their neural link. *We're almost there. Are you in position?*

Ready and waiting, Gunny, Malik returned *Just say the word*.

Alex took a deep breath, steeling himself for what was to come. This was it. The culmination of their mission, the moment that would determine whether all their sacrifices had been worth it.

Alright, he continued. *I'll go in first, draw their fire. Once they're focused on me, hit them hard from your side.*

Copy that, Malik acknowledged. *We've got your back.*

Alex turned to his team. "This is it. Whatever happens in there, remember your training. Remember why we're here. I'll go in first. Stay behind me and provide cover."

With nods from his team, Alex activated his jump jets, propelling himself around the final corner towards the CIC's entrance. As expected, a hail of weapons fire greeted him. He returned fire, more to protect his team behind him and to draw their attention away from Malik's team than with any real expectation of hitting them. His true purpose was to be the bright, shiny target that drew all their attention.

It worked. The CIC's defenders focused all their fire-power on Alex, whose armor absorbed the bulk of the attack, leaving them completely unprepared for Malik's assault from the opposite direction.

With the neural augmentation, Malik had targeting data from Alex's view of the scene and aimed with uncanny accuracy. Two energy grenades arced through the air, their trajectory perfect. The grenades detonated among the defenders, the flash and arcs of energy momentarily stunning them. It was just the opening Alex and Malik needed.

Both teams stormed forward, their combined firepower overwhelming the dazed SF troops. The defenders fought bravely, but they were outmatched and outmaneuvered.

In no time, the area outside the CIC was secure.

Alex approached the sealed doors of the command center, his weapon at the ready. *Five, we need a way in. Can Aster work his magic one more time?*

Zoe's neural reply came back almost immediately. *He says he thought you'd never ask. Just say when. And hurry up in there. Three's got us covered in the passageway, but we can't leave here until you can come rescue us.*

Understood. Standby. He turned to the gathered Marines behind him and Malik. "Watch your fire in there. We don't want to hit any of the electronics."

"Maybe it's better if you wait outside," Malik said to the Marines.

They've got this. "Mal and I will go in first and draw their fire," Alex said out loud. "Cover each other. Watch your targets." And then, to Zoe, *Okay, go ahead. Have Aster open the doors.*

Copy that, she replied.

With a hiss of hydraulics, the heavy doors began to slide open. Alex tensed, ready for whatever resistance they might face inside.

As the opening widened, a barrage of weapons fire erupted from within. "Take them down!" Alex ordered, charging forward into the barrage.

Malik stormed in beside him, equally deadly with his rifle. The Marines brought up the rear, picking off targets as they rose from cover to take short, controlled bursts in an effort to not hit any of the consoles or workstations. Rounds continued bouncing off his and Malik's armor, the crews' small arms no match for the composite. They shot back at the enemy, picking up targets through their implants, allowing them to aim and fire with barely a glance at the tangos in their reticles.

Alex had hoped they might be able to take some of the crew alive, to gather intelligence. But it quickly became clear that wasn't going to happen. The SF personnel fought with the desperation of those who knew they had nothing left to lose.

A security officer charged Alex, his sidearm blazing. Before Alex could react, a second officer rose from cover and fired, not at Alex or his team, but at the guard. He hit the man in the neck, knocking him to the deck clutching at the blood spurting from his throat.

"Don't shoot!" the second officer cried when Alex turned his rifle on him.

"All clear, Gunny," Malik reported. "CIC is secure."

"Drop your weapon!" Alex barked at the officer.

To his surprise, the man immediately complied, raising his hands in surrender. "Don't shoot!" he repeated. "My name is Lieutenant Commander Marcus Reeves, FUP Intelligence. I have an urgent message for Admiral Yarborough!"

CHAPTER 29

The Wraith shuddered under another barrage of enemy fire. The viewscreen was a chaotic display of streaking missiles and railgun rounds, punctuated by the occasional brilliant flash of a detonation against their shields.

"Shields down to fifty percent, Captain," Keira reported, her voice tense but steady.

Soren nodded, his eyes never leaving the sensor grid. They were taking a beating, but his gambit was working. The bulk of the enemy's firepower was now focused on the Wraith, giving the remaining Hooligans some much needed breathing room and the FUP ships time to arrive, which he felt certain they should have by now.

"Come on, Jane," he muttered under his breath. "Where are you?"

As if in answer to his silent plea, a cluster of new contacts finally appeared at the edge of their sensor range. Soren felt a surge of relief, quickly tempered by confusion.

"Captain," Mark called out, "I've got FUP signatures...but only about half the fleet is incoming."

"What the hell is she doing?" Jack wondered aloud, even as the leading ships in the FUP's diminished fleet began launching missiles at the strike force Komodos. "They're at the far edge of effective range," Jack added, even more confused. "Those aren't going to hit anything."

Before Soren could respond, another group of contacts winked into existence on the opposite side of the battle zone, much closer to the SF strike force. The enemy ships, caught off guard and still focused on the Wraith, were suddenly caught in a devastating crossfire.

Soren's eyes widened as he realized the brilliance of Yarborough's strategy. By splitting her forces and executing a pincer movement, she had taken the enemy by surprise. It was a risky move since the ships that had folded in close to the enemy were now at a dead stop, vulnerable to counter-attack. But with the SF's attention divided, their firepower focused on the Wraith, it appeared that it would pay off.

"Clever," Jack murmured, clearly impressed.

Chaos erupted around them as the FUP ships opened fire. Railgun rounds and missiles streaked across the void, hammering the SF strike force from multiple angles. The Komodos, caught in the center of the assault, took the brunt of the attack. Their shields flared brilliantly under the onslaught, struggling to repel the concentrated firepower.

Soren watched in awe as the battle unfolded. FUP Valkyries unleashed swarms of missiles, their payloads overwhelming the enemy. The SF ships, slow to adjust to this new threat, were pounded before they could react, two of them breaking apart, destroyed within the opening salvos. The others scrambled to change their vectors and firing solutions, taking the pressure off the Wraith as they opened up on the FUP ships.

"Keira, target that Valkyrie," Soren ordered, marking it on his control surface. "Sang, bring us twelve degrees to starboard, cut mains to fifteen percent. Fire port vectoring thrusters and pitch down ten degrees, yaw right thirty."

Sang guided the Wraith on the path Soren ordered,

shifting to face the embattled SF fleet, approaching the Valkyrie at an angle that would allow most of the railguns to fire on it while staying away from the enemy's guns.

The Valkyrie, already damaged from the FUP's surprise attack, couldn't withstand the additional assault. Its shields collapsed, flickering and dying in a cascade of blue-white energy. Subsequent hits tore into its hull, armor plating buckling and peeling away under the intense barrage. Secondary explosions blossomed along its length, atmosphere venting from multiple breaches. With a final, spectacular detonation, the ship went dark, drifting life-lessly in space.

"Target destroyed," Keira announced.

Soren eyed the grid, picking another target and passing orders to his crew as the battle raged on. A swirling melee of ships and weapons fire, both FUP and SF ships maneu-vered frantically, each trying to gain the upper hand.

A Komodo-class vessel, its hull already scarred from previous engagements, found itself caught between two FUP Komodos. The crossfire was devastating, tearing through its defenses in a matter of seconds. The enemy ship went dark, trailing debris and bodies as it drifted away from the battlefield.

It was a solid kill, but the FUP wasn't having it all their way. An SF ship that resembled a Rhino, its heavy armor allowing it to weather the initial surprise attack, was laying down punishing fire on the FUP's lighter vessels. Soren watched as a FUP Valkyrie, overwhelmed by the Rhino's superior firepower, broke apart under the assault.

While the larger capital ships duked it out, smaller craft wove intricate patterns between them, like schools of deadly fish navigating a reef of sharks.

Soren noticed on the secondary viewscreen that two Pilums had executed a perfect scissor maneuver, catching a Scutum between them. The fighters approached from opposite angles, their paths crossing just as they reached weapons range. Their combined firepower overwhelmed the patrol ship's defenses, punching through shields and armor. The Scutum's reactor went critical, turning the bulky vessel into an expanding cloud of superheated gas and debris. The Pilums emerged from the explosion, their shields flickering as they shed the blast's energy.

The Hooligans weaved through the chaos with practiced ease, their movements fluid and unpredictable. They danced between capital ships and through debris fields, using every scrap of cover to their advantage. The SF fighters struggled to keep up, often finding themselves outflanked or caught in devastating crossfires.

The battle continued to rage, with neither side able to gain a decisive advantage. The FUP Navy fleet, while putting up a valiant fight, was taking heavy losses. But the outnumbered SF paid a heavy price for every ship they took down. The surprise attack had devastated their strike force, leaving them off-balance and struggling to regroup.

Or rather, to escape.

"Captain, the SF ships are decelerating," Mark announced. "I think they're going to jump."

"Keira, target those ships. We can't let them escape!"

But it was too late. The surviving SF vessels, recognizing the battle was lost, began to disappear one by one. In seconds, only wreckage and disabled ships remained of the once formidable enemy force.

A ragged cheer from the bridge crew went up, but Soren didn't join in. His eyes were fixed on the sensor readings from the FUP fleet. They had won, yes, but at a steep cost. Multiple FUP ships were adrift, and their systems were offline or barely functioning. At least three ships had been destroyed, their debris mingling with that of their enemies in a somber cloud of twisted metal and frozen corpses.

"Captain," Samira said. "Incoming transmission from the station. It's Scorpion One."

Soren exhaled, glad that Alex was okay. "Put him through."

Alex's tense, breathless voice filled the bridge. "Captain, I need you to patch me through to Admiral Yarborough immediately."

"Alex? What's going on? Are you alright?"

"I'm fine, but there's no time to explain. We need to talk to Yarborough now, Captain. Hurry," Alex pressed, an edge of desperation in his voice.

Soren didn't hesitate. "Samira, get me the Admiral."

Moments later, Yarborough's voice came over the comms, her signal broken and choppy, suggesting damage to Spirit of War's comms array. "Captain Strickland... good...out there. We..."

"Admiral," Alex cut in, "we have a situation. We've captured the CIC, but one of the officers here claims to be FUP Intelligence. He says he has urgent information for you."

Soren sat forward in his seat, glancing at Jack, who seemed equally surprised.

"Put...on," Yarborough replied.

A new voice came through, breathless and panicked. "Admiral Yarborough, this is Lieutenant Commander Marcus Reeves, FUP Intelligence. You need to get your fleet out of here immediately. There's a spy in the FUP. Grand Admiral Strickland knew you were coming."

"What?" Yarborough's face paled. "How is that possible?"

"I don't have all the details," Reeves continued, his words tumbling out in a rush. "But Strickland moved additional resources to the station to bolster its defenses. But that's not the worst of it. He has a contingency plan in case the station falls. You need to leave! Now, before it's too late!"

"Too late for what?" Yarborough demanded, her voice sharp.

As if in answer to her question, Mark's voice rang out. "Captain! New contact detected. It's...it's massive."

Soren's eyes snapped to the sensor grid. His blood ran cold at what he saw. A colossal ship had just dropped out of fold space, dwarfing even the largest vessels in the FUP fleet. It was easily twice the size of the largest Komodo-class battleship, its hull dark and ragged. But what truly caught his attention was the gaping maw at its bow—unmistakably the housing for one or more vortex cannons.

The monstrosity's sudden appearance sent ripples of panic through the battered FUP fleet. Ships moving to assist damaged allies suddenly began to slow in preparation to jump.

When Yarborough spoke, her voice was shrill, quivering with fear. "All ships, emergency fold! Retreat! We need to get out of here, now!"

"Wait!" Soren shouted, his heart racing. "Admiral, my son is still on that station. We can't just—"

"I'm sorry, Captain," Yarborough cut him off, genuine anguish in her tone. "There's nothing we can do for them now. Save your ship if you can. Live to fight another day." With that, her transmission cut out, leaving Soren staring at a blank screen.

Soren watched helplessly as the FUP ships began to vanish, folding away to safety. His eyes were drawn back to the monster of a ship that now dominated their sensors. The front of the vessel had become distorted, signaling an energy buildup for what would undoubtedly be a catastrophic discharge.

Time seemed to slow as Soren grappled with an impossible choice. Every fiber of his being screamed at him to stay, to find some way to save Alex and the others. But the rational part of his mind knew that such an attempt would be suicide. If they stayed, they would all die—and with them, any hope of stopping the Convergence.

With a heavy heart that felt as if it were rending in two, Soren made his decision.

"Bobby," he said, his voice hollow, "set a course for the rendezvous point. Sang, all stop. Prepare for emergency fold." He switched comm channels on his control surface. "Minh, fall back immediately. Full retreat."

"Copy that," the Hooligan leader answered.

"Aye, Captain," Sang replied softly.

"Soren, what about—" Jack started.

"There's no time to save them!" Soren snapped back, every ounce of his pain audible in his voice.

The Wraith flipped over again, main thrusters slowing them as the Pilums shot toward the ship like bees returning to the hive. Thankfully, there were no enemy ships left to give chase.

They had all cleared the area as well.

"Coordinates set, Captain," Bobby said. "Ready to fold on your command."

The enemy dreadnought's bow was now blazing with barely contained energy. The vortex cannon at its heart seemed to be sucking up the darkness as though it were gathering the very fabric of spacetime around it.

In the next instant, it fired.

A beam of distorted spacetime erupted from the massive vortex cannon, expanding rapidly as it crossed the distance between them. Unlike the focused beam of their own weapon, this blast spread out in a cone, engulfing everything in its path. Soren watched in horror as it washed over the FUP ships that had yet to fold. Shields flickered and died, thrusters went out, and life support systems failed, leaving the vessels nothing but lifeless husks adrift in space.

As the wave passed over the station, the lights along its surface blinked out one by one. Soren couldn't tear his mind off Alex, his squad, and the other Marines trapped inside as the station's systems failed around them.

But he had to make a decision, the only decision he could make as the leading edge of the disruption field raced towards them, warping the stars behind it.

"Fold now!" Soren roared.

And in a flash of light, the Wraith disappeared.

CHAPTER 30

The Wraith's bridge was deathly quiet. Soren sat motionless at the command station, his mind reeling.

They had escaped with their lives, yes. But at what cost? Without the ships docked at the station. Without the supplies and ammunition the FUP would need to keep fighting. Without Alex…

He lowered his head into his hands, needing all of his willpower to keep himself together in front of his crew. He could hardly believe how quickly their fortunes had turned. The spy, Reeves, had said Grand Admiral Strickland knew they were coming, which meant someone had sold them out.

Someone who was likely still with Admiral Yarborough and what remained of her fleet.

And what of Alex and the Scorpions? Soren's eyes clenched tighter, trying to will reality to warp and change so that his boy was back on the ship with him.

A strong hand squeezed his shoulder. "Soren, I'm sorry."

Soren didn't reply. Didn't move. And then he finally blinked. The vortex cannon on the SF ship…it was different from theirs. More like a spacetime warping EMP than an annihilating tornado that ripped apart everything it touched. The space station hadn't been destroyed; it just went dark. As long as it hadn't been breached, that meant a breathable atmosphere remained trapped inside. At least for a time. And the Scorpions' powered armor was EVA capable, with four hours of compressed air supply. No doubt, the blast had taken the powered part of the armor offline, but the breathing system had manual redundancy for exactly this kind of catastrophe.

Soren lifted his head, sitting upright and looking at Jack. "He's not dead," he said. "The Scorpions can survive the loss of power. They don't need the station's life support."

"Soren—" Jack began.

"Bobby, wait an hour and then deactivate the fold drive," Soren said. "We're going back."

"Soren—" Jack started again.

"We're going back, Jack," Soren insisted. "Even if the station is venting its atmosphere, the Karuta armor has four hours of air. We jump one hour, we wait one hour, we jump back. With any luck, we find Alex and his team waiting for us."

"What if we find that ship waiting for us?" Jack asked. "We won't be able to fold soon enough to escape it a second time."

"They're still alive, Jack!" Soren barked. "If we leave them, they'll either run out of air, or the SF will kill them or take them prisoner. I don't know which is worse. We can go back and help them. We have to take that chance."

"Soren," Jack said gently. "You know we can't go back, not now. It will put our entire mission at risk."

"He's my son!" Soren shouted. "I'd put every universe at risk for him. The only reason we left is because I knew we couldn't withstand that ship's vortex cannon. You saw what it did. We would be just as dead in space as the rest of them if we had stayed."

"I know," Jack said, his soft expression reflecting Soren's pain and guilt. "You made the right decision. The only one you could make as captain of this ship, and I understand why you want to go back immediately. I would want to do the same for my boy. Hell, he's the reason I'm out here. But unlike my son, Alex is SpecOps. If the enemy lingers near the station, he'll find another source of oxygen, or pull a tank from an enemy Marine's armor. Even if it's not the same, his team will find a way to make it work. We can go back, but we need to give it more time. Reduce the risk to all of us. To the Wraith. The rendezvous point is eight hours out. Let's finish the fold, regroup with the Admiral, and then return to the station. Okay?"

Soren stared at Jack. He could see the care and concern in his old friend's eyes. He knew what Jack was saying made sense. Alex and his team had survived on Jungle. They could handle a day inside a dead space station.

"Okay," Soren replied at last. "Bobby, belay the prior order. We'll complete the fold."

"Aye, Captain."

"Minh," Soren said next, over the comms. "Status report."

"We lost six fighters, sir," Minh reported, his voice strained as he fought to contain his own emotions. "Pilums Three, Five, Seven, Nine, Twelve, and Fifteen. We're down to nine birds. We would have lost more if you hadn't turned around to draw the enemy's fire. I'll never forget that, sir."

Six pilots, six lives snuffed out in the chaos of battle. Soren knew each of them by name, and had shared meals with them. Now they were gone, like so many others.

"They were good pilots, all of them."

"They were, sir. Every damn one of them."

"I'm sorry, Minh," Soren said softly, his voice heavy with regret. "I know how close you were to them."

"Thank you, sir," Minh replied. "But they knew the risks. We all do. And they died heroes, fighting for something bigger than themselves."

Soren managed a small, sad smile. "That they did, Captain. That they did." He paused, collecting his thoughts. "We'll hold a proper memorial service once we've regrouped with the fleet. For now, make sure the remaining pilots get some rest and anything else they need."

"Understood, sir," Minh said. "Pham out."

As the bridge fell silent, Soren's mind drifted. How many more would they lose before this was over?

Samira's voice again cut through the silence before he could spiral further into his dark thoughts. "Captain, Dr. Mitchell wants to speak to you. He says it's urgent."

Soren suppressed a sigh. "Put him through."

"Captain! I'm glad I caught you. I've been analyzing the sensor data from just before we folded, and I think I've made a breakthrough!"

Soren felt a pang of irritation at Lukas's enthusiasm. He had to remind himself that the scientist didn't know about Alex yet. Knowing the man, he probably hadn't even known they were duking it out in the middle of a war zone while he was studying his numbers. "What have you found, Doctor?"

"Well, sir, I was hoping you could tell me more about what created that massive distortion field we encountered just before we folded," Lukas said, his words tumbling out in a rush. "The readings are…wow. Off the chart."

Soren's jaw tightened as he recalled the monstrous ship and its devastating weapon. "It was a vortex cannon, Lukas. But on a scale we've never encountered before. The ship that fired it was massive. At least twice the size of a Komodo-class."

"A vortex cannon? But that's...that's it! Captain, I think we've found it!"

"Found what?" Soren asked, confusion momentarily overriding his grief.

"The source of the instability!" Lukas exclaimed. "The trigger for the Convergence!"

Soren was taken aback. "But Lukas, you said it would take something far more powerful. Your example was a hundred vortex cannons firing simultaneously. That might have been a big one, maybe the size of five, but it was only one."

"I understand, Captain. But now that I see these readings...I think I was looking at it all wrong. I'll have to start over to confirm it, of course, but what I'm seeing suggests it's not all about raw power. It's about the specific way spacetime is being manipulated. I've gone over the data from the Eye so many times I see it in my sleep. The patterns from the cannon's discharge match, almost identically, to the edges of the dilations inside the Eye. The resonance is almost perfect. I think this weapon, or weapons like it, are what's causing the instability between dimensions. Each discharge is like...like plucking a cosmic string. And if they keep doing it..."

"The string breaks," Soren finished, the implications dawning on him.

"Exactly!" Lukas nodded vigorously. "I'll need more time to confirm my findings. But I really think this is it, Captain."

Soren felt a glimmer of hope amidst the darkness that had settled over him. If Lukas was right, they were one step closer to understanding the Convergence—and potentially stopping it. If the mission had revealed the source and they couldn't get Alex back, at least his sacrifice would have been for something.

Right now, he had to believe his son was still alive and

that they would get him back. But if he were dead, he would have his vengeance, one way or another.

"You have eight hours, Doctor," Soren said. "That's how long until we rendezvous with the fleet. I want a full report by then."

"Understood, sir," Lukas replied. "I'll get right on it."

"One more thing, Lukas," Soren added. "Could you ask Dana to meet me in my ready room?"

"Of course, Captain," Lukas said. "Is everything alright?"

Soren managed a weak smile. He wasn't going to give Lukas the news before her. "I just need to discuss something with her. Soren out."

As the communication ended, Soren turned to Jack. "You have the conn. I'll be in my ready room."

Jack nodded, understanding in his eyes. "Take all the time you need."

Soren made his way to his ready room, each step feeling heavier than the last. He settled into his chair, his eyes falling on the holo-image of his family that sat on his desk. On Jane's smile, Dana's laughter, Alex's mischievous grin—a moment frozen in time, from a simpler, happier era.

The door chimed, pulling him from his reverie. "Enter," he called out.

Dana stepped inside, her face clouding with concern as she took in her father's demeanor. "Dad? What's wrong?"

Soren gestured for her to sit, struggling to find the right words. "Dana, sweetheart...there's something I need to tell you."

Dana sank into the chair, her eyes never leaving her father's face. "It's Alex, isn't it?" she asked, her voice barely above a whisper.

Soren nodded, feeling his composure start to crumble. "H...he and his squad were trapped on the station. I had to leave them when that SF dreadnought appeared and took out half the Admiral's fleet, We had to leave. I had to leave him behind."

Alone in the ready room with family, the admission was more than Soren could take. His eyes burned as they welled, his bottom lip quivering when he was trying so hard to be strong. But he was still human. Still a father.

Dana's face crumpled, tears welling up in her eyes, too. "No," she whispered. "No, no, no..."

In an instant, Soren was around the desk, pulling his daughter up into a tight embrace. They clung to each other, their shared grief pouring out in silent sobs. For a long moment, they stayed like that, father and daughter united in their pain.

Finally, Dana pulled back slightly, wiping at her eyes. "Is he... do you think he's...?"

"He's alive," Soren said firmly, as much to convince himself as her. "I have to believe that. Your brother...he's resourceful. He'll find a way to survive."

Dana nodded, sniffling. "Of course he will. He's a Strickland, after all."

Despite everything, Soren felt a slight smile tug at his lips. "That he is." He took a deep breath, gently squeezing Dana's shoulders. "We're going back for him as soon as we can. I promise you, we're not abandoning him."

"When?" Dana asked, a hint of her usual determination creeping back into her voice.

"We need to rendezvous with the fleet first," Soren explained. "Regroup, assess our situation. But as soon as we can, we're heading back to that station."

Her eyes met his. "I know you feel guilty, Dad. But you shouldn't. You did what you had to do. I know it, and everyone else on this ship knows it. And when we get Alex back, he'll know it, too."

Soren exhaled and nodded. "I'm trying to accept that. I appreciate you saying it."

"Is there anything else I can do to help?"

"Keep doing what you're doing. I don't know if Lukas told you already, but he thinks he's made a breakthrough regarding the Convergence. Something to do with the vortex cannon on the SF dreadnought."

"I heard him telling you about it," Dana said, standing up. "We'll have the report ready in time." She hesitated for a moment, then hugged her father again. "We'll get him back, Dad. We have to."

"We will," Soren agreed, holding her tight. "No matter what it takes."

CHAPTER 31

Alex floated in the Command and Information Center, still trying to make sense of the sudden, chaotic shift in their situation. One moment, they were in control, the station secured, their mission seemingly accomplished. The next, everything went to hell.

The memory of that moment replayed in his mind. A shuddering vibration that threatened to tear the station apart, followed immediately by an eerie silence as every system aboard the massive structure shut down simultaneously. The gentle hum of life support, the soft beeping of consoles, the barely perceptible vibration of the station's reactor—all gone in an instant, leaving behind a void that seemed to swallow sound itself.

And with it, gravity vanished.

Alex's stomach had lurched as he found himself suddenly weightless, drifting away from the deck. If not for filters in his neural implants, he would have been blind as well. Thankfully, the augments seemed unaffected by the attack, though he had no clue how or why.

Around him, unsecured objects began to float. Datapads, styluses, even droplets of blood from the recent firefight, forming perfect crimson spheres in the zero-g environment. Both the living and the dead had lifted off the deck, his fellow Marines searching for purchase or one another with outstretched hands, blind in the pitch black.

Whatever hit them had taken out his Karuta armor as well. He had felt the servos lock up, the suit becoming a rigid shell around him, lifting off the deck as the electro-magnets in his boots lost power. He should have had emergency backup, but that was gone too. Whatever hit them, it was like a massive EMP that didn't care about how much protective shielding their equipment had.

Gunny, what the hell just happened? Malik's voice came through the neural link, tinged with panic and confusion. *My suit's dead. I can't move!*

Stay calm, Alex ordered. *Scorpions sound off. Status report.*

One by one, his team checked in, their thoughts a jumble of fear, confusion, and resolve.

Five here, Zoe replied. *Suit's offline, but I'm unharmed. Three is with me.*

Present and accounted for, Jackson chimed in, his usual bravado slightly subdued. *Gotta say, Gunny, this wasn't in the mission brief.*

What's the status on those tangos you were tangling with before things went to hell? Alex asked.

They're as confused as we are, Zoe replied. *Maybe more so. They retreated as soon as the gravity went out.*

I'm not in much of a fighting mood right now either, Malik said. *Four reporting, ready for your orders, Gunny.*

A chill ran through Alex, the status reports a stark reminder of Sarah's absence. He couldn't afford to linger on the thought. Four of them were still alive, but he doubted they were safe.

Three, Five, stay put. Four and I will lead our units to you. We'll regroup at the network relay.

Maybe we should meet you on the bridge, Zoe suggested.

Negative. If they send a boarding party over, this is the first place they'll look for survivors. We don't want to be easily discovered.

Copy that.

Alex turned his attention to Reeves, the FUP Intelligence officer who had warned them of the impending attack. The man was clinging to a console, eyes wide with fear and resignation.

"What the hell was that?" Alex demanded, his voice sharper than he intended.

Reeves swallowed hard. "The dreadnought," he said, his voice barely above a whisper. "It must have fired its disruptor cannon."

"Disruptor cannon?" Alex repeated. "That thing knocked out power to the entire station?"

"Yes. It uses spacetime distortion to disable all electronics in its path. Unlike an EMP, it can't be shielded against. We never thought they'd use it on their own station."

Alex considered the implications. If the disruptor cannon had disabled the entire station, that meant life support was offline. They had air for now, but it wouldn't be replenished. And without power, they couldn't send a distress signal or contact the Wraith.

"Why didn't you warn us sooner that the enemy knew we were coming?" Alex demanded, frustration boiling over. He pushed off from a nearby console to float in closer to Reeves. "We could have called off the attack, damn it!"

"I couldn't," Reeves said, his voice cracking. "There was no opportunity. The strike force only brought the additional Marines in an hour before your attack. By then, it was too late. I...I'm sorry."

Alex bit back a curse, forcing himself to take a deep breath. Anger wouldn't help them now. "What happens next?" he asked, his voice low and controlled.

Reeves seemed to shrink in on himself, his shoulders hunching. "They'll dock the dreadnought to the station," he explained, his words coming out in a rush. "Recover any survivors. Probably salvage what they can of the station's tech and data cores."

Alex's jaw clenched, his mind already working on their next move. If the enemy was on the way here, then they didn't have much time.

Malik, he called out through the neural link. *We need to get out of these suits. The armor's just dead weight now.*

Copy that, Gunny, Malik replied.

Alex managed to release the emergency seal on his armor with some effort. He carefully extracted himself from the powered suit, clinging to it as they drifted across the CIC together. Pushing bodies, datapads, and other debris aside, they recovered their suits' air supplies and their rifles. When Alex came in contact with one of his Marines, he announced himself and told the man to stand by for orders.

Without his frozen armor, Alex steadied himself against the overhead. "Listen up, Marines. You too, Reeves," he added to include the FUP spy. "My Scorpion Squad has eyes in the darkness. We're going to lead you away from the CIC to regroup with the remainder of our forces. Keep a hand on the Marine in front of you. If you lose contact, shout out to make it known. I know we're in a bit of trouble right now, but if we stay calm, we'll get out of it. Understood?"

A ragged round of oorahs echoed in the dark compartment.

Four, help me get these Marines oriented, Alex said through the implant.

Copy that, Malik replied.

The two of them began navigating to the individual Marines from their units, taking them by the shoulder and guiding them to one another. Once all of the Marines were floating together, Malik grabbed the hand of one to lead him while Alex took point, ready for trouble he hoped they wouldn't run into on the way out of there.

Moving in zero-g was challenging, especially trailing eight blind Marines, but they made steady progress through the station's corridors. Occasionally, they'd encounter floating debris or the occasional body—somber reminders of the battle that had raged just minutes ago.

"Stay sharp," Alex whispered as they approached an intersection. "There could still be hostiles." Grateful for all their zero-g training in the sims, he used the deck to propel himself forward, planting his hand and using friction to slow him as he neared the corner ahead of Malik. Leading with his rifle, he followed it around the bulkhead.

Four SF crew members floated static in the passageway, having heard their approach but as blind as the others.

"This is Scorpion One of the FUP Marines," Alex said, knowing that using his name would confuse the enemy. "You can't see me, but I can see you. If you want to keep breathing, I suggest you surrender."

"We…we surrender," a young lieutenant with a nasty gash across his forehead replied.

"We can't see a damn thing," another added. "We're no threat to you."

"Just keep that in mind," Alex replied. "What's your situation?"

"We… we can't believe it," the lieutenant said, his voice a mix of shock and betrayal. "They fired on us. They used the disruptor cannon on the station. On their own people!"

The raw emotion in the man's voice was palpable. Alex couldn't help sympathizing. He knew a little bit about what it was like to be betrayed by leadership.

"Have you encountered any other survivors?" Alex asked.

The lieutenant nodded, wincing slightly at the movement. "A few. We were trying to make our way to the bridge, to see if emergency comms were active, but without power..."

"Comms are dead," Alex said. "Everything is dead except us. If you've had a change of heart about fighting for an evil bastard who shoots at his own, you're welcome to follow. Otherwise, just stay out of our way."

"You don't stand a chance against the Strickland Federation," the lieutenant said. "It's you who should surrender to us."

"I'd rather die," Alex replied flatly.

"Suit yourself. We're going to check on the bridge, just in case you're lying."

The SF personnel drifted forward along the top right corner of the passageway, bypassing the other Marines as they made for the CIC.

"Good luck," Malik said to them as they passed.

Alex and the Marines continued their journey through the station, with Alex using his implant's HUD to keep track of their position relative to the other Scorpions. It was harder to do without the map loaded into his armor, but he'd prepared for the mission, memorizing most of the route through the station.

The eerie silence of the dark station was broken only by their labored breathing and an occasional creak of resettling superstructure. Alex tried not to think about the fact that every breath was depleting their limited air supply. The station was big enough that they should have at least twelve hours.

After a long, dark float, they finally reached the area where Zoe's team had been attempting to reach the fire control systems. Alex followed the passageways to their marks on his HUD, entering another corridor and spotting what remained of their two units of Marines—six in total now—standing with their rifles pointed in his direction, even though they couldn't see him if they wanted to.

Three, we're here. Call off your dogs, Alex said through the implant.

A shrill whistle immediately followed. "The rest of our platoon is in front of you," Jackson said. "Stand down."

The Marines lowered their weapons, their postures a little looser now that the rest of the team had joined them.

Alex floated over the Marines while Malik helped the two groups mingle, guiding them to one another. He found Zoe and Jackson floating just outside the network relay compartment. Both looked worse for wear, their armor dead and useless as Alex's. But they were alive, and that was all that mattered right now.

"Damn, are we glad to see you," Jackson said, his usual bravado tempered by noticeable relief. "I was starting to think we'd be permanent space station decor."

"What's the situation?" Zoe asked, her voice all business despite the circumstances. As Alex and Malik helped them out of their suits, salvaging their air supplies, Alex quickly filled them in on what had happened. The disruptor cannon. The impending arrival of the SF dreadnought. And their limited options.

"So what's the plan, Gunny?" Jackson asked, his voice a mix of anticipation and trepidation. "Please tell me you have one of your crazy, brilliant ideas up your sleeve."

Alex took a deep breath, considering their options. They were trapped on a powerless station with limited air and an unknown number of hostiles. The smart move would be to surrender when the SF forces arrived and hope for decent treatment as prisoners of war.

But Alex Strickland had never been one for making the smart move. He never gave up. When things went to shit, he liked throwing the book out and going his own way.

"We're going to take that dreadnought," he said, his voice low and determined.

The others stared at him in disbelief.

"You're joking, right?" Malik asked.

Alex shook his head, a wicked smile playing at the corners of his mouth. "Think about it," he said. "That ship is our only way off this station. And if Reeves is right about its capabilities, it would be a damn valuable asset to put into the FUP's hands."

"And how exactly do you propose we take control of a ship that size?" Zoe asked, skepticism evident in her voice and thoughts. But beneath that, Alex could sense a growing spark of hope.

"We use their own plan against them," Alex replied, his confidence growing as the plan took shape in his mind. "They'll be expecting to find survivors, maybe some resistance. But they won't be prepared for a coordinated assault from inside the station."

"It's insane," Jackson said, his voice tinged with awe. Then, a grin spread across his face, and he chuckled, the sound mirrored in the burst of excitement Alex felt through their link. "I love it."

Zoe and Malik exchanged glances, then nodded their agreement, their determination flowing through the neural link and bolstering Alex's resolve.

"Alright," Alex said. "Here's what we're going to do..."

As Alex outlined his audacious plan, he pushed aside thoughts of the Wraith, of his father and sister. He had to believe they had survived and would come back for him. But right now, he couldn't afford to wait for rescue.

It was time for Scorpion Squad to get to work.

CHAPTER 32

Alex and the Scorpions returned to the other Marines once they finished finalizing the details of their plan. For any part of it to work, they needed to prepare—and to prepare, they needed to move fast—before the SF dreadnought docked and flooded the station with reinforcements.

"Reeves," Alex said to the FUP spy. "You know this station better than anyone here. How long do you think it'll take the dreadnought to dock?"

Reeves considered for a moment. "They won't complete a formal docking cycle without power. They'll come up alongside and connect to one of the arms without clamping. It's a less stable hold, but they don't intend to stay long. I'd say twenty minutes."

"Except I locked all the docking clamps closed before the power went out," Aster reminded them. "They'll need to be manually released to allow the dreadnought to get close enough to make the interlock connection."

"How long will that take them?" Alex asked.

"Best guess? At least an hour, maybe two. They'll have to send EVA teams to manually override each clamp."

Alex nodded, a flicker of relief passing through him. It

wasn't much, but it was something. "That gives us a window, but we need to move. Now."

He turned to his team, his voice low but firm. "Scorpions, we're heading out. The rest of you," he addressed the Marines, Aster, and Reeves, "stay put. We'll be back with supplies and a plan to get us all out of here."

Without waiting for acknowledgment, Alex pushed off from the bulkhead, propelling himself down the corridor. The other Scorpions followed close behind, their movements fluid and synchronized even in the zero-g environment.

They made their way through the darkened passageways. As they approached the hangar bay, Alex raised a hand, signaling the others to halt. He peered around the corner, his enhanced vision piercing the darkness.

The hangar was a scene of eerie stillness. Most of the starfighters sat clamped to the deck, but a few that had been prepping for launch when the distortion field hit were floating with everything else from blood droplets to ordnance loaders and more. And there, amidst the detritus, Alex spotted what he had come for.

"Sarah," he whispered, his voice thick with emotion.

Her body floated near the center of the hangar, a stark reminder of the cost of their mission. Alex swallowed hard, pushing down the surge of grief and anger that threatened to overwhelm him all over again.

"Let's move," he said, his voice tight. "Four, Five, gather whatever supplies you can find. Three, you're with me."

They spread out, working quickly and efficiently. Alex made his way to Sarah's body, Jackson close behind. He shuddered when he reached her, unable to reconstruct her face past the damage the bullets had done to it. A furious fire ignited in his chest, leaving him more resolved than ever to get his Marines off this station and back with his father.

"We're taking her with us," Alex said. "We can't leave her behind."

Jackson nodded solemnly, helping Alex maneuver Sarah's body towards the hangar exit.

Meanwhile, Zoe and Malik had been scouring the floating debris. They picked the rifles and ammo from the dead power armored SF Marines, along with a couple of flashlights drifting loose with everything else.

Finishing quickly, Alex and Jackson led the way, guiding Sarah's body through the corridors.

The other Marines were excited at their return, but when Zoe flipped on one of the flashlights and finally restored their vision, their pleased outbursts went silent quickly. "Is that...?" one of the Marines began, his voice barely above a whisper.

"Corporal Sarah Chen," Alex confirmed, his voice tight. "One of the best damn Marines any of us have ever had the honor to serve with."

"Semper Fi," the Marines responded, doing their best to come to attention and salute in the zero-g environment as Alex and Jackson brought her past.

They carefully secured Sarah's body in a corner of the relay compartment.

He turned to the assembled group, his eyes hard. "We need to make sure she gets home. But right now, we need to focus on the mission. We're going back out. There are more supplies we need, and we have a dreadnought to capture. Stay alert, stay quiet. We'll be back soon."

With that, Alex led the Scorpions back into the station in search of the needed equipment. They headed to the site of Alex's earlier skirmish. The corridor was littered with debris and the lifeless forms of SF Marines, their Karuta armor rendering them massive, intimidating shapes in the gloom.

"You did this all yourself, Gunny?" Malik asked, impressed with the scene.

"These are the bastards who killed Sarah," he replied. "They had it coming. Let's move. Rifles, Moonbeams, ammo, grenades."

The Scorpions spread out, working quickly and efficiently. Alex made his way to the nearest Karuta-armored corpse. He had to boost his strength to pry the Marine's fingers open and retrieve his high-powered rifle, a more capable weapon than the Marines' standard issue and one they didn't have enough of on the Wraith. He also opened the suit's storage compartments to see what he could find.

"Jackpot," he announced, coming up with two spare magazines, a flashlight that clipped onto the rifle barrel and a grenade.

The others made similar declarations as they scavenged what they could. Within minutes, they had amassed a small but powerful arsenal: four high-powered rifles, a dozen magazines, eight grenades, and enough flashlights for half their personnel.

"Time to go," Alex said. "Back to the others."

They retraced their path through the station, moving as quickly as they dared while laden with their newly acquired gear. A subtle tremor ran through the station as they neared their makeshift base. Alex's stomach clenched. That shudder likely meant that the dreadnought had arrived.

"We're back, bearing gifts," Alex announced as they entered the relay area. The tired yet eager Marines had been busy checking their weapons and mentally cataloging their remaining magazines. As he began distributing the supplies, handing one of the rifles to Reeves, another, stronger vibration shuddered through the station.

"They're here," Reeves said, a somber tone to his voice.

"What do we do now, Gunny?" one of the Marines asked.

Alex ground his teeth together for a moment. "Now, we take the fight to the bastards." He quickly outlined the plan, emphasizing the need for stealth and precision. The Marines listened intently, their earlier jitters giving way to firm resolve. "Any questions?" he asked when he finished.

Silence greeted him. He nodded, satisfied. "Alright. Scorpions, you're with me. The rest of you, stay put and stay quiet. We'll be back for you as soon as we can. If anyone shows up that isn't us, kill 'em."

Using their enhanced vision, Alex once more led his team into the station's dark and winding corridors. This time, they were headed for the central hub where the docking arms connected. It was a vast, cavernous space dotted with cargo containers and secured equipment. He signaled for them to slow and approach cautiously as they neared it. *Scan for any signs of movement*, he ordered through their neural network.

Alex spotted an ideal observation position behind a cluster of crates. The spot would provide cover while giving them a clear view of the docking arm entrances. *There*. He signaled to the others, leading them to the spot he'd chosen. Their gentle pushes and pulls took them through the weightless environment toward the docking arm where the dreadnought was docked. Once in position, they didn't have to wait long for something to happen.

Movement caught Alex's eye as a group of SF crew members emerged from one of the corridors. Their movements in the zero-g environment were frantic and uncoordinated as they pushed clumsily off the bulkheads and grabbed hold of grooves in the deck. They were obviously headed for the docking arm where the dreadnought waited.

Alex's gaze shifted as one of the docking arm doors ground open, its hinges squealing a need of lubricant. And then his blood ran cold. SF Marines in Karuta armor emerged from one of the arm entrances, their helmet lamps cutting through the darkness. Behind them came regular Marines equipped with flashlights.

Lamps mean no augments, Jackson said silently.

Let's hope so, Alex replied. *We'll wait for them to clear the area.*

They watched as the Marine leader approached one of the struggling crew members. The woman looked up at him from where she levitated along the deck, trying to keep her grip on it. "Sergeant," she said, her voice filled with relief. Thank you for coming for us."

"Are any of the FUP scum still alive in here?" the SF Gunnery Sergeant demanded.

"I...I think so."

"Have you seen them?" the sergeant asked impatiently.

"Y-yes, I passed a group in the passageways. They were heading for the bridge."

Alex silently cursed himself for sparing the station's crew. It had been a short-sighted, overly compassionate decision considering the circumstances.

The sergeant motioned toward the dreadnought. "Get to the ship. We'll handle the intruders."

The crew didn't need to be told twice. They scrambled for the docking arm, disappearing through the open hatch. Meanwhile, the Marines began to move deeper into the station.

Malik's voice came through the neural link, tense with suppressed energy. *Why don't we go for the ship while all those Marines are on the station?*

We need to get our people off first, Alex replied. *And hiding them here when they aren't very adept at zero-g would have been a problem. We equipped them for when we got onto the dreadnought. The station is our playing field.*

Don't you mean killing field, Gunny? Jackson said.

Same difference, Alex replied. *We'll follow them and pick them off, one at a time if we have to. Slow and steady.*

Oorah! the other three replied.

They moved out, trailing the SF Marines at a safe distance. Their augmented vision gave them an advantage, allowing them to easily navigate the darkness while their enemies relied on their limited light sources.

After a few minutes, the SF force split into two groups. Without hesitation, Alex divided his team as well. *Zoe, Jackson, take the left group,* he said through his implant. *Malik, you're with me on the right.*

Alex and Malik followed their target group, who soon encountered another group of SF crew members. One of the Karuta Marines detached from the main group, apparently tasked with escorting the support personnel back to the ship.

Perfect, Alex said. *Let's follow them.*

He and Malik shadowed the Karuta Marine and the crew members as they returned to the docking arm. As they neared a junction, they got their opportunity to attack.

Now, Alex snapped silently to Malik. Pulling a grenade from his belt, he armed and threw it all in one fluid motion into the middle of the group. The detonation created a blinding light, the shockwave amplified by the lack of gravity. Half of the crew were killed instantly, while the Karuta Marine tumbled across the corridor. His armor absorbed much of the energy, but bowling him over disoriented him long enough for Alex and Malik to open fire.

Their rifles barked before the survivors could pull their handguns, the recoil pushing them backward into the bulkhead. They kept firing, and within seconds, it was over. Every crew member and the Marine floated lifelessly in the zero-g.

Move! Alex ordered, pushing off the bulkhead and

propelling himself down an adjacent corridor. Malik followed close behind. They barely made it around the corner when the sound of heavy boots approached, The other group of the SF Marines had no doubt heard their rifle reports.

Up, he said, indicating a maintenance hatch he'd spotted in the overhead. Alex boosted his strength to force it open, and they pulled themselves up and through the hatch, closing it behind them just as the enemy Marines rounded the corner.

Through the thin metal of the hatch, Alex could hear the Marines' angry exclamations as they discovered the bodies of their comrades. Orders were exchanged, and the sound of several sets of boots running down the corridor indicated that just some of the Marines were continuing down the corridor while others remained behind.

Alex waited, his breathing slow and controlled, until more of the Marines followed the others. Then, moving with deliberate care, he eased the hatch open and peered out. Four Marines remained, their helmet lamps sweeping the area as they searched for clues as to where the attackers might have gone. Unfortunately for them, their backs were to the hatch. Alex didn't hesitate. He pushed silently out, Malik right behind him. Before the SF Marines could react, the two Scorpions stung their prey.

The fight was brief and brutal. Enhanced by their neural augments, Alex and Malik moved with superhuman speed and precision. In the zero-g environment, they launched off the walls and ceiling, coming at the SF Marines from unexpected angles.

Within moments, it was over, the Marines glued to the floor by their magboots, upright but dead. Alex shoved them hard enough to dislodge them, and proceeded to take their boots.

These should help our guys, Alex said. *Five, sitrep.*

Zoe's response came back immediately. *We've taken out six so far. No casualties on our end.*

Make sure you grab their magboots.

Copy that.

Alex did a quick mental tally. The enemy had started with thirty-two. They were down to twenty-four, and the Scorpions were just getting started. Alex couldn't help wondering how many Marines they had on that ship.

However many they sent over was however many he would kill.

Over the next hour, Alex and his team became ghosts in the station, striking from the shadows and disappearing before the enemy could mount an effective response. Their superior mobility in zero-g and augmented capabilities overwhelmed the SF Marines at every turn.

By the time they had eliminated the last of the initial force, Alex was breathing hard, adrenaline coursing through his veins. But there was no time to rest.

"Back to base," he ordered. "We need to get our people ready for the next phase."

They made their way back to where they had left the other Marines and Reeves, moving as quickly as caution would allow. Upon arrival, Alex wasted no time in distributing the additional supplies they had collected.

"Listen up," he said, his voice carrying the weight of command. "The situation has changed. We've eliminated the first wave of hostiles, but there will be more coming. Now that you can all see, now that you can all stand, now that you all have full ordnance, you can all fight. It's time to take this battle to the enemy."

"What's the plan, sir?" one of the Marines asked, his voice steady despite the circumstances.

Alex allowed himself a smile. "We go for the ship. It's time for round two. Let's make the Strickland Federation regret the day they decided to mess with us."

CHAPTER 33

"One more thing," Alex said, his gaze sweeping over the assembled Marines. "Before we move out, we need to go over some key points about fighting in zero gravity. I'm sure you went through this in basic, but it's probably been a while, so it's good to be reminded of proper technique. I need someone to demonstrate."

Corporal Richards stepped forward to volunteer. "I remember this, Gunny." He dropped into the proper stance, shifting his center of gravity low over his magboots, legs spread, left leg forward, knees slightly bent.

"The main thing...keep your body low and your legs apart," Alex instructed. "Otherwise, the recoil will try to push you back, so brace yourself against it. You'll need to use your core muscles more than usual to maintain your position when firing." Alex picked up one of the heavy rifles they'd scavenged from the armored SF Marines they had killed. "These pack a hell of a punch," he warned. "In zero-g, that means you have to be extra careful they don't throw you off balance. Short, controlled bursts are key. Let the weapon's weight work for you, using it as a counterbalance to your movements. Questions?"

One Marine raised his hand. "Gunny, what about moving and shooting at the same time?"

"Good question," Alex nodded. "Best advice, don't if you can at all help it. Otherwise, make sure you're in a posture closest to static as you maneuver. There's a specific walk, but we don't have time for you to learn it. It's time to move out. Aster, Reeves—you two, stay with with Sarah's body. Treat her with respect."

The FUP spy and the hacker nodded solemnly, moving to guide Sarah's body forward. Alex watched for a moment, another pang of grief and anger tightening his chest. He pushed it down, focusing on the task at hand.

"Remember," he addressed the group one last time, "we're not just fighting for ourselves here. We're fighting for billions of people across three universes. And we're fighting to get home. Let's make it count."

With that, they moved out, a resolute silence falling over the group as they made their way through the station. Alex took point, his augmented vision scanning for any sign of movement or danger. The rest of the Scorpions spread out among the Marines, ready to provide support where needed.

As they neared the central hub, Alex held up a fist, signaling the group to halt. He cocked his head, listening intently. The sound of boots on metal deck plating echoed faintly through the station.

"Enemy incoming," he said. "Fall back and spread out. We'll use the side corridors to our advantage."

The Marines quickly complied, breaking into their original groups with a Scorpion at their head and taking up positions in the adjoining passageways. Alex floated against the overhead at the intersection, his rifle at the ready. Through his neural link, he would convey positions and targets to the other Scorpions, coordinating their defense without a word.

Moments later, a squad of SF Marines rounded the corner, their flashlights cutting through the darkness ahead of them. At their head were two power-armored figures, their heavy footsteps echoing on the deck. Alex captured their advance through his implant before pushing away, taking cover behind a bulkhead, his eyes on the spot he wanted the enemy to reach.

Alex waited until they were fully in the kill zone before silently giving the order, the other Scorpions passing it along with hand gestures.

The corridor erupted in a storm of gunfire as the Marines laid down a deadly barrage. The heavy, long-range rifles they'd scavenged proved their worth, punching through the standard body armor of the SF troops with ease.

The Karuta-armored Marines returned fire, their own heavy weapons blazing. But Alex and his team had the advantage of surprise and position. Jackson and Zoe focused their fire on one of the armored foes, their coordinated assault peppering his helmet and eventually punching through, dropping him to the deck. Seconds later, the other armored Marine joined him. Soon enough, so did the rest of the initial SF force.

"Push forward!" Alex yelled, shoving hard off the bulkhead for the momentum to lead a charge down the corridor. The Marines followed, their confidence bolstered by their initial success.

But the enemy wasn't done yet.

More troops poured in from adjoining passageways, slowing the advance. The Marines comported themselves well, holding their formations, remaining in the right posture, and maintaining short, steady bursts of fire despite the incoming storm.

Alex saw one of his Marines take a hit, the man's magboots losing their grip and sending him spinning away trailing globules of blood. Another went down under a burst of fire from a Karuta-armored Marine, the heavy rounds shredding his body.

Three, Four, flank left! Alex ordered through the neural link. *Five, with me!*

The Scorpions moved with practiced efficiency, their augmented reflexes and coordination giving them a decisive edge. They carved through the enemy ranks, their heavy rifles making short work of anyone foolish enough to get in their way.

As the two forces closed ranks, the battle devolved into a series of intense, close-quarter engagements. Alex found himself grappling with an SF Marine, the two of them spinning through the air as they struggled for control. He managed to get his hands around the man's head. Planting against the bulkhead and pushing off, he slammed the enemy's head into the opposite bulkhead, his neck breaking from the impact. Alex let go of him in time to swing his rifle down and fire on a tango beneath him. The combined recoil and motion pushed him in an upward spiral. He straightened, bending his knees as his feet—his magboots deactivated—hit the overhead. Pushing off hard, he brought himself down, feet first on top of another SF Marine.

A similar whirlwind of destruction, Zoe bounced off overheads and bulkheads to come at the enemy from unexpected angles, Her rifle barked in short, controlled bursts as she efficiently cut down opponents. One after another. Jackson and Malik focused on leading the rest of the Marines in, picking off the greatest threats with brutal accuracy.

Another pair of Karuta-armored Marines joined the fracas, shrugging off most of the rifle fire coming their way as they powered into the fight. What they didn't expect was the coordinated response from Alex and his team. They quickly focused their full firepower on the faceplate of one. He put an armored hand up to help deflect the assault, only to have it chewed apart by the overpowering barrage.

The second Karuta-armored Marine had time to grab one of Alex's Marines by the throat, crushing his windpipe before tossing the body aside like a rag doll. It was all the damage he had time to do before the Scorpions combined forces to bring him down the same way they had the first.

For several intense minutes, the battle raged. The corridor filled with globs of blood, spent casings, and ravaged bodies. In the fog of war, it was hard for Alex to tell who was winning, but he knew his side was putting up a hell of a fight.

And then, the tide of battle began to turn in their favor. The SF troops, caught off guard by the ferocity and tight coordination of the attack, started falling back.

"Don't let up!" he called out. "We've got them on the run!"

The Marines responded, pressing their advantage with a chorus of battle cries and surging forward with renewed vigor. They pursued the retreating SF forces, cutting down anyone who tried to stop and make a stand.

Finally, the last of the SF Marines fell. Alex did a quick head count, his heart heavy as he tallied their losses. They'd lost six Marines in the fight, with several others wounded. But they'd won, and the path to the central hub was clear.

"Regroup and reload," Alex ordered. "We push for the ship now, while we have the momentum."

The surviving Marines quickly complied, salvaging ammo and weapons from the fallen. With little respite, they pressed on. The central hub loomed before them, pristine compared to the corridors leading to it, where so many had died. Alex could see the docking arm where the SF dreadnought waited, their ticket home if they could just reach it.

"There's the prize," he called out. "Let's take it!"

They surged forward, charging across the open space. For a moment, it seemed like they might make it without further resistance. That the enemy's fighting force had been fully depleted.

Then, before they could reach the docking arm, a new wave of SF forces emerged from the interlock between the dreadnought and the station, led by a squad of Karuta-armored Marines. The sheer number of them threatened to break their advance.

Not only that, Alex immediately sensed that these new Karuta-armored Marines were something different. Something more than the Marines who wore the enemy's black Karuta armor. The suits these new SpecOps Marines wore were a deep, midnight blue, the chest emblazoned with the clenched fist emblem of the Strickland Federation. They moved with a fluid grace that spoke of extensive training and experience, their jump jets shooting them forward to cut off Alex's force before they could clear the hub.

With their advance stalling, Alex and his Marines stood firm and opened fire on this powerful, new threat. Managing to move so quickly that none of the rounds hit their helmets, they fired back. And all around Alex, FUP Marines began to fall, cut down by the precise, devastating fire from these elite troops.

"Fall back!" Alex yelled, desperately trying to salvage the sudden reversal. "Find cover!"

The Marines broke ranks, scattering across the central hub, desperate for cover. Alex and the Scorpions moved to the flanks, silently working together as they awaited the enemy.

The first of the special Marines entered the hub backward, floating through with his sights already set on the Scorpions. Alex pushed off, angling toward the overhead, just in time to avoid the burst of rounds fired at him. He couldn't afford to spend too much time drifting, or these crack fighters would get a bead on him before he could react.

He hit the overhead and bounced off at an angle, opening fire as the rest of the special Marines entered the hub. His rounds peppered the enemy, pushing him backward toward the compartment's rear. He scored a hit on the faceplate of one of the fighters, leaving a scuff in the reflective transparency but nothing more.

Meanwhile, the other Scorpions pushed away from their positions, firing on these new threats. The same one continued tracking them, his rounds whistling past, not missing by much, and impacting the bulkheads and overhead.

Alex hit the back bulkhead and flexed his legs against it, boosting the power of his push-off. He rocketed downward at an angle, rolling and planting his feet again as he landed, the momentum exerting heavy strain on his legs. He lunged at the blue-armored Marine, rifle tucked against his chest.

Caught off guard, the man saw him at the last moment and whirled to target him. The move played right into Alex's hands, the Marine's face turning right into line with his rifle. His finger froze momentarily on the trigger as Malik's face stared back at him, his eyes wide with surprise.

The hesitation almost cost Alex. Shaking off his initial shock, he opened fire, catching the enemy Malik squarely in the faceplate with multiple rounds. The barrage chewed through the transparency and into his head. Alex collided with the body, using it as an anchor to press off and rise back up toward…

An armored hand suddenly wrapped around his ankle, jerking him to an abrupt stop before roughly dragging him back down to the deck. He landed on his back with enough force to knock the air out of his lungs.

Sudden realization hit him. If the Marine he'd killed was

Malik, then the one standing over him with his boot on his chest had to be…

"Surrender," an all too familiar voice ordered. "Or die."

Alex used his implant to see through Zoe's eyes. She had found cover behind the crates, but the fight was clearly over. Their Marines, including Reeves and Aster, were all eliminated. Jackson and Malik were pinned against the bulkhead, rifles trained on them.

And he was under the heel of Alexander Strickland.

"Well?" Alexander asked. "What will it be?"

We need to surrender, Gunny, Zoe said. *It's over. We lost.*

Alex swallowed hard. "We surrender," he croaked out.

The boot immediately left his chest. "Let go of your weapon."

Alex let go of it, and it drifted away.

Alexander's boot left his chest. "Stand up."

He did as he was told, rising to his feet, his reactivated magboots clamping onto the deck as he stared through his faceplate and that of his doppelgänger. Although the face that stared back at him was his own, it wasn't like his at all. It was harder, more angular, with eyes that held no warmth or compassion.

"Interesting," Alexander said. "Is this some kind of FUP trick? You look just like me."

"It isn't just him," another familiar voice said, coming from the Marine with her rifle trained on Jackson. "This one's you, Jackie."

"What the hell is this?" Jackie replied. "Where's your twin, Sarah?"

"Gunny," the enemy Zoe said, crouched beside the body of their dead Malik. "Mal's dead. Your dupe killed him."

Alexander's eyes narrowed on Alex, the fury visible in his expression.

"You killed my Sarah," Alex said. "That makes us even."

Alexander grew even more enraged, but he didn't lash out. "I would kill you where you stand if I wasn't sure my father would want to have a word with you about...this." He waved his hand at Alex's appearance. "Did you think you could fool your way on board this station? Is that what this is?"

"No," Alex replied. "Actually, it's nothing like that...at all."

Alexander smirked. "I'll admit, I'm impressed you managed to do as much damage as you did. Especially that you brought down Mal without powered armor of your own. But you're mine now." He motioned toward Malik and Jackson. "Get them down."

Three, Four, stand down, Alex ordered silently. The two Scorpions complied, pushing off from their positions overhead and drifting down to where Alex stood, their magboots locking onto the deck.

"Where's your Zoe?" the Zoe copy asked.

"Here," Zoe replied, emerging from cover, unarmed with her hands up.

"Don't you wish you still had that pretty face, Zee?" Jackie asked the SF Zoe.

"Shut up, asshole," she replied, her face, plainly visible through her faceplate, bearing the healed scorch marks of plasma fire.

"Our Sarah is over there," Alex said, jerking his chin to where her body drifted in the hub. "I'd appreciate it if you'd treat her with the respect due a fallen Marine."

"I'm sure you would," Alexander replied. "Well, seeing that we're brothers, I suppose I can grant that request. There's just one other thing I need to do first."

Before Alex could even start to wonder what that was, Alexander turned his rifle on Malik and squeezed the trigger, sending a single round between the Scorpion's eyes.

"No!" the other Scorpions cried as one, quickly subdued by weapons pointed at their chests.

"You son of a bitch," Alex growled, white hot fury burning in his chest.

"Now we're even," Alexander replied coldly before pointing toward the docking arm. "Let's go."

CHAPTER 34

The Wraith emerged from folded space, joining a cluster of battered FUP ships materializing against the backdrop of unfamiliar stars. Soren stood on the bridge, eyes fixed on the viewscreen. He had agreed to complete the jump and rejoin the FUP's forces, but he was already eager to be on his way back to the SF space station.

Back to his son.

"Twenty-two ships, Captain," Mark reported. "Out of thirty."

Soren's gaze swept across the fleet. They had lost eight in the fighting. Nearly a third of their original force, and they had nothing to show for it. What had promised to be a game-changer for the resistance had quickly turned into a potential game-ender.

"Samira, open a channel to the Spirit of War," Soren ordered.

"Aye, Captain," she replied.

"Captain Strickland. I'm relieved to see you made it," Admiral Yarborough said. She sounded tired and frustrated, despite the time she had to recover during the fold. Since she was so much like his Jane, Soren knew she had spent the time reliving every decision, not because she could change what happened, but so that she would do better the next time.

"Likewise, Admiral," Soren answered. "Though I wish the circumstances were better."

"Captain, I'm sorry about your son. If there had been any way to get him and his Marines off the station in time, believe me, I would have done it."

"I do believe you. I wanted to do the same. My XO convinced me to get out while we still could, and it was the right call." He glanced at Jack, who nodded in support. "With that being said, my intention is to return to the station as soon as possible to rescue him."

"Back to the station?" Yarborough questioned. "Captain, surely you can't be—"

"I can, Admiral," Soren interrupted. "And I will. If my son is still alive on that station, I'm going to bring him home."

"Captain, I understand how you feel, but are you sure you want to do that? That dreadnought may still be there when you arrive, and we're in no condition to offer you any kind of support."

"I'm not asking for your fleet's support, Admiral. I'm telling you what I'm planning to do."

Yarborough sighed. "I can't stop you, of course, but I strongly advise against this course of action. We need to regroup, assess our losses, and plan our next move carefully."

"And you should. But I won't abandon my son."

Jack spoke up, trying to move the conversation forward. "Admiral, what can you tell us about your intelligence network? And the Strickland Federation's? It seemed the enemy knew we were coming long enough to roll out the welcome mat."

"Obviously, we have a leak, and that's deeply troubling

to me. We have protocols around all of our tranSat communications, along with full encryption. We also monitor all ground activities and inspect every supply we purchase or steal in a raid. For someone to get a warning out to the SF in a matter of days, and within our primary strike force..." She trailed off, likely thinking more about it. "The good news is that I can narrow down possible suspects to the ships that knew about the upcoming attack. The bad news is that it's possible the ship the leak was on didn't make it back here. They might already be dead."

"Isn't that good news?" Jack asked.

"No," Soren replied. "Because if they don't turn anyone up, it could mean they're dead or it could mean they're still here, and still passing intel to the Federation."

"Which means we can't afford to give up the search," Yarborough added. "Even if it comes up empty, which would be a tremendous waste of time and resources. Nevertheless…"

"Just as important," Soren said, "it's possible the leak provided the SF with this location as well. They could be here any minute."

The statement sent a chill over the comms and caused a brief silence on the bridge as his crew considered the implications.

"That's a concerning thought," Yarborough said, biting her lower lip while her mind worked. Soren couldn't help seeing his Jane in the response. He knew when she was ready to speak because she stopped chewing at her lip and opened her mouth. "I think another fold is in order, new coordinates, passed only to the captains of the remaining ships—just to be safe. We can't afford to be caught off guard again."

"That sounds prudent," Soren agreed. "Do you mind providing me with the coordinates once you've settled on them?"

"Not at all. I'll transmit them securely once we've decided on a location."

"Thank you, Admiral. I have one other question. What can you tell me about the vortex cannon on the ship that attacked us?"

"The Fist of Justice," Yarborough said quietly.

"The what?" Jack asked.

"The dreadnought. Soren gifted it to my son. I can tell you that he's used that cannon on entire cities, wiping out their infrastructure in seconds and sending them back to the Stone Age."

"And he used it on his own station. His own people." Soren shook his head in disbelief.

"I wish I could say I was surprised," Yarborough replied. "But Alexander...he's relentless. Cruel. He has no moral limitations, no line he won't cross in his father's name."

"How could he become like that?"

Yarborough's voice carried a mixture of anger and profound sadness. "He's not the son I raised. He's the son my Soren turned him into."

"I wouldn't say using that weapon on their own assets is a terrible strategy," Jack said, surprising both Soren and the Admiral. He put up his hands defensively when he noticed Soren's glare. "I'm not condoning it, but the weapon acts as an unstoppable EMP. He didn't kill anyone on the station or the ships. I know that's only half the equation, but still."

"Believe me, Commander Harper," Yarborough replied. "What happened at the station may not be the best example of what he's capable of, but he is capable of achieving great things through great cruelty. Do you think he'll stay to pick up the starfighter pilots stranded in their powerless spacecraft? And what do you think will happen to the FUP ships he disabled? What do you think might happen to the

Marines we left behind? I'm sorry to say it, Captain Strickland, but Alex and his team had better hope my son doesn't find them in there, or you'll go back to discover their corpses."

The hard words sent a chill down Soren's spine, hands tensing on his armrests as he considered the possibility. If the enemy dreadnought did dock with the station to pick up the surviving crew, would he also hunt for Alex and the Marines? Would Alex hide, knowing he would come back for him? Or would he try to fight?

He hoped not.

"There's only one way for me to find out what happened after we left," Soren said, voice strained. "That's why we have to go back."

Before anyone else could speak, Soren's comm chirped. "Captain," Dana's voice came through, "the report you requested is ready."

Soren took a deep breath, regrouping his thoughts. He had to handle one thing at a time, and trust in Alex to stay safe. "Admiral, would you like to be patched in for this? It concerns the Fist's vortex cannon and its potential connection to the Convergence."

"Absolutely," Yarborough replied. "And Captain?"

"Yes?"

"I apologize. I should have mentioned the Fist of Justice and its primary weapon sooner. I never made the connection between it and the other ships' weapons. I've personally never even seen it in use."

"You almost did," Jack said. "It's better that you didn't."

"Admiral, stand by, we're going to move to my ready room," Soren said.

"Of course, Captain."

"Dana, bring Lukas up to my ready room with your report."

"Yes, sir."

"Keira, you have the conn."

"Aye, Captain. I have the conn," she replied, moving to the command station as Soren and Jack both stood to exit the bridge.

Soren and Jack made the short walk to the ready room. Dana and Lukas joined them soon after. Sitting at his desk, Soren transferred Admiral Yarborough's comm to the room.

"Admiral," he said. "I have Jack, Dana, and Lukas here with me."

"Dana," the Admiral said. "We haven't had the pleasure of meeting yet, which is a shame. I hope we can, soon."

Soren watched Dana's face. He could see her struggling with her composure to speak to the woman who was a copy of her mother. "I hope so too, Admiral. After we get my brother back."

"Of course. I truly hope that you do."

"Lukas," Soren said. "Go ahead."

"Captain, Admiral," he began, "I've completed my analysis of the data from the dreadnought's weapon. I cross-referenced it with our observations from the Eye. As I initially suspected, the patterns are an exact match."

"What does that mean, exactly?" Yarborough asked.

"It means we've found the smoking gun, almost literally." He laughed nervously. None of the others joined him. "Right. In any case, I'm highly confident that the vortex cannon, or more specifically, the way it manipulates space-time to create its EMP-like effect is almost certainly the cause of the instability leading to the Convergence."

"Almost certainly?" Jack pressed.

"Science is rarely about absolutes, but I'd stake my reputation on this. Moreover, I believe each use of the weapon pushes us closer to the tipping point."

"So destroying the dreadnought should solve the problem," Soren said.

"Only if the dreadnought is the only ship with that

weapon. And only if they can never construct another one. And only if they don't come up with something similar but more powerful."

"In other words," Dana said, "we'd need to destroy every instance of the weapon across all dimensions, plus any data on how to build it in order to fully assure the Convergence won't re-occur."

A heavy silence fell over the room as the implications sank in.

"Well, the vortex cannon on the Wraith is one of a kind," Jack said. "And the only plans for it are inside the ship's data banks. So we're safe there."

"The Wraith's cannon has no effect on the instability," Lukas said. "It's using the wrong distortion algorithms."

"But could we modify it to use the right ones?" Soren asked.

"Yes. I believe we could, now that I've identified the pattern."

"Not that we'd want to," Dana said.

"My dimension doesn't have the vortex cannon," Lukas said. "Ours had a fatal flaw that caused it to explode. My FUP never pursued it after that."

"How do you know it wasn't the explosion that caused the rifts?" Soren asked.

"Because it occurred after they were already present. But there is a chance it made things worse."

"That leaves this dimension's version," Jack said.

"We would need to defeat the entire Strickland Federation to do what you're saying needs to be done," Yarborough said. "But with what we have left...it's impossible."

Jack turned to Soren. "Impossible is what the Wraith does best."

Soren allowed himself a small smile. "We'll start with rescuing Alex and destroying that dreadnought. Then we'll worry about doing the impossible." He turned back to

Yarborough. "Admiral, I know you can't commit much, but any help you can provide would be appreciated."

Yarborough considered it for a moment. "As long as it's against the SF, I'll do what I can. I'll transmit the coordinates for our next rendezvous point within the next few minutes. And I promise you, I'll work tirelessly to root out the source of our leak and gather whatever intel I can that may be useful to you. Beyond that, we can't do much. We needed that station. And we needed the ships we lost trying to take it."

"I understand," Soren said. "Thank you for whatever help you can provide, Admiral. We'll be in touch."

He disconnected the comms and looked at Lukas. "You're sure about this? You've been wrong before."

"Too many times," Lukas admitted. "But it's not like there's precedent for any of this. We're doing the best we can to figure it all out as we go along."

"That we are," Soren agreed, getting to his feet. "If you'll excuse me, I need to get us headed back in the right direction."

CHAPTER 35

Soren's footsteps echoed in the empty corridor as he made his way from his quarters down to the hangar bay. Six hours had passed since they'd left the FUP fleet, six hours of torment as he imagined what might have happened to Alex and the other Marines they'd left behind. He'd tried to busy himself with reports and planning, but his mind kept drifting back to his son.

A soft chime from his comm unit broke through his brooding thoughts. "Captain," Samira's voice came through, "The memorial service is set to begin in fifteen minutes."

"Thank you, Samira," Soren replied. "I'm on my way right now."

He picked up his pace a little, a sense of coldness seeping into him in response to the barren corridor. The whole ship felt so much emptier now. They'd lost good people in the battle, and while hope remained for Alex and the others left on the station, the pilots who'd fallen were beyond saving.

Soren finally reached the hangar bay, where the rest of the crew had already gathered. The atmosphere in the cavernous space was uncommonly somber, the usual bustle of activity replaced by a respectful silence. As he entered, all eyes turned to him.

He took his place at the front of the assembled crew, facing the six empty flight suits arranged in a row. Each bore the name and rank of a fallen Hooligan pilot. After offering his silent respects to them for a few minutes, he stood and turned to face the crew.

"We are gathered here today," Soren began, his voice carrying across the hangar, "to honor the memory of six brave souls who gave their lives in service of a cause greater than themselves. They flew into the heart of danger, knowing the risks, because they believed in our mission."

He paused, letting his words sink in. "These pilots weren't just skilled warriors. They were our friends, our comrades, our family. Each of them had dreams, hopes, and loved ones waiting for them back home. And each of them chose to put those dreams on hold to fight for something they believed in."

Soren's gaze fell on Minh, who stood at rigid attention, his face a mask of carefully controlled grief. "Captain Pham, would you like to say a few words about your pilots?"

Minh stepped forward, his voice steady despite the emotion evident in his eyes. "They were the best of us," he said. "Each one of them flew like they were born in the cockpit. But more than that, they were good people. Loyal friends. The kind of people you'd want watching your six in a dogfight or sharing a drink with after a long day."

He went on to share a brief story about each fallen pilot, painting a picture of their personalities and the bonds they'd formed. As he spoke, Soren could see the impact on the crew. Tears were shed, small smiles appeared as fond memories were recalled, and the sense of shared loss deepened.

When Minh finished, Soren stepped forward again. "We honor their sacrifice by continuing our mission," he said. "By fighting for what's right, by protecting those who cannot protect themselves, and by never forgetting the cost of the freedom we fight for."

He nodded to Keira, who stood near a control panel. At his signal, she activated the hangar bay's external doors. They opened slowly, revealing the overhang that kept the bay hidden while cloaked.

"In accordance with naval tradition," Soren continued, "we commit them to the void. May they find peace among the stars."

Minh and five other Hooligans stood, each gathering one of the flight suits. The crew stood at attention and saluted them as they carried the flight suits to one bay door and threw them out, where they vanished below the doors and disintegrated as they met the edges of folded space.

Once the Hooligans returned to their places, Soren spoke again. "Let us also not forget those we left behind on the station. Hope remains for their safe return, and we will do everything in our power to bring them home. For now, let us carry the memory of our fallen comrades in our hearts as we continue our mission."

As the ceremony concluded, the crew began to disperse. Soren made his way over to Minh, placing a hand on the pilot's shoulder. "They were damn good pilots, Minh. We couldn't have asked for better."

Minh nodded, his composure cracking slightly. "Thank you, sir. I just... I can't help feeling like I failed them somehow."

"You didn't fail anyone," Soren said firmly. "You led them well, and they knew the risks. We'll make sure their sacrifice wasn't in vain."

Minh straightened, a flicker of determination replacing

the grief in his eyes. "Aye, sir. The Hooligans will be ready for whatever comes next."

Soren nodded, then made his way out of the hangar and back up to the bridge. Once there, he claimed the conn from Vic and settled into the command station. "Ethan, Keira, status report," he said. "How do we look?"

Ethan spoke first, his fingers dancing over his console. "All systems are green, Captain. The fold drive is operating at peak efficiency, and we've managed to squeeze a bit more power out of the reactors. Shields have regenerated to ninety-eight percent capacity."

"Excellent work, Ethan," Soren said. He turned his attention to Keira. "What about our weapons systems?"

Keira's expression was less enthused as she delivered her report. "We're not in as good shape there, Captain. We expended over fifty percent of our railgun ammunition and seventy percent of our missiles during the assault. We've got enough for another fight, but we'll need to be a lot more conservative with our firing solutions."

Soren leaned back in his chair. They'd burned through a significant portion of their firepower with little to show for it. But dwelling on past mistakes wouldn't help them now. "Understood. Make sure all batteries are loaded and ready, just in case. We don't know what we'll find when we arrive."

"Aye, Captain," Keira replied, turning back to her station to carry out his orders.

As the minutes ticked by, Soren found his thoughts drifting back to Alex. Was he still alive? Had he managed to evade capture somehow? Or was he now a prisoner of the Strickland Federation? The uncertainty gnawed at him, making each passing moment feel like an eternity.

"Two minutes until exit," Bobby announced from the helm.

Soren straightened in his seat, pushing aside his

personal concerns to focus on the now. "All hands to ready stations," he ordered over the shipwide comm. "We don't know what we'll find on the other side, so stay alert."

The bridge crew tensed, hands hovering over consoles as they prepared for potential combat. Soren's eyes shifted to the main viewscreen.

With a flash of light, the Wraith emerged into normal space. The station loomed before them, a massive structure against the backdrop of unfamiliar stars.

"Keira, engage the cloak," Soren ordered immediately.

"Cloak engaged, Captain," Keira replied.

"Mark, what are you seeing on sensors?"

Mark didn't answer right away, waiting to analyze the incoming data. "The station appears intact, Captain. But there's a significant debris field surrounding it. It looks like the remains of the ships that were destroyed in the fighting, as well as the ships disabled by the cannon, both FUP and SF. The dreadnought blasted everything still intact except the station."

"Completely unnecessary," Jack said. "Those ships were all out of the fight."

"Any sign of the dreadnought?" Soren asked.

"Negative, sir. No other ships within sensor range."

Soren allowed himself a small measure of relief. At least they wouldn't have to face that monster again. Not yet, anyway. "Keira, since we're alone out here, let's switch from cloak to shields. We'll need the protection to navigate through that mess."

As Keira made the switch, Soren contacted Phoebe. "Prepare a drone for launch. We need eyes inside that station."

"Aye, Captain," Phoebe replied.

"Bastian, launch the drone as soon as it's ready," Soren ordered. A few moments later, Bastian announced the launch.

"Put the feed up on the primary viewscreen."

"Aye, Captain."

Soren returned his attention to the main viewscreen, where the feed from the drone was now displayed. Expertly piloted by Bastian, the small craft entered the debris field.

"Sang, bring us in as close as possible," Soren said. "Be careful about disturbing the debris."

"Aye, Captain," she replied as the drone reached the station. The Wraith began to slowly accelerate toward the station.

"I don't see any way inside," Bastian said.

"We'll have to make one then," Soren replied.

"What if the Marines are alive in there?" Jack asked.

"Alex will make sure they're prepared for a potential hull breach," Soren confidently replied. "Keira, target the station hull with a single missile."

"Aye, Captain," she replied. Then, a few seconds later, "Target locked."

"Fire."

The single projectile streaked away from the Wraith, winding around the debris in its path. It hit the station's hull and detonated, creating a large hole while also giving the station a small push.

Bastian guided the drone to the hole, where it slipped inside, its camera sweeping the darkened corridors.

"Head for the bridge," Soren said.

"Aye, sir," Bastian replied.

The drone drifted through the station. Soren heard Jack gasp as the probe turned into a corridor, its light illuminating the first bodies. They were SF Marines, their armor scarred and broken.

"Keep going," Soren urged, his eyes searching for any sign of Alex or the other Scorpions.

The Wraith closed the distance on the station as the drone progressed deeper inside.

"Captain," Mark said. "I'm noticing something odd about the docking clamps. They're all closed except for one set."

"That must be where the dreadnought docked," Soren realized. "Bastian, guide the drone to the docking arms. Working backwards from there should provide faster answers."

The drone continued through the station, slowly navigating around more corpses, including the first few FUP Marine bodies. Though he'd expected casualties, Soren's face darkened when he saw them.

When the drone entered the central docking hub, Soren's heart sank. The space was littered with bodies, the majority wearing FUP Marine armor. Among them, he spotted a figure in Karuta armor, its faceplate shattered beyond recognition.

"No," Soren breathed, leaning forward in his chair. "It can't be." His hands gripped his armrests tightly, not ready to accept that Alex was dead and upset that, if not Alex, at least one of the Scorpions had fallen.

"Captain," Kiera said, "sensors identify this Scorpion as Corporal Sarah Chen."

Soren let out a breath he hadn't realized he was holding, and then he closed his eyes, remembering the sound of Sarah's laughter, something he would never hear again.

The drone continued its sweep, and suddenly, Soren spotted a familiar face. "Malik," he said, his voice barely above a whisper. The Scorpion drifted gently, a single gunshot wound to his forehead.

Either the fighter who had killed him was a perfect shot, or he had been executed. Soren shuddered at the thought. And Alex would never have left any of his team behind. But if Sarah and Malik were here, where were the others? Where was his son?

The drone continued forward toward an open hatch

leading to one of the docking arms. As the drone moved into the narrow passageway, Soren held his breath. He needed answers, needed to know what had happened to Alex and the other Scorpions.

Suddenly, the drone's feed erupted into static.

"What happened?" Soren demanded.

Before anyone could respond, a blinding flash filled the viewscreen. The station seemed to bulge for a moment, then exploded outward in a massive fireball.

"No!" Soren shouted, rising from his chair as he watched the destruction unfold. The station disintegrated before their eyes, fragments of metal and other debris spinning away as the fireball quickly dissipated. The objects impacted the Wraith a few seconds later, peppering the shields with everything from body parts to all kinds of detritus.

As the initial shock wore off, Soren's mind began to process what he'd just witnessed. Alexander had set a trap, waiting to destroy anyone who came looking for survivors.

"Soren," Jack said softly, placing a hand on his friend's shoulder. "I'm so sorry."

But Soren shook his head, his eyes never leaving the screen. "He's not dead, Jack."

"Soren, with everything we've seen—"

"We didn't see his body," Soren interrupted. "Or Zoe's. Or Jackson's. And Alex wouldn't have left Malik and Sarah behind." He turned to face Jack, anger and determination blazing in his eyes. "They're not dead. They're prisoners. I'm sure of it."

Jack hesitated, clearly torn between wanting to support his friend and facing what he saw as the harsh reality of the situation. "Even if that's true, how do we get them back? We don't know where they've been taken, or even if they're still..."

"We'll find a way," Soren cut him off. "Any way we can.

I didn't give up on Dana, and I'm not giving up on my son, Jack. Not now, not ever. All roads lead to the Fist of Justice. We'll need Admiral Yarborough's help to locate the ship, and hopefully find Alex."

"I feel like we're running in circles," Jack said.

"Not quite. We need to rendezvous with the Admiral. Bobby, set a return course and execute."

CHAPTER 36

Are we there yet? Jackson asked through his implant.

What are you, five? Zoe replied silently.

No, you're Five. I'm bored.

Alex allowed himself the smallest of smirks at the silent exchange. It seemed wrong to joke at a time like this. With Sarah and Malik dead. With the three of them confined to the dreadnought's brig.

Right now, joking was all they had.

He had felt the vibrations through the ship's structure when the railguns opened fire, in quick bursts with short delays. He guessed from the cadence that Alexander was busy blasting all the ships he had disabled, which he had only even known about because the arrogant asshole couldn't stop himself from showing off his handiwork to them before locking them behind bars. He had to assume Alexander had destroyed the station, too. When his father came back to look for him—and he had zero doubt that he would—he would find no survivors. He would have no choice but to assume the worst. He'd be forced to give up on them and move on.

That's what Alex wanted him to do. He still had a

mission to complete, and the Scorpions were only a small part of that. Just like on Jungle, they were completely on their own. But unlike on Jungle, there were only three of them now.

And that hurt more than anything.

At least the enemy didn't seem to have the means to turn off the neural implants. The three of them could still communicate without risk of giving anything away.

Hey Gunny, Jackson burst out silently. *We haven't done sitreps in a while. Do you want to hear mine?*

Alex knew instinctively this would be another of Jackson's attempts at humor. They were all close, but he and Malik had been especially tight, and he was taking what had happened especially hard. Alex felt extra guilty for that. It was his fault Malik was dead. His smartass remark when he should have been compliant; he wished he could take that moment back.

Go ahead, Three, Alex replied. He had to give Jackson a chance to depressurize, and this had always been the Marine's way.

No change on my end, Jackson said. *Still locked up tight. The bastards haven't even let us out for recreation since they stuck us in here. At least the accommodations are better than that bootleg Hell sim we did. Remember that one? I still can't believe we got away with running that program.*

Still the only sim not all of us survived, Zoe said.

That's an understatement. None of us survived.

Yeah, but we were fighting Satan, after all.

I thought Alex would beat Satan.

I know. I lost a hundred bucks on that wager.

Sorry, Alex chimed in. *Maybe if they hadn't given Satan power armor and a comically oversized railgun.*

I can still smell the sulfur whenever I think about that one, Jackson said. *Though I'd take that over our charming hosts any day.*

Same here, Zoe added. *I've been mapping out every detail I can see. It might come in handy if we get a chance to move. Did you notice the terminal at the guard station? I've been watching whenever anyone uses it. I think I have the first four alphanumerics of the passcode, out of twelve. If I can get the whole thing, and we can get out of here, who knows? Maybe we can raise some hell.*

Good thinking, Alex approved. *If we're going to get out of this, even the smallest detail could be crucial. What about the guards? Any patterns to their movements?*

They're pretty disciplined, Jackson reported. *Shift changes every four hours.* There was a pause before Jackson spoke again. *Any ideas on where they're taking us, Gunny? I mean, I know we're not exactly on a pleasure cruise, but it'd be nice to know if we should be preparing for a tropical climate or packing our winter gear.*

My best guess is Earth, Alex replied. *According to the intel we got from Yarborough, that's where Grand Admiral Strickland is based. Though I doubt we'll be seeing much of the scenery.*

Maybe we can convince them to take us to Vegas before they start the interrogations, Zoe offered, her joke falling flat.

We'll get out of this, Alex assured them, projecting more confidence than he felt. *We just have to play it smart, stay patient, memorize every detail we can, and then come up with a plan.*

Copy that, Zoe replied. *Though I have to say, if this is another one of your elaborate training exercises, Gunny, you've really outdone yourself this time.*

Alex was about to reply when he picked up the sound of heavy footsteps in the corridor outside. *Heads up,* he warned the others. *We've got company.*

The footsteps stopped outside the brig. There was a brief pause, then the door slid open with a soft hiss. Alexander Strickland strode in, flanked by two guards. His eyes swept over the cells, finally settling on Alex.

"Well, well," Alexander said, his voice dripping with false cordiality. "How are you enjoying your accommodations? I do hope everything is to your liking. We rarely get visitors these days, and especially not visitors with such unique appearances."

Alex remained silent, staring back at his doppelgänger with an impassive expression.

"Not very talkative, are we?" Alexander continued, undeterred by Alex's silence. "That's fine. I'm sure we'll have plenty of time to get acquainted once we reach our destination. I hear the interrogation facilities are to die for. Get it?" He grinned.

Alex remained stoic. Jackson chuckled through the neural implant. *Asshole.*

Alexander stepped closer to Alex's cell, studying him intently. "You know, it's uncanny. You really do look just like me. I have to admit, I'm curious about how that's possible. Some kind of cloning experiment gone wrong, perhaps? Or maybe you used to be an ugly duckling, and agreed to be part of a mission to...what? Replace me? Was that your plan? Am I close? Just say cold, room temperature, warm or hot."

When Alex still didn't respond, Alexander's tone sharpened slightly. "I've heard some interesting rumors about you and your friends. About an unidentified ship that was seen near the cosmic disturbance, then at Wolf, and finally at FOB Alpha. They say it came from another dimension." He let out a short, humorless laugh. "Sounds like something out of a child's bedtime story if you ask me. But I have to wonder..."

He trailed off, waiting for Alex to take the bait. When no response came, he continued, his voice taking on an edge of irritation. "Come now, surely you have something to say? Some explanation for your appearances? For your fighting prowess? I'm not trying to trick you into giving up any valuable intel. I'm just genuinely curious. It's not often we encounter opposition with any real competence."

Alex remained motionless, his eyes never leaving Alexander's face.

Alexander turned away from Alex's cell and strode over to where Jackson was being held. "Perhaps you'd like to share your thoughts?" he asked, his tone deceptively light. "If you're anything like my Jackie, you're a big talker. And a big joker, too? I'd love to hear your take on our current situation. Maybe you could provide me some clarity on either situation? You can choose. The unidentified ship, or the fact that we're all body doubles."

Jackson met his gaze steadily but said nothing, his usual wit held firmly in check.

Alexander's jaw tightened almost imperceptibly. He moved to Zoe's cell next. "And you? Any insights you'd care to offer?"

Zoe's only response was to narrow her eyes, her face set in a mask of defiance.

"No?" Alexander said, his voice dripping with mock disappointment. "Such a shame. And here I thought we could have a civilized conversation. I even had the chef prepare a special meal for us to share while we chatted. My Zee and Jackie will be happy to eat them for you."

He spun back toward Alex. In an instant, his facade of civility dropped away, replaced by cold fury. "Let me make something very clear to you," he snarled, leaning in close to the forcefield. "Your silence won't protect you. I've already killed one member of your pathetic little squad. How about we make it two? I wonder which of your friends you'd miss more? The comedian or the pretty blonde?"

Alex felt a surge of rage at the casual mention of Malik's execution and the threat to his remaining teammates, but he forced it down. It was one of the hardest things he'd ever done, but he knew Alexander was trying to provoke a reaction, and he refused to give him the satisfaction.

Alexander glared at him for a long moment, then let out a frustrated growl. "Fine. Have it your way. But know this —my father may want you delivered in one piece, but once he's done with you, all bets are off. And I promise you, in repayment for killing Mal, I will personally ensure that your suffering is prolonged and exquisite. Maybe I'll even let you watch as I work on your friends. I've always wondered if it's possible to turn a person inside out while keeping them alive. This might be my chance to find out."

With that final threat, Alexander turned and stormed out of the brig, his guards following close behind. The door slid shut with a definitive clang, leaving the Scorpions alone once more.

As soon as he was sure they were gone, Jackson's voice filled Alex's mind. *Well, that was pleasant. Think he likes us? I was hoping for at least a fruit basket to welcome us aboard. Maybe some complimentary slippers or a nice thick bathrobe.*

Zoe's mental snort was almost audible. *Oh yeah, we're definitely his new best friends. I can't wait for the slumber party. Maybe we can play Twister.*

I'd love to twist him, Jackson returned.

Despite the gravity of their situation, Alex felt a small smile tug at the corners of his mouth. *We need to focus. What did you make of his questions about the ship?*

He seems interested in the idea of us coming from another dimension, Zoe observed. *But he's skeptical. Like he wants to believe it but can't quite wrap his head around the concept.*

Jackson's thoughts took on a more serious tone. *It could be an advantage, Gunny. If they don't fully understand what they're dealing with, if they don't want to believe it, we might be able to make up some bullshit story to feed them. It could buy us some time and save us some pain.*

Not a bad thought, Alex agreed. *We have plenty of time to* cook up something completely inaccurate. *And since we can make it up together, we can keep all our details straight.*

Alexander keeps mentioning some plot to replace him, Zoe said. *Paranoid much? Maybe we should build off that.*

Good idea, Alex replied. *We'll continue looking out for opportunities to bust out of here, but for now, let's get to work on our story.*

CHAPTER 37

"Computer, increase the volume ten percent," Soren said, seeking the calm he needed to sleep.

"Confirmed," the lifelike voice replied as the volume of the rainfall sounds filling his quarters increased. He stared at the nearest display, watching the rain drip off the needles of hemlock and fir trees and hit the flatter leaves of the thick growth beneath. He tracked one specific drop as it slid from a leaf and just happened to land in a tiny bare spot on the forest floor where it sent ripples through an existing puddle.

He leaned back in his chair, rubbing his temples, fighting for a reprieve from a headache nothing had been able to remedy. Patience had never been his strong suit. Struggling to keep himself focused and calm was tearing him apart. He'd originally come back to space in search of Dana—and had found her under starkly different circum-stances—and he would do the same for Alex. Somehow.

But what if he couldn't?

He wasn't ready to accept that. Not even close. But in the back of his mind, he knew it was a long shot that the Stricklands of this dimension would keep his son alive for long. If they did, it would be to use him as leverage. Maybe to draw him into a situation he couldn't escape. And with the fate of multiple universes at stake, how could he in good conscience make any kind of deal that didn't complete his mission?

He sighed, standing and heading for his desk to get the last of the whiskey Harry had given him. The knots in his stomach hadn't allowed him to stop off at the chow hall en route to his quarters, so he knew the whiskey would go straight to his head, hopefully calming his thoughts and maybe even his headache. Right now, his mind was racing way too far ahead, way too fast. The future would make itself known when it became the present. In the meantime…

A soft chime from the door interrupted his lonely, forlorn thoughts. "Enter," he called out, turning to face the door.

Harry stepped inside, his usual no-nonsense expression softened by a hint of concern. "Evening, Captain. Hope I'm not interrupting anything important."

"No. I was just trying to…I don't know…calm my thoughts. Maybe knock myself out with the last of the whiskey you gave me so I can get some sleep. What can I do for you, Harry?"

The quartermaster shifted his weight, a bit of nervousness creeping into his normally unflappable demeanor. "It's funny that you mentioned you're struggling to calm your thoughts. I've arranged a bit of a surprise. A potential remedy for that. If you're up for it, that is."

Soren raised an eyebrow. "A surprise? Harry, I'm not sure this is the best time for—"

"With all due respect, sir," Harry interrupted, "I think it's exactly the right time. I understand the stress you're under. You shouldn't deal with it all alone. It's not good for you, and what's not good for you is ultimately not good for the crew."

"I appreciate your concern, Harry, but I'm not really in the mood. We're in the middle of a crisis. Alex is most likely being held prisoner, we've lost too many good people, and we're no closer to stopping the Convergence."

Harry took a step closer, his voice softening. "That's precisely why you need this, Soren. I'm not trying to cheer you up—I know that's not possible right now. But you shouldn't be so isolated. This might be a military ship now, but it wasn't when we all boarded. We joined you because we're your friends. And right now, you need your friends."

Soren studied Harry's face for a long moment, seeing the genuine concern there. He sighed, realizing that the quartermaster had a point. "Okay, Harry. You've convinced me, as usual. Lead the way."

They started out walking the corridors in silence, but it didn't last long. "Do you remember back when we served together on the Fortitude?" Harry asked.

Thinking back, the hint of a smile edged one side of Soren's mouth. "You're going back a long time, Harry. That was before the war. Before I was captured. When we first met."

"We were both brash young ensigns just out of the Academy," Harry said. "Well, I was almost two years ahead of you. But I was still brash at that point." He laughed, patting his stomach. "And a lot thinner."

Soren couldn't stop himself from laughing. "We met because some administrative snafu put me in your bunk. I remember coming onboard and heading to berthing, only to find it already occupied. You were sound asleep."

"I'm just glad you didn't go get a bucket of water and dump it on me. Bureaucracy being what it is, it took almost an entire day to get things sorted out."

"And meanwhile, I had nowhere to sleep. You let me crash in your bunk while you were on duty, and you helped me straighten everything out, even though you didn't know me."

"How else would I get to know you?" Harry asked. "One of the best decisions I ever made. You've always been a good friend to me."

"And you to me," Soren replied. "So, are you going to give me any hints about this surprise?"

Harry smiled. "Now where would be the fun in that? Don't worry, we're almost there."

They reached the galley, and as the doors slid open, Soren was greeted by a sight that momentarily took his breath away. Gathered around the tables were all of the friends he had recruited to join him on the Wraith, plus the strays he had picked up in the Dregs. Jack, Ethan, Keira, Mark, Sang, Samira, Bobby, Lina, Wilf, Tashi, and Asha turned to face him as he entered.

For a moment, Soren was at a loss for words. He looked from face to face, seeing the warmth and support in their eyes. Finally, he managed to speak. "What's all this?"

Ethan stepped forward, a warm smile on his face. "We thought you could use some company, Captain."

"We've all been working so hard," Keira added. "We figured it was time for a little break, and you need our support right now."

Soren felt a lump form in his throat. He looked around at the faces of his crew—his friends—and saw nothing but support and encouragement. "I don't know what to say."

Sang stepped forward, her usual cool demeanor softened by a gentle smile. "You don't have to say anything, Captain. Just sit down and eat with us. That's all we're asking."

Harry gently nudged Soren towards an empty chair. "Come on, Soren. The food's getting cold, and I didn't go through all this trouble just to let it all go to waste."

As Soren took his seat, the others settled around him. The tension coiled in his chest for days began to loosen just a little. Serving plates were passed around, filled with what looked like real, home-cooked food.

"Harry, I was surprised you pulled this off once. How did you arrange it a second time?"

"You can thank Admiral Yarborough when you see her again," Harry replied. "She asked me how she could thank me for saving them from the loss of lives and ships those damaged parts would've caused. This was my request. And there's more in the freezers. For special occasions only."

"And this qualifies as a special occasion?" Soren asked, raising an eyebrow.

Wilf leaned in. "Any time we're all together like this is special, Captain. Especially given everything that's happened." His fingers nodded in agreement.

As they began to eat, the conversation flowed naturally. At first, they avoided talk of the mission or their current situation, instead sharing stories from their pasts or discussing lighter topics.

"Oh, that reminds me," Lina said, a mischievous glint in her eye. "Do you all remember that time in New York when Ethan tried to impress that city girl?"

Ethan groaned, burying his face in his hands. "I thought we agreed never to speak of that again."

Asha leaned forward, her interest piqued. "Oh no, this I've got to hear. What happened?"

"Well," Lina continued, ignoring Ethan's protests, "Don Juan here decided that the best way to win her heart was to demonstrate the 'amazing capabilities' of his datapad. You know, show off some of his impressive engineering skills."

"That doesn't sound so bad," Asha said, looking confused.

Lina grinned. "It wouldn't have been, except he wasn't exactly sober. So instead of projecting the romantic poetry he saved for just such an occasion, he ended up showing her the results from his last medical exam."

The table erupted in laughter, and Ethan joined in after a moment. Soren found himself chuckling along, the sound feeling foreign after so many days of stress and worry.

"In my defense," Ethan said, "she turned out to be a nurse, so she was more interested in the inside of my colon than my poetry."

"I certainly am," Jack joked. "That poetry of yours was awful."

"Do you still have any of it?" Asha asked. "I'd like to hear it."

"No, you really wouldn't," Ethan said. "Jack's right. It wasn't very good. And to be honest, I didn't write it myself. Though I did program the AI that did write it."

As the laughter died down, Sang spoke up. "If we're sharing embarrassing stories, I've got one that might top that. It was during my early days as a pilot, back when I was still in training..."

She launched into a tale of a training exercise gone spectacularly wrong, involving a malfunctioning simulator, a mistaken evacuation order, and Sang accidentally locking her instructor in a maintenance closet. By the time she finished, the entire table was in stitches.

"I can't believe you got away with that," Mark said, wiping tears of laughter from his eyes.

Sang shrugged, a sly smile on her face. "What can I say? I've always been good at talking my way out of tight spots."

As the meal progressed, more stories were shared. Mark regaled them with tales from his Academy days, painting a picture of a much more awkward and uncertain young man than the confident officer they knew today.

Even Soren shared a few stories from his past, including

some of the misadventures he and Jack had gotten into as young officers.

"Wait, wait," Samira said, holding up a hand. "You're telling me that you and Admiral Harper actually stole a shuttle?"

Soren grinned, the memory bringing a twinkle to his eye. "Borrowed, Samira. We borrowed a shuttle. And in our defense, it was for a good cause."

"Which was?" Ethan prompted, leaning in with interest.

"We don't need to go into so many details," Jack said.

"Of course we do," Keira countered. "I want to hear this."

"Me, too," Tashi said.

"Well, you see, there was this girl Jack was dating," Soren began, launching into the tale of how they'd 'borrowed' a shuttle to help Jack make a grand romantic gesture. The story involved a close call with a patrol ship and a faulty navigation system, and ended with Jack accidentally professing his love to the wrong person.

Keira shook her head in disbelief. "I can't believe you went along with that plan. You always seem so serious."

Jack chuckled. "I wasn't always the straight-laced officer you know now. I used to have a serious rebellious streak."

"I think you still do," Bobby chimed in. "You just hide it better these days."

"This story has a happy ending though," Jack added. "The wrong woman I professed to ended up becoming my wife. Well, until she wasn't."

As the conversation lulled and the meals were finished, a comfortable silence fell over the group. Finally, Soren rose to his feet.

"I can't thank you all enough for this," he said, his voice quivering with gratitude. "Not just for the meal or the company, but for your unwavering support and dedication.

We've faced impossible odds before, and we've always come out on top. This time will be no different."

"Damn straight," Sang said, raising her glass in a toast. The others followed suit, a chorus of agreement filling the galley.

As the crew finally began to disperse, each adjourning to their quarters or returning to their duties, Soren felt a hand on his shoulder. He turned to find Harry standing there, a knowing look in his eyes.

"Feeling better, Captain?" the quartermaster asked.

Soren nodded, a small smile playing at his lips. "I am. Thank you, Harry. For all of this. I didn't realize how much I needed it."

"Don't mention it, sir," Harry replied, his usual gruff demeanor softening slightly. "Just doing my job. Making sure everyone on this ship has what they need to keep going."

With that, Harry left Soren alone in the galley. The captain stood there momentarily, taking in the lingering warmth of the gathering. For the first time in days, he felt a spark of genuine hope ignite in his chest.

CHAPTER 38

Soren stood on the bridge of the Wraith as the ship emerged from its fold. The familiar flash of light faded, revealing a cluster of ships. The FUP fleet. Only, it looked to have grown.

"Twenty-eight ships, Captain," Mark reported from his station. "And one of them appears to be the SF vessel we watched them disable in the Wolf system."

Soren leaned forward, his interest piqued. "The Valkyrie? How did they manage to fix her so quickly?"

Before Mark could respond, Samira's voice cut in. "Incoming transmission from the Spirit of War, Captain."

"Put it through," Soren ordered.

Admiral Yarborough's face appeared on the screen. "Welcome back, Captain Strickland."

"Thank you, Admiral," Soren replied. "You seem to be full of surprises. I thought you said you brought all of your ships into play at the station."

"All of my available ships," she corrected. "The additions you see were under repairs at the time."

"So you have a repair station?"

"Sadly, no. But we do have a second, civilian fleet that

works with us to put these military ships back in action. Three of the ships involved in the fighting at the SF station will be headed back for repairs soon. But enough about that. How did your search go?"

Soren's expression darkened. "Not well. As you suggested, all of the disabled ships were destroyed, their crews killed."

"And your son? Did you find him?"

"No," Soren replied. "We sent a drone onto the station. We discovered the bodies of two members of his unit. Alexander rigged the station. It exploded before we had a chance to recover our dead."

Yarborough's face fell. "Oh, Soren. I'm so sorry."

"I'm confident Alex is alive," Soren said firmly. "We had evidence the dreadnought docked with the station, and since we found his squadmates' bodies near the docking arm, I firmly believe he and the remaining members of his squad were taken prisoner. If that's the case, what do you think might happen to them now?"

Yarborough was quiet for a moment. "If I know my son —and unfortunately, I do—he'll likely bring them to Soren on Earth. I'm sure the so-called Grand Admiral would love to interrogate them."

"You mean torture?" Soren asked.

"That depends on your son."

"There's no chance any of the Scorpions would freely give up any information that would harm the FUP or the Wraith and her crew."

"Then yes, I hate to say it, but torture is likely."

Fury churned in Soren's gut at the thought of it. "I need to reach him before that can happen." Unfortunately, he knew very well what torture was like from his own days in captivity.

"We're too far from Earth for that to be possible," Yarborough said. "Besides, even with a cloak, there's zero chance of you rescuing your people there. The defenses are heavy enough they'll shoot a spread of weapon's fire into space until they find your position. I hate to say this, but your best hope is for Alex to give my ex-husband what he wants before he's beaten to death."

"That's not really the kind of hope I want to hold onto."

"But it may be your best shot at recovering your people. Once Soren's done with Alex, there's a chance he'll be sent to a penal colony for FUP prisoners of war on Teegarden b. He's young and strong, he'll survive there. So will what's left of his unit."

"I don't see how being tortured and then going to a prison colony is our best case scenario," Jack mentioned beside Soren.

"Regardless, that may offer us our best chance to recover the prisoners," Yarborough explained. "And it's a lot better than the alternative. Would you prefer him beaten and alive, or straight up dead?"

Soren shuddered at the bluntness of the Admirals' question. "Definitely alive. But did you say our best chance?"

"I did, if you're open to the arrangement. It's in the best interests of the FUP to try to free some of our people, and with the Wraith, I believe we could do it."

"No offense, Admiral," Soren said. "But you said something similar about the space station."

"You know the reason our mission failed. It wasn't due to a lack of skill or firepower."

"The leak," Soren said. "Speaking of which, we can't plan any kind of rescue if the enemy will know about it ahead of time."

"You're the only one who knows about this plan right now," Yarborough assured him. "In any case, we've identified the mole."

"Don't keep me in suspense, Admiral."

"We believe Major Gray is the traitor."

Soren frowned. "Gray? The same Gray who ran the operation in the Wolf system?"

"The very same," Yarborough confirmed. "If you recall the faulty parts your man Harry found. We believe they were left for him, and he planned to bring them on board to intentionally sabotage our ships."

"That's an interesting theory," Soren muttered. "But how can you be sure?"

"Second Lieutenant Moss," Yarborough said. "One of our communications officers. She was previously assigned to the Ever Valiant. She and Gray became involved with one another, and apparently Gray convinced her to send unmarked and unlogged transmissions. She was reassigned to the Fearless, the SF Valkyrie we captured, to help get the comms up and running. As soon as the ship arrived here and she heard about our losses, she came to me and confessed."

"That's rather convenient," Jack said. "How do you know she isn't setting Gray up?"

"Opportunity," the Admiral replied. "And some circumstantial evidence. For example, there was a reason the defenses were so light on Wolf. And, Gray had access to the SF comms and tranSat at the installation, without any oversight. He had every opportunity to inform the enemy of our plans before, during, and after the mission."

"That's still not really evidence," Jack pressed.

"Not in the traditional sense perhaps. But this is war, a war we're losing. We can't risk more lives on the idea of *innocent until proven guilty*. It's rather the reverse. In any case, we can't bring Gray in for questioning. He's gone missing."

"Missing?" Soren asked. "How? Didn't he go back to the Ever Valiant?"

"We aren't sure. He may have slipped through the cracks at the Wolf station."

"Fantastic," Soren said, his voice dripping with sarcasm. "Your people completely dropped the ball on this one, Admiral."

She exhaled in frustration. "I know. Believe me, I'm not happy about it, either. I can't babysit my entire Navy. I'm sure you understand."

"It's not the first time, Admiral," Jack said. "You should have told us about the Fist of Justice before it showed up and blasted the fleet. You should have told us about its primary weapon."

Soren expected the Admiral to argue her case. Instead, she lowered her head. "I know. It was an error in judgement. A complete failure on my part. Maybe I was subconsciously trying to protect my son. I can't say for sure. But I'm sorry."

"To be fair," Soren said. "We had no reason to suspect the Fist would be anywhere near FOB Alpha. While you should have divulged the nature of the ship when we met the first time, it wouldn't have changed the outcome." He paused a moment to let things cool a little. "What's done is done, and can't be changed. Let's focus on what we can control. Are there any other surprises we should know about?"

"If there is, it'll be a surprise to me, too. But there is a bit of good news. A silver lining as it were. There's little reason for the Fist to fire its cannon again right now, so the threat of the instability collapsing should be diminished for the time being."

"That's something, I suppose," Soren conceded. "But it's not enough. The FUP from Lukas' dimension is still attacking my universe. Every day we burn means more people are dying."

"I understand your frustration. But there's nothing more we can do right now except prepare." She paused, her expression hardening with resolve. "So tell me what you need."

Soren considered for a moment. "First and foremost, we need intelligence. Any information you can get on the penal colony—their defenses, patrol schedules, the works. We need to know exactly what we're up against."

"I'll put our best people on it immediately, and get you whatever I can. Though I have to say, just because we may have identified a mole, doesn't mean we've rooted out all of the leaks. It also doesn't mean the Strickland Federation won't set a trap for us at Teegarden."

"At least this time we can plan for that possibility," Soren said.

"Agreed. What else do you need?"

"Ordnance," Soren continued. "The Wraith is formidable, but we burned through a lot of our ammunition in the last engagement. If we're planning to get into a fight against the Fist of Justice, we'll need full stores."

"That's a bigger ask than intel right now, but I'll approve a transfer of some of the ordnance we captured with Fearless to the Wraith. It might not bring you back to capacity, but it should help."

"I appreciate that, Admiral. As a longer term goal, we need to think about how to neutralize the threat of more cannons like the Fist's. Defeating the Strickland Federation is unfortunately not realistic. So what are our other options?"

"I haven't given up on defeating the SF," Yarborough said. "Or I would have already surrendered. It may be difficult, but I believe my people are up to the task, even after our latest setback. Rescuing POWs from Teegarden will boost morale and replenish our crews."

"And then what, Admiral? Where would you strike next?"

"One fight at a time, Captain," she replied, slightly annoyed by his question. "One target at a time."

Soren glanced at Jack. The FUP resistance was already on its back foot, and after the debacle at the station it was clear their odds of pushing the SF's advances back were slim to none. It was one thing to attempt the impossible, another to refuse to admit there was no real long-term plan beyond survival.

Was there any way to change the FUP's fortunes for the better? Right now, he didn't see one. At the same time, they were the ally he needed if he was going to get Alex back and complete his mission.

"The question remains, Admiral," he said. "How might we eliminate the risk of additional cannons creating dire consequences?"

Yarborough was quiet for a moment. "I understand the question. I'll bring it to my people so we can work on an answer."

"As will we," Jack said.

"In the meantime, we should focus on the rescue operation."

"Fair enough," Soren agreed. "We'll start preparations immediately. And Admiral? Thank you. For everything. Including the food you gifted to Harry. It was a welcome change from our standard chow."

"Don't thank me yet, Soren," Yarborough said, her voice softening. "We still have a long way to go."

"I'm afraid truer words have never been spoken," Soren replied. "But I'm not giving up either. Not now. Not ever. Strickland out."

CHAPTER 39

Alex leaned against the cold metal wall of his cell, his eyes closed as he focused on the subtle vibrations coursing through the ship's structure. After three weeks of confinement aboard the Fist of Justice, he had attuned himself to every nuance of the massive vessel's operational resonance. The steady, light pulsing had been a constant companion against the back of his head, but now there was a change, a shift in the harmonics that could only mean one thing.

They had exited fold space.

His eyes snapped open, meeting Jackson's gaze in the adjacent cell. A silent understanding passed between them. This was it. The moment they had been preparing for had finally arrived.

Zoe, he called out through their neural link. *Did you feel that?*

Oh yeah, she replied, her mental voice tinged with anticipation. *Looks like we've reached our destination.*

Earth, Jackson chimed in. *For how long it took, it has to be.*

They all knew what that meant. Soon, guards would come to escort them off the ship—likely to face interrogation, probably torture, and eventual transfer to a prison colony. But the Scorpions had other plans.

For three weeks, they'd bided their time. Observing. Planning. Waiting for the right moment. And now, he knew that moment had finally come.

Get ready, he communicated silently to his team. *This is our shot.*

A pair of mental affirmatives came back to him. They were as ready as they'd ever be.

Alex's muscles tensed as he heard the sound of heavy boots approaching. A part of him hoped it would be his twisted doppelgänger leading the guard detail. The thought of finally getting his hands on that smug bastard sent a surge of adrenaline through his system. With their augments still active, Alex knew he could tear the son of a bitch apart.

But as the brig door slid open, Alex's hopes were dashed. Six Marines in full combat gear filed in, their weapons at the ready. Before the door closed, he caught a glimpse of at least six more waiting in the corridor outside.

No sign of Alexander.

Still, they couldn't afford to wait for a better opportunity. This was their best—and possibly only—shot at escape.

One of the Marines, a sergeant by his insignia, stepped forward. "On your feet," he barked. "Hands where we can see them."

Alex complied slowly, his eyes never leaving the sergeant's face. He knew Jackson and Zoe would be doing the same in their cells.

He's an ugly one, isn't he? Jackson passed silently.

He'll be even uglier in a minute, Alex replied.

The Marines moved with practiced efficiency. They approached Zoe's cell first, deactivating the force field and quickly securing her wrists with handcuffs.

Jackson was next, offering no resistance as they bound his hands. Finally, they came for Alex.

"Don't try anything stupid," the sergeant warned as the force field dropped.

Alex allowed himself a small, humorless smile. "Wouldn't dream of it."

As the cold metal of the cuffs clicked shut around his wrists, Alex sent out a final mental command to his team.

On my mark.

The Marines began herding them toward the exit. Alex remained calm, waiting for just the right moment. They had to time this perfectly.

Now!

The three Scorpions activated their neural augments in perfect synchronization, flooding their systems with enhanced strength. The cuffs never stood a chance. With a series of sharp cracks, the links of the restraints popped, freeing their hands.

Before the Marines could react, Alex was in motion. He drove his elbow into the nearest guard's solar plexus, doubling him over. He grabbed the man's head in the same fluid movement and brought it down hard against his rising knee. The Marine crumpled to the floor, unconscious.

Jackson had already taken down two guards to his left, his augmented speed making him a blur of precise strikes. Zoe, meanwhile, had disarmed one Marine and was choking another into submission.

The sergeant, recovering from his initial shock, reached for his sidearm. Alex didn't give him the chance to draw it. He twisted the sergeant's wrist, bending his arm back at an unnatural angle. The man's gun clattered to the floor as a quick chop to the throat silenced his cry of pain. A follow-up strike to the temple put him down for the count.

The entire exchange had taken less than ten seconds.

"Clear," Jackson announced, standing over the last of the fallen Marines.

Alex nodded. "Zoe, the terminal. Now."

Without a word, Zoe sprinted to the guard station. Her fingers rocketed across the keypad, inputting the passcode she had painstakingly memorized over weeks of careful observation.

"I'm in," she reported after a moment. "Deactivating alarms and opening a path to the hangar bay."

"How long will that hold?" Alex asked, already moving to collect weapons from the fallen Marines.

"Not long. Maybe five minutes before someone notices and overrides it."

"Then we move fast," Alex decided. He tossed a rifle to Jackson and another to Zoe. "What about the ship's layout?"

"Got it," Zoe confirmed, capturing a feed of the screen through her implant. "Sending it to your HUDs now."

Alex blinked as a schematic of the Fist of Justice overlaid his vision. It was a massive vessel, but they had a clear path to the hangar bay. They might have a chance if they could reach it in time.

"Alright, Scorpions," Alex said, hefting his rifle. "Let's go introduce ourselves."

They moved swiftly into the corridor, where the remaining Marines were just beginning to realize something was wrong. The Scorpions didn't give them time to raise the alarm. They opened fire, their augmented reflexes guiding each shot with deadly precision. The Marines went down before they could even bring their weapons to bear.

"Move!" he shouted, already sprinting down the corridor.

They raced through the ship's passageways, guided by the capture of the ship's schematics in their HUDs. They encountered crew members a few times, caught off guard by their presence, eyes drawn to their orange prisoner jumpsuits. Rather than give them a chance to raise a verbal alarm, the Scorpions ruthlessly cut through them.

There's the elevator, Zoe passed through the implants as they rounded a corner.

We've got company, Gunny, Jackson said, bringing up the rear a short distance behind them. *I guess someone heard the shots. They're probably freaking out, wondering why there aren't any klaxons.*

Jackson, covering fire, he ordered. *Zoe, with me.*

They made a mad dash for the elevator while Jackson paused at the entrance. The moment their pursuers came into few, Jackson opened up with suppressing fire, killing one of the incoming Marines and forcing the rest to take cover. Alex slammed the call button repeatedly. "Come on, come on," he muttered, willing the doors to open faster.

Just as the elevator arrived with a soft chime, the Marines broke cover in a suicidal advance into Jackson's defense.

Three, fall back! Alex ordered.

The three Scorpions piled into the elevator, shooting back at the Marines, taking down two more while bullets bit into the closing elevator doors. Finally, the elevator began to descend.

"Well," Jackson said, "that was fun."

Alex allowed himself a grim smile. "We're not out of this yet."

As if to punctuate his words, alarms began blaring inside the elevator. Zoe cursed under her breath.

"They finally caught on to my changes," she reported.

"We need to beat Alexander and his squad to the hangar bay," Alex said. "I'm sure they'll be on their way."

The elevator stopped, and Alex tensed, ready for another fight. But when the doors slid open, they revealed an empty corridor.

"This way," he said, already moving. "The hangar's not far."

They had barely made it halfway down the passageway when two full squads of Marines rounded opposite corners, blocking their path in both directions.

"Drop your weapons!" one of the Marine leaders shouted. "Surrender now, and you won't be harmed!"

Alex's mind raced, assessing their options in a fraction of a second. They were outnumbered, outgunned, and cornered. But they also had one advantage the enemy didn't know about.

Without a word, he sent a single command through the neural link.

Maximum boost. Now.

The world seemed to slow down as their augments kicked into overdrive. Alex could see individual droplets of sweat on the face of the nearest Marine, and could track the minute adjustments of their aim as they tried to keep the Scorpions in their sights.

Then, chaos erupted.

The three Scorpions exploded into action, moving faster than the human eye could track. Alex charged the squad in front of them, his rifle spitting death with inhuman accuracy. Three Marines fell before they could even register what was happening.

Jackson and Zoe glanced over their shoulders, holding their rifles in one hand and aiming at the Marines behind them. Augmented strength kept their arms steady against the recoil, the targeting reticle on their HUDs providing perfect aim despite the awkward shooting position. Their bullets tore into the Marines, killing them like swatted flies.

Alex threw himself to the left as bullets split the air between him and Zoe. He pushed off the bulkhead and lunged forward, bowling over the remaining trio of Marines. Rolling to his feet, he side-kicked one in the face, breaking his neck, and shot a second point-blank. Jackson hit the third before he had time to spin fully around.

"Clear," Alex gasped, the explosion of violence over in seconds. Both Marine squads lay broken and battered on the deck, victims of the Scorpions' augmented assault, but the boost had taken its toll on them, their breathing coming in short gasps and their muscles burning from the massive exertion. Maximum boost had been a much-needed last resort, even knowing they would pay for it later.

"That's gonna leave a mark," Jackson groaned, glancing at his shoulder where a stray round had grazed him.

"We need to move," Zoe urged. "The hangar's just ahead."

They pressed on, their pace threatened by fatigue but driven by desperation. They reached the hangar doors at a full run, Zoe stepping ahead to hit the control panel and open them.

Alex and Jackson waited at the center for the doors to open, ready to slip through when they had enough room. Exhausted but ready for a final push, Alex tensed as the doors began to part.. They were almost there. Almost out. All they had to do was commandeer a fold-capable shuttle and blast open the hangar bay doors, and they would be home free.

Zoe stepped in behind them as the doors slid aside. All three Scorpions immediately froze.

Son of a bitch, Alex cursed through the implant.

Between them and potential freedom stood five Marines in dark blue Karuta armor, a black fist emblazoned across their chests. And at their center, looking infuriatingly smug, was Alexander.

For a brief moment, Alex considered maximum boosting again and going down in a blaze of glory. Maybe that would have been the best option. A heroic end, and at least he could try to take his counterpart down with him.

But escape had always been a long shot. A desperate hope, driven by desire. And in the back of his mind, something told him not to give up. Not to quit. That it wasn't the Strickland way. His father had survived years as a prisoner of war, had made it back to the frontlines to help turn the tide against the Coalition of Independent Planets. Maybe he could do the same here, against this enemy.

But not if he was dead.

With a resigned sigh, Alex dropped his rifle and stepped out into the open, his hands raised. Jackson and Zoe followed suit, their expressions a mix of frustration and defeat.

Alexander's laughter echoed through the hangar as he approached, slow and deliberate. "Well, well," he said, his voice dripping with mock admiration. "It's about time you got here. We've been waiting for you. That was quite a show you put on. I have to say, I'm impressed."

He stopped a few paces away from Alex, his eyes roving over the three Scorpions with undisguised curiosity. "So much like me," he mused, "but not quite as smart. I asked myself, if the rumors are true, and there is some ship from another dimension captained by a man who looks just like my father, what would his warrior son who looks just like me and thinks like me, do? Well, try to escape of course. If you were just some FUP scum who happened to look like me, you'd be very happy in your cell. And very happy to sing once the interrogation starts. I'm still struggling to understand what's happening here, but I am starting to believe the rumors."

Alex bit back the urge to offer another sarcastic retort. He'd learned his lesson about the consequences of running his mouth. Instead, he remained silent, meeting Alexander's gaze with defiant stoicism.

"Nothing to say?" Alexander asked. "That's okay. We don't need to be friends." He turned, gesturing expansively toward the hangar bay. "You might be wondering why I let you get this far if I knew you would try to escape. The truth is, I wanted to see what you were made of. And I must say, you didn't disappoint. The way you tore through my Marines? Magnificent. It serves as further proof to me that you are who Gray says you are. Simply incredible."

Alexander's praise felt like acid in Alex's ears. He clenched his fists, fighting the urge to lash out despite the futility of it. And Gray? Could he mean the same Gray they had met on Wolf?

That traitorous bastard, Jackson passed silently through his implant.

"Now then," Alexander continued, "if you'll step forward."

Alex did as he was told, entering the hangar bay and coming to a stop right in front of Alexander. To his surprise, Jackson broke their combined silence.

"What happens now?" he asked.

"That happens," Alexander replied, motioning toward the open bay doors leading out into space. A shuttle came into view, escorted by a pair of starfighters. The three ships maneuvered into the hangar, touching down with practiced ease.

Alex's stomach churned with a mixture of dread and anticipation. He had a feeling he knew exactly who was on that shuttle.

The ship's engines wound down, and for a moment, there was silence. Then, with a hiss of equalizing pressure, the main hatch began to open.

Alex held his breath. His fists clenched as every muscle in his body tensed like coiled springs. As the hatch lowered to form a ramp, a figure emerged from the shuttle's interior.

Tall and imposing, with graying hair and piercing eyes that seemed to cut right through Alex. The man's uniform was immaculate, adorned with various medals and insignia that spoke of a long, distinguished career. But it was his face that sent a chill down Alex's spine.

It was his father's face. Older, harder than his father's, with lines etched by years of command and the weight of an empire. But unmistakably, undeniably, the face of Soren Strickland.

Grand Admiral Strickland stepped onto the deck of the Fist of Justice, his gaze sweeping over the assembled Marines before settling on Alex and his team. As he approached, a small, cold smile played at the corners of his mouth.

"Well," Grand Admiral Strickland said. His familiar voice sent conflicting waves of comfort and revulsion through Alex. "What do we have here?"

————

Thank you for reading! I hope you enjoyed the book! For more information on the next installment in the series, please visit mrforbes.com/convergencewar4

OTHER BOOKS BY M.R FORBES

Want more M.R. Forbes? Of course you do!
View my complete catalog here
mrforbes.com/books
Or on Amazon:
mrforbes.com/amazon

Starship For Sale (Starship For Sale)
mrforbes.com/starshipforsale

When Ben Murdock receives a text message offering a fully operational starship for sale, he's certain it has to be a joke.

Already trapped in the worst day of his life and desperate for a way out, he decides to play along. Except there is no joke. The starship is real. And Ben's life is going to change in ways he never dreamed possible.

All he has to do is sign the contract.

Joined by his streetwise best friend and a bizarre tenant with an unseverable lease, he'll soon discover that the universe is more volatile, treacherous, and awesome than he ever imagined.

And the only thing harder than owning a starship is staying alive.

Forgotten (The Forgotten)
mrforbes.com / theforgotten
Complete series box set:
mrforbes.com / theforgottentrilogy

Some things are better off FORGOTTEN.

Sheriff Hayden Duke was born on the Pilgrim, and he expects to die on the Pilgrim, like his father, and his father before him.

That's the way things are on a generation starship centuries from home. He's never questioned it. Never thought about it. And why bother? Access points to the ship's controls are sealed, the systems that guide her automated and out of reach. It isn't perfect, but he has all he needs to be content.

Until a malfunction forces his wife to the edge of the habitable zone to inspect the damage.

Until she contacts him, breathless and terrified, to tell him she found a body, and it doesn't belong to anyone on board.

Until he arrives at the scene and discovers both his wife and the body are gone.

The only clue? A bloody handprint beneath a hatch that hasn't opened in hundreds of years.

Until now.

Deliverance (Forgotten Colony)
mrforbes.com / deliverance
Complete series box set:

The war is over. Earth is lost. Running is the only option.

It may already be too late.

Caleb is a former Marine Raider and commander of the Vultures, a search and rescue team that's spent the last two years pulling high-value targets out of alien-ravaged cities and shipping them off-world.

When his new orders call for him to join forty-thousand survivors aboard the last starship out, he thinks his days of fighting are over. The Deliverance represents a fresh start and a chance to leave the war behind for good.

Except the war won't be as easy to escape as he thought.

And the colony will need a man like Caleb more than he ever imagined...

Man of War (Rebellion)

mrforbes.com/manofwar
Complete series box set:
mrforbes.com/rebellion-web

In the year 2280, an alien fleet attacked the Earth.

Their weapons were unstoppable, their defenses unbreakable.

Our technology was inferior, our militaries overwhelmed.

Only one starship escaped before civilization fell.

Earth was lost.

It was never forgotten.

Fifty-two years have passed.

A message from home has been received.

The time to fight for what is ours has come.

Welcome to the rebellion.

Hell's Rejects (Chaos of the Covenant)

mrforbes.com/hellsrejects

The most powerful starships ever constructed are gone. Thousands are dead. A fleet is in ruins. The attackers are unknown. The orders are clear: *Recover the ships. Bury the bastards who stole them.*

Lieutenant Abigail Cage never expected to find herself in Hell. As a Highly Specialized Operational Combatant, she was one of the most respected Marines in the military. Now she's doing hard labor on the most miserable planet in the universe.

Not for long.

The Earth Republic is looking for the most dangerous individuals it can control. The best of the worst, and Abbey happens to be one of them. The deal is simple: *Bring back the starships, earn your freedom. Try to run, you die.* It's a suicide mission, but she has nothing to lose.

The only problem? There's a new threat in the galaxy. One with a power unlike anything anyone has ever seen. One that's been waiting for this moment for a very, very, long time. And they want Abbey, too.

Be careful what you wish for.

They say Hell hath no fury like a woman scorned. They have no idea.

ABOUT THE AUTHOR

M.R. Forbes is the mind behind a growing number of Amazon best-selling science fiction series. Having spent his childhood trying to read every sci-fi novel he could find (and write his own too), play every sci-fi video game he could get his hands on, and see every sci-fi movie that made it into the theater, he has a true love of the genre across every medium. He works hard to bring that same energy to his own stories, with a continuing goal to entertain, delight, fascinate, and surprise.

He maintains a true appreciation for his readers and is always happy to hear from them.

To learn more about me or just say hello:

Visit my website:
mrforbes.com

Send me an e-mail:
michael@mrforbes.com

Check out my Facebook page:
facebook.com/mrforbes.author

Join my Facebook fan group:
facebook.com/groups/mrforbes

Follow me on Instagram:

instagram.com/mrforbes_author

Find me on Goodreads:
goodreads.com/mrforbes

Follow me on Bookbub:
bookbub.com/authors/m-r-forbes

Made in United States
Orlando, FL
12 December 2024

55468862R00198